When Forty Blooms

HONEY BLOSSOM PRESS

When Forty Blooms

JACINTA HOWARD

HONEY BLOSSOM PRESS

When Forty Blooms Playlist

OutKast- ATLiens

Lucid Dreams - Leon Thomas featuring Masego

Kiss of Life- Sade

When I'm In Your Arms - Cleo Sol

Kissing In Public- Destin Conrad

OutKast- SpottieOttieDopalisticAngel

Another Star - Stevie Wonder

The Other Side- Moonchild

Life Is Changing - Destin Conrad

Didn't Cha Know- Erykah Badu

Nipsey Hussle - Hussle & Motivate

I Can't Help It- Michael Jackson

Red Room- Hiatus Kaiyote

Belongs To - Jerome Thomas

Love You - Sir

Another Life- D'Angelo

I Want You - Marvin Gaye

Fight For Love- Sault

Golden Pt. 2- Berhana, Mereba

Float- Amerie

Wherever- Alex Isley featuring Gorden Campbell, Terrace Martin

& Then Some- Kenyon Dixon, Alex Isley

Lovers Rock - Sade

Before

TWO YEARS AGO

"I DON'T KNOW HOW TO *do this. I don't know how to do life without you—this...*"

Jackson stops, gathering his lower lip between his teeth as he shakes his head and stares at me. His chest heaves slightly, and I find myself mirroring his breathing.

I'm at his new house, the one he's renting a few miles from our old home, where I'm still living with our thirteen-year-old son, Caleb. I've just dropped Caleb off with Jackson for the first time since he moved. We're outside on Jackson's small lawn, speaking in hushed tones in case Caleb decides to come back out of the house. I lick my dry lips, and Jackson's gaze lingers there before he meets my eyes again, shaking his head.

"Jackson, we said we wouldn't do th—"

"Fuck what we said, Simone." Jackson's voice is deep and raspy, like rocks scraping against the ocean floor. He takes a half step toward me. "This can't be us. This can't be our life."

He pushes up the brim of his baseball cap, his jaw tight. His eyes are the color of dark rum and just as potent when they're trained on me.

I swallow hard, the tears that've been lodged in my stomach traveling to my chest, where they lodge, making me feel as if I can't breathe.

"How'd we get here, baby?" he asks, staring at the curb before he looks at me.

It's the first time he's asked the question, one I've asked myself over and over since filing for divorce.

I expected signing those papers to feel like a lifeline, but instead, I feel heavy, as if my limbs have been sewn together. Each movement requires extreme effort, like I'm wading through deep water.

He places his hands on the top of his head and releases a sigh that seems to go on forever, drifting between our bodies, weaving itself into my skin and worming its way into my chest, wrapping itself around my tears. I tug at the sleeves on my faded Prince sweatshirt, toeing the ground with my boots.

Jackson stares at me for a beat longer, then finally drops his arms to his sides. "I'm sorry," he says after long minutes. "I shouldn't've done this."

I open my mouth then close it.

"I'll have Caleb ready at three on Sunday," he says.

He looks at me one last time before turning and striding toward the house.

I manage to get home and pull into the driveway before the tears finally dislodge themselves, and I sob.

NOW

THERE'S SOMETHING SOOTHING ABOUT HOME Depot at two p.m. on a Thursday. Maybe it's the paint smells in the air, the hum of the overhead fans. The smell of lumber.

I shouldn't be here. I should be prepping for a meeting discussing Dillon McCarthy's potential contract with a new sports drink that's launching next quarter. It's supposedly made with açaí berries and adaptogenic mushrooms, which sounds suspect and overhyped, but that's par for the course in my line of work. A deal with the sports drink makes him look caring and down to earth, which, with his ice-blue eyes, wheat-blond hair, and a smile that always teeters on the edge of smug, is needed.

But fuck Dillon McCarthy.

After the video his ex-girlfriend, Jenna, just sent me, threatening to post it online, Sage Athletic will have to seriously reconsider representing him. The two-minute clip showed Dillon, red-faced and yelling, calling Jenna a "worthless cunt bitch" and a "piece of shit" for questioning his whereabouts. His massive frame, looming over her as she argued back, made my stomach churn. I was tempted to drive over to his place and karate kick him in the left kneecap. Lucky for him, Home Depot was closer.

My phone buzzes in the back pocket of my jeans as I walk down the paint aisle, toward the garden section.

You saw that video?

Before I can respond to Tristan's text, I see the dots bouncing on my cracked screen.

Caleb is always on me about replacing my phone, but there's only a tiny crack at the top and my phone is only two years old. I choose not to live my life at the mercy of Apple's product cycles, unlike my teenage son, who seems to need a new device every time I blink. I stop next to the paintbrushes, waiting for Tristan's text to come through. Instead, the phone starts buzzing in my hand.

"What're you thinkin'?" Tristan asks the second I answer, his deep voice tinged with concern.

As Sage's VP of operations/strategy, he's always trying to keep the peace between our more volatile athletes and the agency. He already knows the answer to that question. He's always saying I'm a "reactionary empath," some phrase he made up when he studied psych in undergrad.

"I'm thinking Dillon needs to find somebody else to represent him." My voice echoes slightly in the cavernous aisle.

"Simone."

"You saw the video, dude," I reply, moving down the long aisle once more, trying to keep my voice low as I pass a crew of men with paint-splattered t-shirts.

"I did. And I'm not saying it's okay."

"That's actually kinda exactly what you're saying. That's what *we'll* be saying if we continue to work with him."

Tristan's sigh is mostly silent, but I feel it like it's in my own chest anyway.

"You've already made up your mind about this."

"You should've too, the second you saw it," I say, unable to hide the disappointment in my voice.

"It was just words," he says on a sigh. "Fucked-up words, true. But words. From two years ago. And the fact that she held on to that video to use against buddy whenever they get in an argument honestly might speak to her character too."

I've already thought about that. But Jenna's actions don't negate Dillon's. And I'll admit, the fact that he's six-one and two-sixty doesn't do him any favors. That Dillon's temper could get hot enough to say such foul things is more than a red flag, especially in this line of work, where his image will be used to peddle shit like mushroom-infused water.

"What's bigger than a flag?" I ask as I turn out of the aisle and head toward the back of the huge store, to my current favorite place.

"A blanket," Tristan answers without missing a beat, his voice carrying a hint of the playful banter we've shared since our college days.

"Exactly. This is a big-ass red blanket."

"Dropping him would affect a lot," Tristan says needlessly.

"I know." I inhale and let the breath out slowly. "I know."

"I think we need to think about this, at least for another few days. We gotta be smart about this, Simmy," he says, reverting to his old nickname for me. "We need to at least have a conversat—" He pauses for a moment, mid-sentence. "Hold up, where are you?" Before I can even reply, Tristan guesses, "You're at Home Depot, ain't you?"

I consider lying just as a clerk's loud voice booms over the intercom for help at the return desk.

"Simmy." Everyone thinks Tristan sounds like Dennis Haysbert, but I've always leaned toward *Shawshank Redemption* Morgan Freeman, especially when he's in lecture mode.

"What? I needed to think," I say, hating how defensive I sound.

I walk faster, past the garden hoses and outdoor tables that are dusty from sitting on the massive shelves, and slip through the door into the garden area. The smell of damp soil and fertilizer wraps around me.

Warmth hits my face the second I step into the open room, and I inhale deeply, making my way toward the succulents, where the light from the sun has left a pattern of shadows over their fleshy leaves.

"Home Depot is like…"

"Your therapy, I know," Tristan says.

He falls silent, and I know he's measuring his words, a thing he's done with more frequency over the past couple of years.

"I'm fine, Tristan."

I never should've told anyone about my weird thing with Home Depot and the rows of plants that calm me. It feels like lately everyone is trying to solve me. Or tiptoe around me, as if I might shatter.

I imagine Tristan picking at his hair the way he's done since junior year at Clark Atlanta University, back when he played small forward for the basketball team. That's how we met—I covered the games for the school paper, convinced I'd become a sports reporter. We quickly became friends, and after I introduced him to my best friend Logan, he decided he was in love and started hanging around all the time. Tristan is one of the rare people I've met in Atlanta who was actually born and raised here, and on weekends, we'd hang out at his parents' huge house in Cascade Heights, letting his sweet mom fuss over us and feed us. Nearly twenty years, kids, marriages, and divorces later, we all still know and like each other. In this world, littered with the kind of people who seem intent on ruining it, that's a miracle.

"You talk to Lo?" he finally asks.

"Not in a couple of days," I answer, accepting his subject change because for the moment, I'm tired of thinking about Dillon, his outburst, and the complications we'll face if we keep representing him.

"You still holdin' out on the beach trip?" he asks. I hear his car door open, and Scarface's voice booms loudly for a split second before Tristan turns down the music. He's probably on his way to pick up his daughter, Bella, from pre-K.

"I love Logan, but this trip sounds incredibly corny," I admit as Tristan laughs.

"Damn, Simone."

"I'm just sayin'. I love Lo to death, and I appreciate her. But I'm just turning forty. Is it necessary for me to do the same exact thing every other woman does to celebrate it? Go to a beach, do the feet-in-the-sand picture, then a picture of my fruity, too-sweet rum drink and post it on social media to show everyone how fantastically carefree and fun my life is? It feels narcissistic."

Tristan laughs again. "You ain't using that word right."

I roll my eyes. "For real. All the 'Hey, look at me! It's my birthday, so everyone must drop everything to bow down to my existence and also fly halfway across the world to acknowledge it' is so self-indulgent."

"Jamaica is a two-hour flight from Atlanta."

"That isn't the point," I say, lowering my voice when an older woman looks up from her cart of daffodils at me. "Time is a construct anyway." I move away from the daffodils, toward the indoor plant section.

"Here you go," Tristan says, and I know he's rolling his eyes.

"Who cares that I'm turning forty?" I press on, tugging at my curly bush of a ponytail that sits in the middle of my head. "Why is it any different than when I turned thirty-nine?"

Tristan laughs. "Aight, Simone. You're on one right now. But aight."

"I'm just irritated. And don't go repeating what I said to you about the whole birthday thing being corny to Logan, either."

"You should take the trip, Simone," he says, ignoring me. "Forget that you're turning forty and just look at it like a vacation."

"I don't have time for all that. Especially now with Dillon trying to fuck up everything I—" I stop and sigh, shaking my head.

"What's going on right now is even more reason for you to take a minute and get away. You need to make time for that. You've been going way too hard lately."

"According to you."

"According to everybody."

"And who is everybody?" I demand, brow wrinkled.

"Me, Lo, Caleb—even Jackson thinks a break might be good for you."

I pause, my hand hovering over a small succulent. "You talked to Jackson about this? You can't be—"

"Yo, chill. It wasn't like that. Logan called and talked about the trip to me while I was with Jackson at Atlantucky," he says, referencing the popular brewery that sits on the edge of downtown. "You been over there lately? They have a new IPA on tap that—"

"Don't try to change the subject, Tristan. You know it's weird when you and Jackson sit around having conversations about me."

"What's weird is your insisting that we have conversations about you when I just told you that wasn't the case. It's okay for a person to care about you, Simone."

The dull ache behind my eyes intensifies. I swallow and release a breath. "I know," I say after a long second. "I'm doing too much. I'm sorry."

"It's all good. Just think about the trip, for real. And at least buy something if you're gonna be hanging out at gotdamn Home Depot."

"You know I kill everything I bring into my house, so that's a no-go, homie."

Tristan is chuckling when we hang up. I run my hand along the bright orange and green leaves of a croton, feeling the smooth texture against my skin after I slide my phone back into my pocket. I stop in the bedding plant aisle of the garden center, staring blindly at the trays of pansies, fighting off a wave of emotions. I'm tired. And I don't feel like I have the mental stamina to deal with this Dillon thing, or anything else going on in my life, if I'm honest.

I look up and see the elderly woman from earlier struggling to lift a tall plant into her cart, and I hurry over to help her.

"Thank you, baby." She offers me a smile that I'm sure in her heyday had men beating down her door. Her face is etched with lines, but her brown eyes are bright and observant.

"This is pretty," I say, tracing the leaves on the plant with my finger, the mood ring Caleb gave me when he turned twelve glinting in the sun. According to it, my mood has been "cheerful/energetic" for the past four years.

"It is," she says, tilting her head as she admires the plant. "It'll probably die in a couple of weeks."

She says it so matter-of-factly that I can't stop my burst of laughter.

"I'm terrible with plants," she explains, smiling. "I never did have much of a green thumb."

I raise my brows. "But you still buy them?"

"Of course I do," she answers, squinting a little as if I've said something absurd. "Even if they don't last long, I still can say I had something beautiful in my home. And these days, that's enough for me."

She winks at me and rolls her cart down the aisle to grab a smaller, yellow-flowered plant that she'll apparently probably kill.

I lift my face toward the sun beaming through the greenhouse ceiling. It's a sunny, warmish day in Atlanta, after five straight days of rain, even though it's the end of February. Lately, I keep cycling back to one thought—this is not what I expected my life to look like at almost forty. Me, three weeks away from my birthday, a single mom standing in Home Depot's garden room, staring at flowers I don't dare buy. Me, on the verge of potentially losing one of only three clients that are actually keeping my boutique sports agency afloat. Me, raising a sixteen-year-old son without his dad under the same roof. Me, divorced and trying to figure out what comes next when, two years and some change later, it still sometimes feels as raw as when Jackson and I first split.

I suck in a breath, push the heavy thoughts away. Then I turn and walk back into the garden center. I buy a plant.

Two

LAST NIGHT I DREAMT I was about to fall off the spaghetti junction overpass.

Only this overpass was tall as a skyscraper, and so I didn't dare look over the railing, because to do so felt as if I might go careening over it. Jackson was in the car with me, anchoring me with his quiet calm. It felt so real, his deep voice filling the confines of my old Nissan, his cedar-wood smell, there on all of my inhales. I turned to look at him, and just as I did, the car started to swerve toward the railing. I woke up right before we fell over the edge.

I've had some variation of that dream since I was twenty-two. At first I chalked it up to the time I got stuck up there, on I-85, in the rain. I was heading to Buford Highway, to get my fill of dumplings from one of my favorite Chinese spots, when I ran into a wreck that brought traffic to a *Walking Dead* standstill. I was in the beginning stages of a panic attack. My body broke out into a light sweat, my heart hammering against my ribs. I called Jackson. Even back then, he was my safe space. Just hearing his voice, his deep baritone, repeating "drive, baby, drive, you got this, just drive" was enough to calm me down and get me over the overpass.

When I woke up from the dream at three forty-seven this morning, I reached for him, expecting to feel the warmth of his skin, the evenness of his breaths when I laid my head on his chest. It took a full fifteen seconds for me to remember he hadn't shared my bed in years.

I exhale as I turn into my small cul-de-sac in East Point, pushing the fragments of the dream out of my brain, which is difficult because I'm listening to Jackson's sports podcast, *The Playbook*, right now. He and his co-host, Alisha Wright, are talking about the Atlanta Dream's free agency period, and who the team might pick up, because Lord knows they need a new point guard.

It was our thing when we met my senior year in college at Clark Atlanta, bonding over sports. Jackson is two years older, and was interning at CNN with me, back when I thought I also wanted to be a sports journalist. Only, he wasn't like most guys I knew, super impressed that I not only loved but knew sports. Jackson always just talked to me like I was a human. He acted like I was supposed to know and nerd out over a thing I was interested in. Our sports arguments were epic. Me, saying Barry Sanders was the best running back who ever lived. Jackson, arguing that without Walter Payton, there'd be no Barry. Me, explaining why Hakeem Olajuwon was the most underrated all-around NBA player of all time. Jackson arguing Dominique Wilkins wore that crown. I always teased him that he only felt that way because he's from Brunswick, GA, a little less than five hours from Atlanta.

Fatigue weighs heavily on me as I approach the renovated home I've lived in for the past eight years. It was built in the 1960s, like a lot of the houses in this quiet neighborhood, and was completely renovated just before we bought it.

Everybody was skeptical when Jackson and I told them we were going to buy a house in East Point. Their faces would wrinkle in confusion or their eyes would widen with slightly horrified surprise. *What about the crime? What about the schools?* Which were all codes for asking, *What about the Black people?* Atlanta is a Black city, but the class separation here, even among Black people, is flagrant. Most people with financial means take their talents to suburbs like Dunwoody, Powder Springs, Marietta, Alpharetta.

But East Point offers close access to the city and airport, which means a lot in a city as perpetually clogged with traffic as Atlanta. And more than that, I wanted to live among Black people, especially since I grew up just outside of Austin, Texas, and was still suffering from "only syndrome" when I came to Atlanta—used to being "the only" Black person in most rooms I entered. I liked the friendly neighborhood vibes here, especially on my tranquil street, where all of my neighbors are either retired or close to it. I feel safe knowing that Mr. Jones, Miss Samantha, and the Taylors have my back. It's peaceful here.

As I pull into the driveway, I'm surprised to see Caleb and the girl he's been tutoring, Tiana, sitting outside on the wide porch steps. Their heads are huddled close together as she stares at his phone with him. Tiana's hair is in a bushy ponytail at her nape, her oversized navy-blue hoodie nearly swallowing up her thin frame. I know she plays two-guard for the school, and that she's very, very good.

But I'm still not sure how I feel about Caleb spending so much time with this girl, whom he clearly has a thing for. Tiana offers me a small wave and a shy smile as I climb out of the car, adjusting my bag on my shoulder as I approach, and I feel niggling deep in my belly when our gazes meet. Tiana's issues are not loud. She's not cursing out teachers, or getting into fights, or anything blatant. Instead, her challenges are quieter—she's falling behind in three classes, which is why Caleb's been tutoring her. It's the subtlety that worries me the most.

"She's actually really smart, Mom," Caleb told me before he asked if she could come over to the house to do their studying a few weeks ago. "She just…zones out sometimes."

I asked why Tiana "zones out" and got a shrug in response. It's moments like these that highlight how different Caleb is from how I was at his age.

He already has a bird's-eye view of the world, scoping out everything, all at once, perching in one place for a minute before he flies off to observe something else. He's in a group called Study Buddies, where he tutors other kids, mostly in English and social studies. He's in the CubeSat Engineering Club. I did a lot of extracurricular things too, but not because I enjoyed them. I just wanted to be at home as little as possible.

I shift my heavy bag on my shoulder as I make my way toward them.

"Cheerio, mates, are ye home early, matey?" I say when I reach the steps.

Caleb smirks and rolls his eyes, stuffing his hands in his hoodie pockets. I guess our Irish thing is no longer cool when he's with friends.

"I texted you. Engineering club was canceled." Caleb's voice change is still jarring sometimes. One minute it was cracking and pitchy, the next it sounded like Michael Clarke Duncan's.

I pull my phone out of my pocket and see the missed text glaring on my screen. *Engineering is canceled. Coming home early with Tiana to study.*

"Hi, Miss Simone," Tiana says, meeting my eyes briefly before returning to her notebook.

"Ye studying the pledge o'—"

"Mom," Caleb interjects, raising his eyebrows. "You sound like a pirate."

Tiana covers her laugh with a hand, and Caleb looks over at her, smiling as he scratches his head. He's in the early stages of loc'ing his hair, and the style smooths out his baby face, making him look more like the teenager he is.

"How was your day?" I ask, dropping the act as I push my sunglasses up on my head. "Awesome and productive?"

Caleb shrugs. "It was cool."

"What about you, Tiana?" I ask, offering a wave to Miss Samantha next door, who's just pulling out of her garage.

"It was okay," Tiana answers, pulling at her hoodie sleeves. I study her face for a beat. Her eyes are a little puffy and pink, the tip of her nose bright.

"Just okay?" I press, pushing away the ball of dread that's formed in my stomach.

Tiana nods quickly, but doesn't look up at me.

"Is it okay if Tiana stays for dinner?" Caleb asks without looking up from his phone.

Tiana's head jerks up and she looks at Caleb, eyes wide. "Caleb," she says, her voice quiet. "It's not—"

"I thought you wanted pizza?" Caleb interjects, raising his eyebrows when he glances up from his phone, looking just like Jackson in that moment. "And we usually get pizza on Thursdays anyway. It's cool if she eats with us, right, Mom?"

Tiana gnaws on the inside of her lip, her eyes on her notebook again as she fiddles with her pencil.

"Yep, for sure," I say. "You're more than welcome."

Caleb looks like he won the lottery and Tiana mumbles a soft thank you. I pass Caleb my keys so he can go pick up the pizza from around the corner, which he loves doing, since he got his license a few months ago.

"Oh, Dad's on the way over," he says before he reaches my car, with Tiana following after him. "I left my chemistry book over at his house and he said he'd drop it off. I have a test tomorrow."

"*Tomorrow*, Caleb?"

"Nah, it's good. I already know it. I just need to look over it one more time. Tell Dad not to leave when he gets here—I need to talk to him," he calls as he opens the door for Tiana.

I'd nag him a bit more, but I honestly don't need to. Caleb is harder on himself when it comes to his schoolwork than I'd ever be.

I push inside our house. The renovation gave it an open floor plan. I recently repainted the living room "whispering white," which means it looks mint greenish when the light hits it just right. The furniture is simple beige, complemented by numerous fake plants scattered around. The floors are honey-colored hardwood, giving a soft, golden warmth throughout the space. It was our absolute favorite thing about the house when we bought it.

I head upstairs and take a quick shower, then slip into a pair of baggy sweats and an Atlanta Falcons hoodie. I return downstairs and flick on the TV before popping into the bright kitchen to pour myself a glass of wine. There are dishes in the sink, and some of Caleb's stuff—headphones, books, a baseball cap—scattered on the counters, which I leave for right now because I'm tired.

I've just taken the first sip of my wine when there's a knock at the door. I set my glass down and pad barefoot to open the door for Jackson.

"Hey," he greets me, holding Caleb's thick chemistry book.

Memories from my dream float to the top of my brain the second he speaks, and I draw in a breath, inhaling his warm, woodsy scent. Jackson smells exactly the way he did in my dream last night.

I clear my throat and greet him, stepping back to let him in.

My gaze bounces over his dark jeans, forest-green henley, and distressed black leather jacket that covers his broad shoulders. Jackson is one of the handsomest man I've ever seen in real life. Thick eyebrows sheltered by eyelashes so long they cast shadows on his cheeks. His rich, deep complexion reminds me of sun-warmed earth after a summer rain. His lips are full and expressive, almost pretty if they weren't framed by his beard. The hair on his face is perpetually two hours past a five o'clock shadow, adding to the edge of gruffness he carries with him. He's sexy-gruff without trying. The kind of man that makes you not only look but wonder.

He squints and cocks his head when he catches me staring.

"What's up? You good?" he asks, his gaze sweeping over me, lingering briefly on my lips before trailing up to meet my eyes.

"Yeah, for sure," I say as we linger in the entranceway next to the bench seat that's mostly stuffed with Caleb's sneakers and a few of my flip-flops. "Caleb ran to pick up a pizza with his tutoring buddy, Tiana."

At that, Jackson smirks, a dimple peeking out on one cheek. "I think that little girl is more than his 'tutoring buddy.'"

I sigh, leaning against the wall in the foyer. "He's not calling her his girlfriend or anything to you, is he?"

"Nah. Not yet," he says, grinning. "But she has his nose wide open."

I shake my head and frown, looking down at my bare toes.

"What? You don't like her?"

I look up at Jackson, meeting his eyes on a shrug. "She seems sweet, but she also seems like she has a lot going on. Like, psychological, emotional stuff that's too much for Caleb, who has never even had a real girlfriend."

"What makes you say that?" Jackson is studying me now, in that intense way he often does.

It's the core of his journalistic brilliance. His gaze dissects you, seeing every shard that makes up your whole, piecing you together like a living puzzle. His eyes drink in everything, demand nothing, and that mix has a way of peeling back layers, revealing what's buried beneath a person's silence.

I shrug again. "I dunno. I just… feel it."

Jackson grins, his gaze dropping briefly to the floor before he looks at me again. *"You feel everything, Simone,"* he used to tell me. *"That's your superpower when you don't let it control you."*

"She's too jumpy," I add after a long second. "Too uncomfortable in her skin."

"She's a teenager," Jackson counters, scratching his jaw, his short fingernails raking over the late evening stubble. "Aren't they all uncomfortable in their skin?"

"I know, but this is different. Deeper."

Jackson bites on the inside of his lip, and his dimples make another appearance. "Caleb makes good choices," he says after a beat.

"He does. But he's sixteen. With hormones that are raging and impacting his brain. He said hi to me earlier and I thought I was talking to the ghost of James Earl Jones."

Jackson is chuckling when he finally sets Caleb's chemistry book on the entryway table, and I smile too.

"He should be back in a few minutes," I say. "He said to let you know he needed to show you something? I don't know if you have time to stick around or…"

"Yeah, it's good," he says, although I notice he checks his phone before he takes off his sneakers and follows me down the hallway toward the living room, passing the black-and-white family photos in black frames on the wall: Caleb as a fat-cheeked baby, Caleb posing with a trophy at his chess tournaments, Jackson and Caleb on the beach at Tybee Island. Jackson is in a lot of them, mostly because I never wanted Caleb to feel as if our divorce meant that we were no longer a family. A few months ago, Logan asked me if I'd leave up the photos after I started dating.

"You know men are children," she told me matter-of-factly. *"And seeing your ex-husband all over your living room walls is gonna be an issue."*

I told her Jackson's photos weren't in the living room, they were in the hallway, and she stared at me unblinkingly, looking for a response that wasn't going to come because I really didn't have one. I'd have to cross that bridge when the time came, which wouldn't be anytime soon. My focus is on Sage and Caleb. I don't have space for any romantically induced melodrama. Especially considering the men available in Atlanta—or rather, the lack thereof—since most men here, even those who are no longer in their twenties and should ideally be ready to settle down, are not.

"You want a glass of wine?" I ask as Jackson seats himself on the couch. "Or a beer or something?"

"It's not that sweet red wine that tastes like red Kool-Aid, is it?" He looks up at me, his lips twisted into a smirk, and I roll my eyes.

"I brought that home *one time*, dude," I remind him as I head into the kitchen to pour him a glass. "And it was an accident."

Jackson laughs as he shrugs out his jacket, draping it on the back of the couch. "Don't front, Simone. It's all right if you like sweet red wine that tastes like fruit punch."

"Is that what you do, when someone is serving you? Talk shit?" I ask, brow raised when I hand him a glass of pinot.

He meets my eyes as I hover next to him, his dark eyes glinting with amusement, lips twisted into a playful smirk. "Pointing out facts and talkin' shit are two totally different things."

I head over to the adjacent armchair, hiding my smile behind my glass as I take another sip, crossing my legs underneath me. It took about a year for us to get back to some semblance of normal—to be able to share space without it feeling tense, weird, and unbearably heavy.

I wouldn't exactly call us friends now, though. I've seen those Erykah Badu-type couples who can be all mature and progressive with their exes. I admire that, but I'm not about to be delivering any babies for Jackson. My feelings for him surpass simple emotion. Together or not, he's part of my blood cells, the molecules that make up my air. It took a long time for me to square with that.

I still don't know what it means, being divorced yet feeling this way. It's something I live with, like the mole on the inside of my right thigh. It's there. It will never go away. And somehow, I've learned to breathe around it.

"This is actually a new South African blend Logan just started selling," I say.

Logan owns an award-winning wine shop in Atlanta, a dream she made happen a few years ago after spending a decade in the hospitality industry.

"It's good. I need to get by there," Jackson says. "How's she doin'?"

"She's Logan," I answer with a shrug, smiling.

Jackson nods, matching my grin. "Tristan said she's not with ol' dude any more."

"Darren," I supply. "Yeah, for today, at least. She doesn't really even like him. I don't know why she's wasting their time."

"She's just searching," Jackson says, his eyes trailing to *SportsCenter*. "Nothin' wrong with that. Long as you don't start losing yourself while you're doing it."

He doesn't say "unlike you," but I imagine the words hanging unspoken in the air anyway. I look over at him, but his eyes are on the TV. Jackson is not passive-aggressive. When he has something to say, he says it, so I know that once again, I'm probably projecting.

I sigh, following his gaze to the screen, where the anchors are talking about the upcoming WNBA draft in April.

"You really think Danisha Cole would be a better pick over Aari McDonald?" I ask, changing the subject. That was the main topic of Jackson's podcast today.

He raises an eyebrow. "You don't?"

"No. Aari's a firecracker. The Dream looked half-asleep most of last season."

"You sound like Alisha."

I shake my head, resisting the urge to point out that I'm actually nothing at all like his pretty cohost.

"Alisha wants Aari because she'll run up the scoreboard," I say instead. "I think Aari has the energy to bring some life to the team. There's a difference."

Jackson leans back on the couch, stretching out his long legs after moving one of Caleb's baseball caps that I keep telling him not to leave there.

"True, but Danisha's a veteran. She knows how to handle a team mentally, and could mentor the younger players."

"Yeah, but is experience enough?" I ask, watching him over the rim of my glass.

"Sometimes that's all you need," he says, his eyes meeting mine. "Big change isn't always the answer, is it?"

I break eye contact first, focusing on swirling the wine in my glass. "Guess it depends on what you're trying to maintain." My voice is barely above a whisper.

His exhale is heavy before he drinks from his glass again. My phone buzzes on the coffee table, breaking the silence, and I lean forward and grab it.

Whatever you wanna do, I'm down like this... Tristan's text is followed by four flat-tire emojis, and I chuckle before it slips into a sigh. I close my eyes briefly, twisting my lips.

When I open them, Jackson is looking at me.

"Dillon McCarthy," I say, answering his unspoken question. "You know how we signed him a few months ago."

Jackson nods.

"Turns out, he's very, very douchey," I say.

"You knew that already."

I nod. "I did. But now it's biting me in the ass."

I click through my phone and pull up the video Jenna sent over then hand it to Jackson. His fingers brush mine when he takes it from me, and my nerves tingle where our fingers meet. I take another large sip of my wine.

Jackson's face transforms just as I knew it would when Dillon starts cursing at Jenna. He doesn't even finish the video before he passes the phone back to me, shaking his head, disgust etched on his face.

"What are you gonna do?" he asks.

Jackson has intimate knowledge of how long it took me to build my agency, of what a client of Dillon's stature means for the company, financially but also in terms of declaring our place, especially in a field dominated by men. Dillon isn't just another client. He's validation. Proof that I belong in this business.

I lean back in my chair and stare up at my boho wooden ceiling fan, the one I bought during my house-decorating spurt when I was "boho-ing" everything last year. I can hear my mom's voice clear as day in my head, telling me I need to be "twice as good to get half as far as the white men in this business." But the older I get, the more I realize how that entire concept is flawed. Why should I have to overperform to try to be "equal" in a system that's rigged against me?

In a system that was never meant to include me in the first place? It's exhausting. It's *dehumanizing*. It's bullshit.

"You know what I wanna do," I tell Jackson, before crossing my legs under me. "I wanna drop him. But I don't realistically know if I can. Tristan is right—it'd affect a lot if we lost him. And they *were* just words. From two years ago. I do think people can change and grow. You gotta give folks the grace to be human. But I just wonder…"

"What else he's done that wasn't caught on video if he could speak to her that way."

I nod. "Exactly."

I meet his eyes when I say it, and watch him exhale as he leans forward with his elbows on his knees. His sleeves push up on his arms with his movement, revealing the vine tattoo that travels up to his shoulder. He's had it since he was nineteen. Most guys at that age were marking their bodies with silly things. Women's lips. Lion faces. Crowns of fire. Symbols meant to assert their dominance in a world they often felt belittled in. One day, before we started dating, we were at lunch and I asked him what his tattoo meant, reaching out and tracing a finger along his shoulder before I thought about what I was doing. I jerked my hand back, heat flooding my face when he looked up at me, his gaze unreadable, though a small grin was on his face, making his dimples peek out and the flutters that'd become normal whenever I was in his presence wake up.

"It's about connection," he said, meeting my eyes. *"We all share the same life source. And as long as we stay connected to the vine, the branches never die, not really."*

I thought about what he said the rest of the day, the crush I had on him blooming into full-blown infatuation—and more than that, respect and appreciation for who he was, and the man he was clearly already on the way to becoming.

I look over at him now, taking another sip of my wine before I exhale.

"What's your gut telling you?" he asks about the McCarthy situation, just as I knew he would.

I shake my head, letting it plop against the back of the cushion. "To be real? I don't know if I can even trust it anymore."

I can't decipher the look in his eyes when he meets mine again. "What's that mean, Simone?" His deep voice is quieter when he poses the question.

I breathe out, my response caught somewhere deep in my belly as I take another sip of wine. Jackson still hasn't broken eye contact when he bites then releases his lip. He looks like he's about to say something when the front door swings open, and we hear Caleb talking a mile a minute to Tiana.

Caleb's eyes light up when he enters the living room and sees Jackson, even though he was just over there on Sunday. And I feel my usual pang of guilt.

"What's up, Dad."

"What up, kid," Jackson says with a smile, extending his fist to give Caleb a pound as he passes by to put the pizza on the dining room table.

I get up and head to the kitchen, pulling down plates from the cupboard, then pre-made salad from the refrigerator, while Caleb and Tiana return to the living room. I hear Caleb introducing Tiana to Jackson, though I can barely make out her voice, it's so quiet. Her shyness is interesting because she's the opposite on the court. She's commanding there, bossing the other players around, coaching the team, even though she plays shooting guard, not point.

"Are you staying for pizza?" Caleb asks Jackson when they all make their way into the kitchen.

I pass him and Tiana a plate full of salad and slices of cantaloupe, trying to balance the fact that they're eating pizza, which isn't the healthiest. They take a seat at the dining room table as Jackson leans against the counter next to me, his cedar-wood smell invading the space.

"I'm actually on my way to dinner in a minute," Jackson answers, glancing at his phone again.

I avert my gaze when the words leave his lips, concentrating on serving myself a slice of pizza, determined to ignore the slivers of jealousy slicing through my belly. Jealousy I have no right to.

"Your mom said you wanted to holler at me, though."

Caleb nods as he chews, before glancing at me and then Tiana. She's focused on her food, seemingly off in her own world, that fast.

Caleb gets up, nodding toward Jackson, and they move out of sight, into the living room. I can hear the lower tenor of Jackson's voice but can't make out the words.

"So, how is studying coming?" I ask Tiana as she forks up salad. "Are you understanding things better?"

"I mean… It's not like…" She hesitates, her eyes flickering away. "I honestly kinda understood it before," she finally admits, her voice barely above a whisper. "Caleb does help me, though," she adds quickly. "He's… He helps me."

Her face flushes at the mention of Caleb, and I sigh inwardly.

"So, what do you think the issue is with your classes? Teachers? The class is boring?" I prod.

Tiana tugs at her sleeves, picking at an invisible thread. She picks up her fork again, absently stirring the lettuce on her plate. "Mrs. Tucker, my math teacher, she doesn't… approve of me."

I chew slowly, watching Tiana as she shifts in her seat, her gaze fixed on the table. Saying her teacher doesn't "approve" of her is much different than saying the typical teenager "my teacher doesn't like me."

"Everyone at that school is the same," she murmurs, finally meeting my eyes again. "The same hair, the same clothes, the same way of speaking. And everyone is comfortable being that way, and I'm… not." She sighs softly. "She thinks I'm too different, I guess."

I study her for a minute. "There's never anything wrong with being exactly who you are. God made you *you* on purpose."

She smiles a little.

"Caleb showed me a few clips from your games."

She looks up at me, surprise flashing in her eyes.

"You're good. *Really* good."

"Thank you." Her lips twist, and disappointment flashes on her face. "We didn't make the playoffs."

"Yeah, I saw you barely missed them. Think you have a better chance next year?"

She nods. "We're playing better together now. It's the seniors that didn't have chemistry, and they're graduating."

"Think you'd be comfortable playing point? You're really comfortable with the ball. And I can tell from the few clips I saw that you naturally read the court."

"Coach likes me at the two." She shrugs and looks away.

"Yeah, but would you *want* to play point, if the position were offered?"

She sucks in a breath and nods, almost like admitting what she really wants is some sort of betrayal to her coach, even though she knows his guidance isn't serving her well.

"Then you should go for it next year," I tell her, watching as she fidgets in her seat, her brow furrowed as she studies the floor. "Study some film of other point guards you like, get on the court more often, more consistently. You have the raw talent to do it, and I think they're misusing you in the shooting guard position. Sometimes people, even coaches, just need to be nudged to do the right thing."

Tiana nods, her eyes thoughtful when she looks at me again.

"Are you thinking about playing in college?" I ask, taking another bite of pizza.

"I think I so. Maybe." She picks at her salad.

"Then now's the time to start being persistent and telling people what you want, show them who you are."

I stop talking when Jackson and Caleb enter the room again. Caleb offers Tiana a smile, which she returns before ducking her head and picking at the pepperoni on her pizza. I glance at Jackson, whose lips twist into a quick smile before he comes to where I'm standing, setting his glass beside mine.

"Thanks for the wine," he tells me, meeting my eyes for a second before directing his attention to the table. "Nice to meet you, Tiana."

"You too," she says, smiling before studying her pizza again.

"I'll see you tomorrow," he tells Caleb, moving toward the living room.

Jackson grabs his jacket from the back of the couch, and I follow him to the door, watching as he slips his sneakers back on. I want to ask what he talked to Caleb about, but I've learned to back out of their man-to-man time.

"We've gotta be able to have those conversations," Jackson told me months ago.

I'm just about to say forget it, and ask anyway, when Jackson speaks.

"Tiana got suspended from school today."

My eyes widen before I let out a long breath. "She looked like she was crying earlier when I pulled up." I look at the floor, digesting the fact that Caleb didn't feel comfortable enough to tell me what was up. "Do you know what for?" I ask, keeping my voice low.

"Something to do with missing too much class," he says quietly, releasing a humorless half-chuckle. "Kicking a kid out of school for not wanting to be in school makes a lot of sense." He shakes his head again.

We've had many conversations about the failures and goofy idiosyncrasies of the American school system. I even contemplated homeschooling Caleb for a while, especially now that it's all the rage and there are so many different options these days. And after the last school shooting, it just seems like common sense. But I'm way too busy with work to check in with him the way I think I'd need to, and I don't want to just plop a computer on his lap and leave him to it. Plus, I know Caleb thrives on socialization.

"Did he tell you why she's missing so much class?" I ask.

"Nah." Jackson pokes his cheek with his tongue and shakes his head, glancing toward the hallway when Caleb and Tiana's laughter rises in the other room.

"This is about to be a problem," I say, following his gaze. "I wonder why he didn't—"

"He said he didn't want to bring it up to you while Tiana was here," Jackson says, answering my quiet question before I can get it out.

"I think he feels more comfortable talking to you about stuff like this, honestly. And that's okay, as long as he's talking to one of us."

Jackson bites the inside of his cheek but doesn't respond. He watches me as I release another long breath that somehow still feels trapped in my chest.

"There's a lot happening, all at once," I say almost to myself.

Jackson stares at me for a beat. "Wanna know what I really think about the McCarthy thing?" The cloud that's been hanging over me all day when I even think about Dillon returns at the mention of his name. "I think you need to trust yourself." He slides his jacket back on. "Get out of your head, and trust yourself to make a good decision about him."

He checks his phone again when it lights up with a text, and this time, he responds, his big hands sliding over the screen with ease. I run a hand over the back of my neck, massaging it lightly with my fingers.

Jackson watches the movement before meeting my eyes again. "You didn't ask me, but I think you should take that trip with Logan."

My gaze lifts to his, my heart instantly galloping in my chest. "Tristan told me that's what you said."

He meets my eyes. "You only turn forty, on your actual birthday, once. It's a once-in-a-lifetime event, right?"

I chew on the end of my thumbnail and swallow the lump there. Jackson has a way of making me feel five years old again, and then as if I've lived a hundred lifetimes with him in the next breath.

"I'll see you later," he says, turning and slipping out the door, leaving traces of his light cologne in the air.

I'm still staring at the closed door when Caleb's voice rings out from the dining room.

"Oh yeah, Mom, why was there a big plant in the back seat?"

My shoulders sag and I close my eyes. *Shit.* I forgot the dang plant in the car.

I open my eyes again. "Wait, *was?*"

"Yeah, there's dirt all over the floor back there. It was tipped over and it looks like it got completely crushed."

I close my eyes again and sigh.

Three

I'M A LEAP YEAR BABY, born on February 29. When I was little, my mom always tried to make me feel better about my actual birthday technically showing up only once every four years.

"You're the only person who gets to choose their birthday," she'd say, pointing to February 28 and March 1 on the small calendar that hung in our kitchen. "Whichever day you pick is when we'll celebrate. Everyone else's birthday is bor-ing," she'd singsong, drawing out the word. "But you get to decide because you're special."

By the time I turned eleven, the thrill was gone, replaced by apprehension. Would my chosen birthday conflict with anyone's schedule? Would my brother Tyler have a game or something that day and mess things up? Would my mom be tired from work, my chosen birthday something that'd make more work for her? So when I turned thirteen, I decided we'd celebrate my birthday on February 28. Not because I liked it better than March 1, but because it seemed like it was the least fussy choice.

Being in Jamaica lounging on Seven Mile Beach feels like a contradiction to everything I've ever thought about my birthday. And yet I'm here, digging my toes into the soft, warm sand. I let out a breath and feel as if I'm inhaling the sun as its warmth coats my skin. Today is February 28, and tomorrow, February 29, I will turn forty, right here on this beach.

"Thank you again for this trip. I'm dumb sometimes," I say.

"You're not dumb, so don't say that dumb shit," Logan answers, her smoky voice telling me that her eyes are still closed.

I laugh and glance at her. She's smirking, sunglasses covering her eyes, stretched out next to me on a white lounge chair, book in one hand. Her hair is cornrowed and hanging over one shoulder. My hair is basically in the same style, only braided into a long ponytail that brushes my waist, and since we landed, no less than three people have asked us "which one of those R&B groups" we're in. Lo has always looked famous—pouty lips, hooded eyes, deep brown skin that's smooth as stone, and a smile that's always a smart word away from a smirk.

I take another long sip of my dirty banana rum drink, savoring the cool sweetness, the condensation from the glass trickling over my fingers, and close my eyes again. The sun is setting on our first day in Negril.

I haven't felt this relaxed in a very long time, and not just because this is my second drink since we arrived this afternoon. The saltwater air fills my lungs as the ocean brushes against the shore, leaving abstract patterns in its wake. I already know from earlier that the water is bathwater warm. It instantly eased my tight muscles the moment I stepped in.

"I bought a plant a couple weeks ago," I say, eyes still closed.

"For real?" Logan's voice is laced with surprise. She's well aware of my plant-murdering history.

"Yup. And then I killed it the exact same day."

Logan laughs quietly.

"I think it was an omen." I turn my palms upward, allowing the sun to greet the skin on my forearms.

"Good Lord, Simone. It was not an omen."

A slow breath leaves me and I open my eyes, staring out at the turquoise water. "It felt like one. I was kinda proud of myself for buying it, though."

"There, *that*," she says, opening her eyes and turning to point a manicured finger at me. "*That's* the feeling you need to hang on to."

I hum my response, closing my eyes again.

"Know what I was thinking?" she asks after a beat.

I turn my head and look at her. A few feet to her left, a couple has returned from the water, and are digging through their clear beach bags.

"You know how you're all anti-birthday," she begins.

"I'm not 'anti-birthday.' I love birthdays. Caleb's, yours…"

"Okay, well, anti *your* birthday," she clarifies with an eye roll. "I think you should switch it up this year. Like, shake things up, especially since it's the leap year."

I tug at one of the braids hanging over my shoulder. "My life has definitely been shaken up enough over the past couple of years. I'm good."

Logan sighs, her eyes holding a trace of sympathy that I look away from, taking another sip of my drink.

"Can I keep it real with you?"

I chuckle. "When do you ever *not* keep it real with me?"

"I think you're stuck in a cycle that's unhealthy."

Her abrupt words hit me in the stomach. I raise my brows. "Oh wow, doctor. Please continue."

"Shut up," Logan says, rolling her eyes with a smirk. "I'm being serious here. I love you unconditionally. I probably shoulda started with that."

I tug at a braid again, releasing a breath.

"And I'm worried about you, if I'm being honest."

"You're *worried* about me?" I ask, widening my eyes. "Why?"

"Because you're unhappy."

Logan's blunt words hit me in the chest again, and I sit up in my lounge chair and stare at her.

"Don't get all defensive."

"It kinda feels like I need to be defending myself right now."

Logan tilts her head, and I can see her sigh. I exhale too and take another sip of my drink.

"So what is this cycle I'm supposedly trapped in?" I ask after a second, trying to push down the agitation I feel pricking at my nerves.

"I think you're scared of being your whole self. I think you're scared of failing. And I think that fear paralyzes you sometimes. Like you just… check out emotionally."

"Check out emotionally," I repeat, hating the way the words feel heavy on my tongue.

Logan twists her lips, allowing her silence to serve as her confirmation. My body flushes hot in irritation before my stomach tightens and I begin twirling the years-old mood ring on my finger. Is this really how people still see me? Scared? Emotionally stunted, or checked out, or whatever the fuck Lo just said? I stare out at the water as her words sink further into my belly while Jackson's voice slides into my brain.

"You don't talk. You just shut down…"

It was his mantra in our last year of marriage. I push the words away and swallow the rock in my throat.

"So you're telling me I'm a bad mother," I say to Logan after a few beats.

"What?" Her brow is furrowed.

"If I'm 'checked out emotionally,' I'd be a bad mother to my son by default."

"Not with Caleb, Simone. *Damn.* I mean… in other ways." She shakes her head. "I just think you need to focus on you. Just completely and totally on you. And do some stuff that is out of your comfort zone."

"Like what?" I force myself to ask.

"Okay, so I read this article a while ago, and this lady in San Jose went on this year-long 'self-quest'—"

"I'm already not feeling this," I interrupt. "This sounds like a New Age way of justifying being a lightweight narcissist. Everyone is so freakin' *self-indulgent* these days. Me, me, me, I, I, I, my happiness, my peace, my, my my…"

Logan blinks at me. "Can I finish?"

I push out a breath and wave a hand, nodding at her to continue.

"All right, so basically, the lady was unsatisfied with her life. Not depressed but just deeply sad, like in her soul."

My eyes fall to the tie on my purple swimsuit bottoms.

"So on her birthday, her personal New Year, she decided to have an experience. Something she'd never done before. I think she went parasailing or something. And then once a month, for the rest of the year, she did something. She was afraid of water, so she took a swimming lesson. She loved gardening, so she flew to New York and went to the botanical gardens because it's the largest one in the country. She wanted to be a jockey when she was a kid, so she went horseback riding. That kind of thing. But everything she did was in celebration of herself. To just live life to the fullest and look at the world through a different lens. I was thinking that's something that would be cool for you to do."

I roll my tongue in my mouth before meeting Logan's eager eyes. She's a lot of things, but "eager" is rarely one of them, so I know she's serious about this.

"Okay," I say after a long second. "Maybe I will."

Logan smiles and holds her fist out for me to bump it. "Bet. I already have our first experience planned for tomorrow. *Chill*," she adds when I open my mouth to protest. "We're not parasailing or anything." She looks up into the sky, where there's literally a man parasailing over the ocean. "I have us scheduled for a beachside manifestation class."

I press my lips together to keep from asking what the hell a "beachside manifestation" class is, and why she'd think that'd be something we should participate in. Logan is really into this, and she apparently thinks I'm having some sort of mental breakdown, so I'll go to the dang-gone class with her.

"Cool, thank you for doing that," I say, leaning back in my chair.

"I also think you should maybe try therapy again?" She says it tentatively, which again, is not her.

"Damn, Lo," I mumble. "What is this, an intervention?"

She shrugs her response, and once again, I'm frowning on the beach in Jamaica.

I know therapy is all the rage, especially in these post-pandemic days, after everyone was holed up and forced to really be with themselves, only to find out they didn't really like or even know who they were. And I'm not anti-therapy. I actually made Caleb go when Jackson and I divorced. And all of my clients are required to go to "Mindset Conditioning," weekly fifteen- to thirty-minute check-ins for four weeks if they sign with us. But for me? I'm not really feeling it. I know what my issues are. I try to work on them the best way I know how.

"You've been through a lot of shit, Simone," Logan says. "Even before your split from Jackson. Heavy shit that didn't just float away because you hang out at Home Depot."

I stare at her.

"I know Naomi—"

"Natasha," I correct her.

"—*Natasha* wasn't for you."

That's an understatement. I started therapy right after my divorce as well. Therapist Natasha couldn't have been more than twenty-eight, was barely out of grad school, and was a living, talking Instagram meme. I swear, the shit she said showed up on my social media feed hours after I'd had a session with her.

"Self-care isn't selfish," she'd declare as an LED-lit "Good Vibes Only" sign loomed over her hot-pink and gold office chair in the background. Natasha and I lasted three Zoom sessions before I had to kick rocks.

"But that doesn't mean you can't find *someone* to talk to," Logan continues. "And since you refuse to make an appointment with my guy Henry, you should find someone."

I've told Logan repeatedly I'm not sharing a therapist with her, especially not one named *Henry*.

"Okay, Logan," I say, mostly because I'm tired of being lectured in Jamaica. "I'll find someone when we get back to Atlanta. Is the self-care part of our trip over, or may I continue drinking now?"

Logan laughs and flips me the bird. I settle back into my lounge chair, pulling absently at my purple swim bikini strap, Logan's words still swirling in my head.

"This sunset is unreal," I say after long minutes have passed, staring at the horizon, where a huge cloud is splashed across the sky, encircled by deep oranges and reds.

"It really is," Logan agrees, her voice sleepier. "It's gorgeous. Not corny at all."

I stop staring at the sky and look at her. A wry grin is on her face.

"Tristan's Chatty Kathy ass cannot hold water, dude," I exclaim, shaking my head, as Logan laughs. "You know I didn't mean…"

"Girl, shut up," she interrupts, sliding her sunglasses up on her forehead. "I know you, and I know how you are, and how you think.

Which is why I truly did not give a fuck what you told Tristan about not wanting to come."

"I think he kinda wanted to be here too," I say.

Logan sighs. "Then he should've spoken up when I was putting this together. I'm not a mind reader. Tristan needs to learn how to say what he wants."

I raise my brows at the harshness in her tone.

"Besides, why would he be here when Darren isn't?" she asks.

"I thought you two broke up?"

"I'm not in high school. I don't 'break up.' But we're hanging out again." She shrugs.

"And he'd be here instead of Darren because it's Tristan," I continue.

"Whatever. He should've said something. He's been like this since we were nineteen," she says. "Has he not?" Logan doesn't wait for my answer. "That's why he ended up divorced."

"Damn, Lo."

She rolls her eyes. "You know just as well as I do that he shouldn't have ever been with Melissa in the first place."

I can't really argue with that. Tristan and Melissa are polar opposites, and not in the cute "opposites attract" romance-novel way. Their views of the world, and how that perception shapes the way they move in it, are fundamentally opposed to one another.

"And now they have a whole-ass kid together?" Logan says. "So they're bound to each other for *life*. I love Bella down," she adds quickly, referencing Tristan's adorable two-year-old daughter, "but their dysfunctional marriage was the ultimate consequence of Tristan never being able to say what he wants for real. At work, yeah. And with those emotionally unstable athletes you all have to babysit, sure. But in his actual life?" She shakes her head.

"Seems like you've been wanting to get that off your chest for a while, homie," I say before sipping my drink.

Logan smirks. "I love Tristan, but you know I'm not lying. And this is nothing I haven't told him to his face."

"He was just trying to do the right thing with Melissa. I get it."

"And look where 'doing the right thing' instead of doing what he really wanted to do got him," Logan retorts. "In a fucked-up custody arrangement with a Betty Boop ex-wife."

"A who?"

"Wannabe sexy, mentally unstimulating, phony."

My phone buzzes before I can respond to Logan's unnecessary Betty Boop diss. Logan sips from her drink, brows arched when I pick my cell up from the small table that separates our lounge chairs.

"I know, I know. But I can't just leave my phone in the room. Caleb might call."

Of course, it's not Caleb, but Dillon McCarthy, asking about what he should wear to some gala benefiting youth sports diversity initiatives, as if I'm his personal stylist. I ignore his text, sipping more of my drink to avoid the stress ball that bounces in my stomach every time I have to deal with him.

We didn't terminate his contract. We did put him on a thirty-day probation period, which he agreed to, mostly because back when he signed with us, so-called "diversity" was hot, and it was good for his image to be signed to an agency owned by a Black woman. I'm still not comfortable with the decision, but cutting him loose completely would be a huge setback I'm not sure I can handle right now. I also increased his mandatory time in Mindset Conditioning to twice a week, for one hour, though I'm honestly not convinced you can therapy the inherent asshole out of a person.

I stare out toward the ocean. Keeping Dillon goes beyond the fact that he's not a good person. What I really want is to represent more women. We have a few WNBA players on our roster, which is great, especially now that the league is starting to get more attention. Hopefully, that will soon translate to getting paid the money they truly deserve. But I also want to represent women in sports that don't get enough attention. Gymnasts. Soccer players. Hell, even water polo players. But figuring how to get them paid while keeping my agency afloat is an equation I have not been able to solve yet.

"Your whole face just changed," Logan observes. "This is why you should've left your phone."

"It was Dillon," I say, sighing.

"He knows you're here, right? On vacation. For your birthday." She frowns and rolls her eyes. "What a dick. I really wish you could drop him. We're gonna figure out how to get him gone," she vows.

She stops talking when a man approaches, his brown skin creased from the sun, his long locs hanging down past his shoulders. A collection of bracelets are tied to a rope that hangs over his shoulder.

"Good afternoon, lovelies," he greets us in a singsong Jamaican accent reserved for tourists, instead of his native patois. "Where are you from? California? Atlanta?"

We've already met two people from our small villa who are also from Atlanta, so his guess isn't surprising. He says his name is Cliff, and tells us that he made the bracelets himself, which we all know is a lie, since they sell the exact same ones at the gift shop across the street, for two dollars cheaper than what he's offering.

Logan slips into an animated conversation with him anyway. She doesn't get offended by hustlers. *"You can only be hustled if you're goofy enough to be hustled. And I ain't goofy,"* she's always saying.

Cliff's bracelet selling is momentarily forgotten when she begins chatting with him about the book that's lying across her stomach, something about Pan-Africanism and Black people's connectivity across continents through commerce, which she broke down to me on the short flight here. I'm half listening to their conversation when my phone buzzes again.

Have you seen Dad yet? I can practically hear Caleb's eager voice when I read his text.

We probably won't see each other, I tell him for the tenth time, dusting sand off my fingertips so I don't get it all over the phone Caleb gave me for my birthday, just before I left. The gold heart decorated with tiny diamonds he also gave me dangles from my neck. *His flight is early tomorrow and he's working today. I'm not even sure he's in Negril.*

Last week, Jackson was assigned a story by *AndScape* about Delroy Smith, a British soccer star originally from Negril Hills. Jackson has been on the island for the past three days, following Smith for a feature profile, since he's about to sign with the MLS, potentially becoming the highest-paid player in league history when he joins Atlanta United. We weren't sure if we'd be in Negril at the same time, since Jackson's trip was partially spent on the other side of the island, in Kingston, where Delroy used to train.

I didn't need to tell him how incredible it was that we'd both be on the same island for my fortieth birthday— a trip we talked about taking for years. What Logan didn't know, what nobody knew, was that this trip was supposed to be for me and Jackson. I hadn't cared which island we went to; I just wanted to wake up on my actual fortieth birthday steps away from the beach. With him.

He's in Negril now. Just talked to him.

I sit up a little and immediately glance around the beach when I read Caleb's text, then roll my eyes at my own goofiness when I see nobody but the same two couples from earlier—and Cliff the bracelet man, who's still in a deep conversation with Logan.

I haven't talked to him yet, I type. *Are you good?*

Jackson's younger sister, April, and my ten-year-old nephew Tariq drove up from Brunswick to stay with Caleb at my house while we're both away.

Yup, teaching Tariq how to play chess.

OK, hug him for me. Love you.

Have fun, Mom.

My phone is ringing as Caleb's final text comes through, and I smile at the sight of Jackson's name on my screen.

"Yo, I was literally about to hit you up," I say when I answer. "Caleb just texted me and said you were in town."

"That dude," Jackson says, his chuckle gravelly and low. "One thing he's gonna do is report some shit with urgency."

"His dad is a reporter, so…" I laugh, brushing sand off my thighs. "He's just excited."

"Did he tell you the other news?"

"No, what?"

"Delroy's cousin is the property manager at Idle Awhile."

"Shut up," I say, unable to stop my grin. "So…"

"Yeah. So he just booked me there for the night too."

I take another sip of my drink as the words hang between us for a beat.

"They're not gonna care that you switched hotels?" I ask, referencing the team at AndScape, who took care of his reservations.

"Nah, saves them money."

I shrug and nod like he can see me.

"Are you already here on the property, then?" I ask, glancing toward the water once more, like I expect him to materialize from the ocean.

"Not yet. Still running around with him. I'm actually about forty-five minutes outside of town. We went to the hills earlier. I honestly don't know when we'll be back that way."

My lips twist as I tug as one of my braids.

"What are y'all up to later?" Jackson asks after another second.

I shrug. "I dunno. Lo's calling the shots. I'm just here so I don't get fined."

Jackson chuckles as I finish the rest of my drink. "You should enjoy yourself, Simone. You been in the water yet?"

"Yeah, you know that's the first thing I did. The water is so clear here, and, like, bathtub warm."

"So you doing dinner tonight or hanging there?"

"Logan said something about a restaurant called Catch a Falling Star?"

I hear noise in the background, and Jackson's murmuring something.

"Sounds like you need to go," I say.

"Yeah, I gotta run. If it's not too late when I get back, I'll hit you up. Is that okay?"

"Of course. We're both here, it'd be weird to..." I shake my head. "Yeah, for sure. Hit me up."

"Cool."

I set my phone down after we end the call, just as Cliff ambles away, strumming a Bob Marley tune on the guitar he had looped over his back. Logan passes me one of the brightly colored bracelets she bought from him and I laugh, thanking her.

"You do know these are the same exact ones in the gift shop," I say, sliding it on my wrist.

She shrugs. "At least with him I know where my money is going. So that was Jackson?"

I nod, sitting upright in my chair. "Delroy's cousin is the manager here, and so this is where he's staying."

Logan blinks. "Wow. That's very convenient."

I eye her. "What, you think he—"

"No, I don't think he planned it. It's just... funny."

I poke the inside of my cheek with my tongue. "It doesn't matter anyway, because I probably won't see him. He's not even in the city right now. And he leaves early tomorrow, so..." I shrug again.

Logan studies me but says nothing.

"What?"

"Nothing. I'm starving. Wanna get dinner?" she asks abruptly, setting her empty rum glass on the small table that separates our chairs. "Cliff says Catch a Falling Star is the place even locals sometimes go."

The sky has grown weary of the sun and darkness has enveloped all traces of the sunset, and the string lights from the small resort's restaurant are now shining behind us.

"I'm down for whatever." I gather my stuff and we begin walking toward our rooms. "Wait. No." I stop in my tracks. "Actually, I'm very excited, ecstatic even, about eating dinner. See how 'emotionally checked in' I am?"

Logan smirks. "Fuck you, Simone."

I'm laughing as we head toward our rooms.

Four

A LITTLE OVER AN HOUR later, we're seated at the bar at the outdoor restaurant, sipping a Nebbiolo that Logan chose to go with our meal. It's warm outside, but the red wine is light-bodied and soothing.

Cliff was right. This place is gorgeous. It's tiered, and the sunken dining room directly overlooks the ocean, while tiki lights cast the huge restaurant in a glow. Sade plays softly on speakers overhead. I hold my glass up for a toast, and Logan taps her glass against mine lightly.

"You know Betty Boop was actually based on a Black jazz singer named Esther Jones," I say, eyeing Logan over my glass.

She laughs, pulling at the string bracelet she brought earlier on the beach. The yellow in the braiding matches her wispy yellow sundress. "You went to the room and looked it up, huh?"

I grin but say nothing as my phone buzzes.

Are you at dinner already?

Yep.

Did you end up at Catch a Falling Star?

Yep, here now.

Mind if I crash?

Nope. Not at all.

I set my phone back down on the bar and glance at Logan. "Jackson is on the way."

"With that cutie-pie soccer player?"

"I think so."

"How old is he again?"

"Thirty-ish, I think?"

Logan hums in response as she lifts her chin toward the restaurant entrance. "Damn, he must've been standing outside of the restaurant when he texted you," she says.

I follow Logan's gaze to the entrance, framed by palm trees and draped in white lights. Jackson's there, standing next to Delroy, wearing an eggshell-white linen shirt with the sleeves rolled up to his elbows, his tattoos visible against his dark skin. He hasn't shaved, so the hair on his face is thicker, accentuating his mouth.

It takes two seconds for him to spot me, for our gazes to connect. I can't control my smile at the sight of him. He tips his head toward me and, still grinning, leans over to tell Delroy something. A few seconds later, they're making their way toward us at the huge circular bar, which is lit with soft string lights.

"Hey," Jackson says, biting the corner of his lip as he smiles, hovering over my barstool.

"Hi." I smile up at him.

"Happy birthday eve," he says as I slide off my stool and hug him, breathing in his clean scent as he pulls me close. When we separate, his gaze skims over my spaghetti-strap orange beach dress, lingering on the thigh-high slit, before meeting my eyes.

Quick introductions are made, and we settle in at the bar, Jackson between us, Delroy beside Logan.

"What's up, Action Jackson?" Logan asks, swinging her attention back to Jackson. "I thought you were possibly in Kingston?"

"We got back to this side of the island earlier today," Jackson answers, grinning, revealing a dimple. "Been running nonstop since we got here."

"I had to show Jackson all my old spots," Delroy explains in his deep voice carrying a singsong accent. There's an appreciative glint in his eye when he answers Logan. "I gotta give him the true view of my country."

"So what did the 'true view' entail, exactly?" Logan asks, letting her braids fall over her shoulder when she tilts her head to meet Delroy's eyes.

"A few bars, the river we used to swim in. We stopped by my auntie's place about twenty minutes away from the city."

"I had the best oxtails of my life," Jackson tells Logan before glancing at me.

"Nice," I say, as Delroy grins, reminding Jackson he has to put that part about meeting his auntie in his article, otherwise he'll be disowned.

I glance at Jackson when Delroy makes the request, already knowing there's no way Jackson will be told what to put in his stories. It's one of the things that make him so good—his perspective comes through effortlessly, because he observes and absorbs everything, and then sorts and filters it out for others to soak up.

"We've only been here for a few hours, so we haven't seen much besides the beach," Logan says.

"Well, I'm here for another day or so if you'd like a tour," Delroy says, probably in offer to both of us, but he's staring at Logan when he says it.

She flashes a smile. "I actually would love a tour. But it's Simone's birthday, so this trip is all about her."

Delroy raises his brows and looks at me. "You should come let me show you two the real Negril."

I smile. "Okay. I'll let you and Logan set it up."

"My fault for blowin' up y'all's spot," Jackson says, nodding toward my wine glass and our appetizers.

His warm, woodsy scent is there on my inhale.

"Simone was just breaking down the origins of Betty Boop, so you really got here just in time," Logan says, placing her cheek in her palm and making a loud snoring noise.

"Oh, word? That's what we're doing?" I ask as Logan laughs, taking another sip of her wine.

A group seated at the opposite side of the bar glance over at us, some whispering when they recognize Delroy. Two of them slide from their seats and approach him for a quick hello, which he handles smoothly, flashing a practiced smile and signing an autograph before they saunter way.

"So are you ready for Atlanta?" Logan asks, doing a bounce-dance in her seat, causing Delroy to smile at her again.

"I can't wait. I'm ready to get out of London," he confesses as Logan leans forward, interest clearly piqued as the two of them fall into easy conversation.

"Did you all order yet?" Jackson asks.

He signals to the cute bartender after I tell him we haven't. Her eyes are big and round and her dark brown skin appears even smoother with her hair slicked back into a low bun. She smiles at Delroy, then lets her gaze linger on Jackson as she takes our food and drink orders.

"Anything else I can get you?" she asks, her attention focused on Jackson.

"We're good for now. I appreciate it."

She nods and smiles again before heading to the other side of the bar to put in our orders.

"What?" I ask, catching Jackson's gaze as the bartender walks away, a small smile playing at my lips.

His gaze trails over my face, dipping from my lips, which are bare aside from blush-pink lip gloss, to my collarbone, down to my crossed legs.

"Forty looks good on you."

My body warms at the way he's looking at me, and I grin. "I'm technically not forty yet."

He lets his gaze trail over me again. "Then that dress looks good on you."

Our gazes connect and I inhale, then let the breath out slowly. "Thank you."

Jackson has always liked me in orange. I don't want to think about whether I subconsciously wore the color tonight knowing there was a chance I might see him.

"So how you feelin'?" he asks, his gaze perceptive as ever when I lean back in the high-back barstool and suck in the damp island air. The music has switched and now eighties yacht rock is overhead, the watery R&B sounds of Hall & Oates softly floating in the air.

"Not as heavy as before I landed," I answer.

He nods, his gaze skimming over my face again, lingering on my lips for a beat. "Good."

"I had a dream about you the other night," I admit after another second.

He looks at me, brow arched, a trace of amusement dancing in his eyes. I dream a lot. Sometimes the dreams are surreal, a hodgepodge of abstract scenes involving people, sometimes people I've barely even met, in absurd situations, like getting their hair washed over my grandmother's kitchen sink. But sometimes, they border on premonition, a thin outline of things to come, or light sketches that fill in the blanks on past things.

There were many mornings when I'd roll over in bed, eager to share my latest dream with Jackson. Sometimes I didn't even have to say anything. He'd just open his eyes and peer at me sleepily. *"What was it about this time?"* he'd ask, his baritone early-morning groggy, half amused.

"What was I doing in the dream?" he asks now as he takes a swig of his beer.

"We were high up on Spaghetti Junction, and I was having a panic attack. You were trying to talk me down from it."

"What'd I say?"

I shrug. "I don't remember exactly. Something along the lines of 'Drive, baby, just drive, you're okay,'" I say, attempting to mimic his deep voice.

He laughs. "So did it work?"

"No. I woke up just when we were about to fall off the edge."

"Damn," he says, chuckling before he takes another swig. "Did we actually hit the ground?"

"Um, *no*. If you actually ever land when you're falling in a dream, you wake up dead."

Jackson laughs again. "That sounds like some shit you made up."

"Nah, google it."

He rolls his eyes, still smirking when he sets his beer on the bar counter. "So what do you think it means?"

I shrug. "I dunno. Something? Nothing? It was just weird. I actually… I actually dream about you pretty often," I admit, my voice quieter.

Jackson doesn't look up as he wipes condensation from his bottle slowly with his thumb. "And what do you think that means?" He tilts his head when he looks up at me.

"I dunno." I pick up my wine and take another healthy sip. "So how are you feeling about the story?" I ask to break the heavy silence that lingers between the two of us.

I glance at Delroy and Logan as they get up from the bar, heading a few feet away, where there's a view of the darkened ocean just beyond the string-lit railing. Delroy is pointing out toward the water as Logan nods at whatever he's telling her.

"I know you've been running around for the past few days," I say. "Are you tired?"

Jackson's eyes are low, and he drags a hand down his face when I ask the question. "It's been pretty nonstop, and I had some other work to catch up on while I was out here too. It's been a long day."

"You know you didn't have to come here. You probably wanted to crash in your room and—"

I stop talking when Jackson looks at me. He pushes out a breath, and squints out toward the black water splashing softly against the rocks.

"You know what I'm really feeling lately? Restless."

"That's a very specific word choice." I tilt my head and study him, watching the way his jaw works as he considers his next words.

He scratches the thick stubble on his jaw. "Shit just feels… unsettled lately."

"How so?"

He exhales but says nothing as he studies me. It's intense, and I blink, looking down into my wine glass. I need a refill, and before I can even say so, Jackson is signaling the flirty bartender.

"Thank you for the phone and the necklace," I say once I receive the wine.

Jackson's gaze trails to my fingers, where I'm absently toying with the gold chain. "Caleb got you those gifts."

"With your money."

He shakes his head. "Nah, he had a good amount. I just put in the rest for him."

I know Caleb's financial status—broke. "A good amount" means Jackson mostly paid for it.

"So… forty." He grins at me.

"I feel like I should have something super insightful to say about it, but I, unfortunately, do not."

Jackson laughs. "People put way too much on turning forty, anyway, especially in America."

"That's literally what I told Tristan a few weeks ago," I agree. "Time is a construct."

"Then no big plans for tomorrow?"

"I just really wanted to wake up on the beach on my fortieth. That was really always it."

There's a trace of something in Jackson's eyes when they meet mine again. "I remember."

I grab my wine glass, pressing it to my lips. We never talk about the past versions of ourselves, the things we used to say to each other, the things we used to dream out loud to one another, and no one else.

"But I actually am doing something," I say, breaking the heavy moment. "Logan planned a self-realization class—"

"A self-*manifestation* class," Logan interjects as she and Delroy slide back into their seats out of nowhere. I didn't even see them approaching.

"Oh, word?" Jackson grins, leaning back in his seat.

"I'm turning over a new leaf," I say, waving a hand in front of me. "I'm on a new *leap*. Get it? Because it's the leap year."

Jackson chuckles, eyeing me. "I see your corny ain't gone nowhere."

I roll my eyes as I take another sip. "Shut up."

"So how's that work?" he asks.

"My new leap?"

"The class," he clarifies, eyes amused when he looks from me to Logan.

"We'll sit out on the beach and manifest some shit, I guess." Logan shrugs as Jackson chuckles again.

He takes the last swallow of his beer and orders another as the waiter sets our food down.

"This pasta is righteous," I say after a beat, forking up another bite of tender noodles.

"Yeah, this spot is legit," he agrees as he scoops up more rice and peas. I glance out toward the blackened water, inhaling the damp, salty air. When my gaze falls on Jackson, he's already looking at me. I grin, biting on the inside of my lip before forking up more pasta.

"How's it been going so far?" I ask after I swallow a bite, lowering my voice so that Delroy can't hear.

"Dude is somethin' else," Jackson replies. "Had me all over this island. I had to remind buddy I ain't strapped out here."

"*Jackson.*"

"We went to meet up with one of his boys at some house party in Kingston, and he almost got into it with a dude he grew up with."

"Over what?" I ask in a hushed tone.

"I dunno. Some shit that happened when they were teenagers. Who knows. It was looking dicey for a minute, though. Literally, because ol' dude pulled out a knife."

"*Jackson,*" I say again.

"He seems to be good people, though," he says, ignoring my concern. "You might wanna holler at him. He said he wants to work with a smaller agency. Feels like he's being mishandled by the big boys."

I glance over at Delroy, who now is toying with one of Logan's braids as she leans closer to him.

"Maybe I will. I need to think about getting some more things going, because…" I shake my head and frown when I think about Dillon McCarthy.

"Don't do that," Jackson says, reaching out and smoothing a thumb between my eyebrows, where my forehead is creased.

I suck in a breath at his touch and our eyes meet. He drops his hand and picks up his beer, taking another swig as I return my attention to my plate, which is still half full because the portions are huge.

Logan sets down her wine glass and leans forward with that look in her eye that tells me she's about to turn this into A Moment. "Let's do something," she says.

"Since it's Simone's birthday eve, and she's stepping into a new decade—let's each share what we want most for ourselves in the next ten years." Jackson leans back in his chair, meeting my eyes.

"Okay, Ms. Logan, I'll start," Delroy speaks up. He's switched from Red Stripe to what looks like bourbon, and he's now talking a little louder. "First, happy birthday, Simone. I'm glad we met today."

"Thank you," I reply. "Me too."

"Okay, back to the question," Logan prods Delroy, waving a hand in his direction. "In the next ten years, you want…"

"What I want in the next decade is peace," Delroy says, his gaze falling on Logan again. "Everything else—the money, the fame, all of it—doesn't mean a fuckin' thing if you don't have that."

"Oh shit, we're getting deep out here, I see. Hell yeah." Logan offers Delroy a high five as the waitress comes and clears our plates.

"All right, your turn," Delroy says, tilting his chin up at Logan.

"Honestly, I just want a remote control that can pause other people from talking. People need to learn to just shut the hell *up* sometimes."

Delroy laughs as Jackson chuckles beside me.

"Nope," I press Logan. "Delroy is out here baring his soul. You gotta be for real too."

Logan sighs. "All right. What I want is"—she pauses, searching for her words—"depth. I'm tired of feeling like I'm skimming the surface of everything in my life."

Delroy nods as Logan takes another swig of wine, her gaze briefly trailing toward the blackened water crashing softly against the rocks before she looks at Jackson.

"Your turn," she tells him.

"Time," he says immediately. "I always need more of it."

He looks at me, his expression unreadable but heavy.

"Simone?" Logan asks.

"Clarity," I say after a beat. I don't say anything more as we all grow quiet.

"To clarity," Logan finally says, picking up her glass and raising it in a toast.

I meet Jackson's thoughtful gaze as our glasses clink together.

Five

IT'S AFTER MIDNIGHT WHEN WE get back to the villas. Logan says goodnight and heads to her room, flashing me a look before she does. Delroy seemed both mildly disappointed and pleased when we parted ways at the restaurant. I figure he's used to getting women whenever and however he wants. The fact that Logan didn't make herself immediately available to him was probably part of the appeal.

"Thanks again for dinner," I tell Jackson, since he paid for everything when the bill came.

"You're welcome."

"It's so pretty at night here," I say, looking toward the sky, which is dotted with a few stars.

The palm trees cast shadows along our path, small lamps illuminating the way. The air is still balmy, clinging to my skin.

"I kinda wish…"

Jackson looks at me, waiting for me to finish my thought. I kinda wish he didn't have to leave in the morning—that's what I want to say, but even though the wine in my system has been feeling loose and warm, I hold the words in my throat.

"You feel like gettin' in the water with me?" Jackson asks.

"Like, in the ocean?"

Jackson grins and stuffs his hands in his pockets. "Yeah, like in the ocean."

We pause on the walkway, a few feet from my door. I look up at him. "It's almost one in the morning."

Jackson doesn't respond, just looks at me.

"And there are barracudas out at night."

At that, he laughs. "Barracudas?"

I nod, my lips twitching as I attempt to hold in my smile.

"C'mon and get in the water with me," he says, his voice low. He meets my eyes, tilting his head, and I feel a flutter in my belly.

"Okay."

"I'll meet you here in five."

I nod and head to my door, turning to watch as Jackson walks in the opposite direction. The room is cooler than outside, but not by much. I go over to my suitcase and pull out a black swimsuit. It's another two-piece—the one Logan picked out for me because "there ain't no kids on this trip and you don't need to be in mommy mode."

I quickly undress and slide it on, determined not to overthink meeting Jackson in the water. I don't even check myself in the mirror, not wanting to see my reflection and talk myself out of what I'm about to do.

No more than ten minutes later, Jackson and I make our way through the night toward the darkened water. A few twinkles of light dot the coastline.

"It's so beautiful," I say softly.

"It really is," he agrees.

He's holding a bottle of wine and two hotel water cups because our rooms aren't equipped with wine glasses. We reach the warm sand, and he pours me a glass first before pouring one for himself and setting the bottle in the sand. We toast, meeting each other's eyes before I strip off my cover-up, watching as Jackson shrugs out of his t-shirt, dropping it silently in the sand. My gaze automatically travels over the hard planes of his chest, lingering on the new ink just below his breastbone.

"You got a new tattoo?" I ask, stepping closer to get a glimpse of *29:11* written in a small, stark font.

My eyes find his in the dark. It almost feels like a betrayal, like the tattoo is a physical representation of the fact that I no longer know the intimate details that define him.

"What is that? Jeremiah?"

Jackson nods, confirming my assumption that it's his favorite Bible verse.

"When'd you get it?" I ask, trying to conceal the irrational tinge of hurt in my voice.

"A year ago," he says, meeting my eyes. I see his chest rise and fall with his silent exhale.

"It's dope," I say quietly. "I kinda wanna get one still." I turn toward the edge of the water. "A cute, tiny heart."

I go in first, glad the water has retained most of its warmth from earlier in the day, so it only takes a few seconds for me to get used to the temperature. I look up at the black sky, dotted with stars, and smile over my shoulder at Jackson. His gaze slides up from my butt, lingering on my lips before he meets my eyes.

"Where?" he finally asks.

I shrug. "Somewhere nobody can see except me."

I take a sip of the wine I've carried into the water, enjoying the soft hint of cherry notes. I stare up at the stars, the salty water clinging to my skin.

"I talked to Ty earlier today," Jackson tells me after long seconds have passed, referencing my brother, as he sinks down farther into the water, so that it touches the tops of his broad shoulders. "Said he might be in Atlanta next month sometime."

"Yeah, he wants us to have dinner if he ends up coming. I was gonna ask you about it."

My brother did not get the memo that Jackson and I are divorced. Or rather, he ignored the memo that Jackson and I are no longer together because every time he's in town, he wants for all of us to link up.

"He's Caleb's dad and we're still family, ain't we?" is Ty's mantra.

"Would it be weird if I got a tattoo, like right here?" I ask, pointing to the side of my ribcage.

"Yeah," Jackson says. "But you're a little weird, so…" He shrugs, and I splash water at him.

He chuckles, reaching and grabbing my free hand, pulling me closer to him.

"Right here." His thumb traces my wrist, leaving droplets of water. "This is where you should get it."

"You think?"

He tugs my hand, and I sway closer, breathing in salt water and his clean scent. We stare at each for a long minute, with the sound of the water lapping gently against our skin. I let out a slow breath when Jackson's gaze drops to my lips again.

"We should probably get out," I manage. "I'm a little cold."

His gaze trails to where the cold has left its mark beneath my suit. He nods, finally releasing my hand. We gather our things and walk slowly to my room. Jackson's shirt is back on, hands stuffed in his swim trunks as I fish for my key. He stands close behind me—so close his heat and scent overwhelm my senses. The way he's been looking at me all night hasn't helped.

"Simone."

Jackson's voice is a low hum when he says my name. I turn, pressing my back against the door as I look up at him. His gaze dips to my mouth as he steps closer, hands still in his pockets. I take in his face—his long lashes, his growing beard, his full lips. When our eyes meet, the heat in his gaze is almost overwhelming. The air between us feels heavy, damp.

I grab the hem of his shirt. Jackson steps forward, closing the distance between us as I rise on my toes to meet his mouth.

The kiss is hungry and electric. Familiar yet brand new. His tongue parts my lips, demanding and warm. My skin pebbles, my stomach tightens, and it feels as if I can't draw in air. When I do, my inhales are all Jackson, his cedar scent mixing with salt air.

His stubble scratches my skin as he presses me fully against the door, the soft thud echoing in the quiet, his big hand palming one hip. The kiss is hungry and hot, like it's been way too long, and we have to soak each other up as quickly and thoroughly as possible. He bites then sucks on my bottom lip, his groan low when a hungry noise climbs its way from deep in my belly and escapes my lips, floating in the heavy air between us.

His lips slip to the curve of my neck, and he kisses his way down to my collarbone, before replacing lips with tongue. I let out a harsh breath, my hips automatically arching toward him. He moves back up to my mouth, kissing me again. Our breaths are weighted, and I slip my hands beneath his shirt, fingers tracing the taut skin of his stomach. He braces himself with one hand on the door above my head, while the other slides restlessly up over my hip to my ribcage, just below my breast and back down. My skin is on fire everywhere he is touching me, even through the thin material of my cover-up.

He pulls back a little, meeting my eyes, then leans forward again and sucks on my lower lip before kissing me. The kiss is slower and somehow hungrier, and I can't stop the soft noise that rises from my belly. Jackson's groan is low and dark when I make the sound, and he kisses the dent below my lip, the corner of my mouth, then trails his mouth to my jaw and kisses me there before returning to my mouth and parting my lips with his again, sucking lightly on my tongue. My hips are arching toward him, my breasts heavy, nipples straining against the material of my swimsuit. Jackson's thumb is just beneath my breast, tracing the curve, his touch barely there.

He pulls back a fraction, bumping his nose with mine. His eyes are framed by eyelashes so long they tangle at the tips, and his gaze is dark, possessive. He's hovering millimeters from my lips, watching me, waiting to see if I'll come to him.

I do, pressing up on my toes, tugging on the hem of his shirt, brushing my fingers against his stomach muscles. This time, when he leans forward, he doesn't kiss me. He traces his tongue over my bottom lip before he sucks on it. My breaths are heavy and hot, heat pulsing between my legs at the sensation, at how *sexy* Jackson is. I feel his erection pressing against my lower belly, and I drag in another ragged breath when his rough fingers skate over my hip again, pulling me tighter against him.

Jackson turns his head, his lips brushing the shell of my ear. "Tell me what you want."

"I want you," I admit, pushing the door open.

Jackson follows me inside.

Six

THE FIRST TIME JACKSON AND I made love, I knew our connection went beyond the physical. It was more than my twenty-two-year old, inexperienced mind could comprehend at the time. I only knew that it was there, humming beneath my skin, present in my blood cells that jumped to attention when he touched me, swimming through my body, giving me life. Before Jackson, I'd only been with one other guy, Sharif, and our relationship only lasted about a year. But even then, I understood that what Jackson and I shared was marrow-deep, feral, and electric.

It's like that now.

There are no words between us, only damp, tangled sheets, slivers of light peeking between the thick wooden blinds, and the electric chemistry that's always existed between us. As if the years we were together and the years we spent apart have collided, creating something ancient and new, all at once.

He is sucking on my neck and my inner muscles are clenching around him, holding him deep inside me. I tilt my chin toward the ceiling, my lips parted as noises I've never heard myself make escape my chest. Jackson groans darkly, covering my mouth with his again, sucking on my tongue as he yanks on my braids, angling my head another way. The kiss is urgent and hungry, and he pulls on my hair again when another noise leaves my lips. I trail my fingers over his flexed biceps, his damp skin.

I arch up to meet his steady thrusts, and he slides his muscled forearm under my knee, hitching my leg up so that he can get deeper. He's been in control the entire time, contorting my body to fit with his just the way he wants it. Our gazes connect in the darkness of the room again, and goosebumps pebble on my skin at the intensity of his stare. He presses his forehead to mine, breathing hotly against my mouth, his movements inside me in tune with our breathing, and I'm so hot I feel as if I will dissolve.

I moan, digging my nails into his damp back and biting his shoulder, and he buries his head between my neck and collarbone, biting the skin there a little roughly, a deep sound leaving his chest. He moves his head, kissing me again, as he moves faster.

The soft light from the wide patio doors drifts over us, the breeze soft because the windows are cracked, filling the room with the soft scent of salt. My breath is coming in short pants, my muscles clenching around him, and I dig my fingers harder into his back. I can't read his expression when he lifts his head from my neck and stares down at me in the darkened room, and then flips us, holding on to my hips.

I know I won't last long when I sink down on him and start moving. He feels so good, and the acknowledgement tumbles out of my mouth in whisper-groan as I wet my lips, my breaths coming in sharp, short spurts. Jackson looks down to where we're joined, biting on the corner of his lip, before lifting his head and capturing a nipple in his mouth. The sensation makes me lose my balance, and I fall forward as Jackson starts moving, taking control even in this position.

He palms my butt, then slaps it lightly, and my groan matches his. I feel my orgasm climbing from the pit of my belly, and when

Jackson slaps my butt again, that's it. I cry out his name, and it's muffled because he's kissing me again as I violently spasm around him. He flips us again, oblivious to the tangled mess we've made of the light cotton sheets, driving into me faster, hunting down his own orgasm, which comes seconds later, a near-growl escaping his chest, his handsome features contorted in pleasure.

Our breathing is still heavy when he meets my eyes as he hovers over me, and again I can't read what he's thinking. I open my mouth to say something, but he shakes his head, almost imperceptibly, before brushing his nose against mine. He parts my lips with his, then flicks his tongue against mine, before increasing the pressure. For a while, we just kiss, slowly.

Jackson pecks my lips again, then rolls onto his back and pulls me into the crook of his arm. I slide my leg over his thigh. My eyelids are heavy as I inhale his skin, blocking out all thoughts in this moment, allowing his familiar scent to lull me to sleep.

Seven

I WAKE UP GROGGY AND disoriented. It takes a few seconds to remember where I am—to understand why my limbs feel heavy and sated, my skin sticky with sweat, my sheets saturated with Jackson's scent. There's a hollow in the mattress where he should be, and I blink again, scanning the room. It's still mostly dark, with only threads of dawn light creeping through the window. My swimsuit and cover up sits folded neatly in the chair tucked into the corner, not crumpled on the floor where Jackson peeled it off last night. He's perched on the edge of the bed, already fully dressed in joggers, a backward Falcons ball cap, and a t-shirt that stretches across his muscled chest, scrolling through his phone.

I feel the first prickles of panic starting to tingle in my belly. I had sex with Jackson last night. Hot, needy, sweaty, frantic sex with Jackson. My ex-husband. I close my eyes briefly, as the fog that's been hanging over me since last night begins to dissipate. I open my eyes again, and lick my lips, which are swollen from Jackson's kisses and bites.

The blue light from the screen illuminates the strong planes of his face, his facial hair, which is thicker than it was last night.

"Morning," I say, sitting up and rubbing my face.

"Morning," he says, turning to look at me over his shoulder. "Happy birthday."

I release a slow breath. Jackson's gaze travels from my lips down to his undershirt, which I slipped on sometime in the night when I got chilled.

"You've been up for a while," I say, my voice still early-morning quiet.

He nods. "My flight leaves in a few hours."

"What time is the car coming for you?" I ask, since the drive from Negril to the airport at Montego Bay is about an hour and half.

"About thirty minutes."

He bites the inside of his lip as he studies me. A rush of warmth coats my skin all over again, and my breaths increase.

"It's okay," he says, voice calm, reading my expression through slightly narrowed eyes. That's always been Jackson's talent. Reading me, even when I don't want to be read.

I nod quickly, and he returns his attention to his phone, rapidly typing.

"I can't tell what you're thinking anymore," I admit after a long moment of silence. At that, Jackson looks up at me. "Even last night…" I lift a shoulder.

Silence stretches between us, and I watch Jackson release a breath, his broad chest lifting with the movement when he sets his phone down and glances toward the patio door. The blinds are still closed, but tiny slivers of early-morning light are peeking through.

"Last night I was thinking about how much I miss you," he finally says, meeting my eyes. "And how angry I still am that I have to miss you."

My lips part and I breathe in, looking out the half-open window.

"I don't know what to say to that," I admit.

"Caleb texted earlier," he says, breaking the silence that's settled in the room again. "I told him it was okay for him to go ahead and head over to my place, since I'll be back in town this evening."

"Did you make sure he knows he can't have company?" This is exactly how teenagers end up doing things they have no business doing with their teenaged bodies.

"Why would I tell him that?" Jackson's eyes are on his phone again. "He knows what's acceptable behavior and what isn't."

I sigh as I climb out of the bed and head for the bathroom. I use the toilet and brush my teeth and then quickly wash my face. When I emerge Jackson is still seated on the edge of the bed, looking out of the now-open blinds toward the beach, where workers are raking the soft sand into clean lines, ridding the shore of seaweed, preparing it for the day's tourists.

He still hasn't shaved, and his facial hair is approaching a full beard, his plain black t-shirt stretching across his chest, revealing the tattoos on his bicep more clearly. He reaches for me when I hesitate, pulling me to stand in between his open legs. He runs his hands up my thighs, and chill bumps break out on my arms as I exhale, meeting his eyes as he stares up at me. He pulls me by the hips, pressing a kiss to my belly button through my shirt, his thumbs rubbing slow circles on my hips. My heart is racing. I close my eyes, finally allowing myself to lean into him as I run my fingers down the back of his neck.

"Simone," he says against my belly.

I open my eyes and look down at him. "Don't climb so far into your head I can't find you, okay?"

He looks up and meets my eyes.

I open my mouth then close it. Jackson waits for me to speak, still making slow circles with his thumbs on my hips.

"When you talked to Caleb earlier, you didn't tell him we—"

"We what, Simone? What'd we do last night?"

"You didn't tell him you were here with me," I finish.

"No. I didn't."

My relief is palpable, and I swallow.

"But it would've been a problem if I had?" Jackson is still looking up at me, wearing that same new expression he had from last night. It's distant and foreign. Assessing.

"I don't think he needs to know about this, no."

He looks away, shaking his head.

"What? You *do* think he should know the details of…"

I stop talking when Jackson fixes a look on me. "C'mon, Simone. It ain't the details you're worried about, right?"

"I just don't think it's smart to talk to him about our… whatever this was. I mean… we were drinking and there were palm trees, it was my birthday…"

Jackson's expression is flat. "Word? So this was a birthday fuck for you?"

I suck in a breath, my brow wrinkled. "You know me better than that."

I release the breath, and Jackson releases me. It's warm in the room, but my body is instantly colder when I perch myself on the edge of the bed. He gets up and moves to lean against the small wooden desk facing the bed, runs a hand down his face, and exhales heavily as he looks at me.

"I'm sorry I said that." Jackson breaks his gaze when his phone buzzes. He pulls it out of his pocket and sends a text. "The car is outside." He stares at me for a beat. "Shit can't get weird with us, Simone."

"I know. I agree."

He shakes his head again, gnawing on the inside of his lip.

"What, Jackson? Why are you—"

"Because I knew better," he says.

"You *knew better?*"

"But I still haven't figured out how to not—"

"To not what?"

"To not want you," he answers, meeting my eyes squarely.

His words hit me in the chest, and I grab the edge of the mattress as he looks off toward the patio door.

"Shit never *ends* with us," he says almost to himself.

"And what does *that* mean?" My voice is quiet, barely a whisper.

"You've never been sure about this." There's a humorless chuckle in his voice when he says it.

"*What?* I *married* you, Jackson."

"And that took how long, Simone? Ten years after we met? Caleb was already going into first grade before you decided you finally wanted to be for real about this. And that was more so that your last names would match more than anything else."

"Are you for real right now?" I ask, leaning forward.

"The second shit got really real, you were ready to dip. You were *always* ready to—"

"That was *you*, Jackson," I interrupt, shaking my head. "*You're* the one who left."

His shifts his stance where he remains perched on the edge of the desk. "That's what we're still calling it? I *left?*"

My gaze drops to the mattress. "No," I admit. "But you were gone and it was too much…"

"I moved to Charlotte for *us*. We both agreed it was the best temporary move for our family so that we could afford to keep shit going while you built Sage."

"Your taking that gig in Charlotte was never really about me building Sage, and we both know it!" I exclaim. "It was about you feeling like you needed to level up in your career."

"You know what I was doing before Charlotte?" he counters. "Uber-ing, substitute teaching, trying to get steady freelance work."

Jackson stuffs his hands in his sweats pockets and looks at me.

"Yeah, Simone. I did need to take that job. I needed to know that I could take care of us financially, and do it not working bullshit jobs that I hated. So moving to Charlotte for a minute is what made sense for our long game. And you said you were down for that, remember? You said you were onboard."

"Because I didn't want you to resent me!" I scoot to the edge of the bed. "I knew that if I would've told you to turn down that job, you would've ended up resenting me for it and we would've fell apart."

"We did that anyway," Jackson says.

The air between us is thick, heavy in my chest on my inhale. I feel tears welling in my eyes but will them away, pressing my lips together as I look out toward the patio.

"Fuck, Simone." He stares down at the floor, hands still stuffed in his pockets, before he looks at me again. "C'mere," he says, beckoning me to him. "Please?" he tacks on when I don't immediately move.

I get up and pad over to him barefoot, and he widens his stance so I can stand in between his legs. I lean against his body, letting his warmth envelop me as I hold on to the bottom edge of his t-shirt. His hands are still stuffed in his pockets, but he drops his head, nuzzling the top of my ear with his nose, his facial hair scratching the skin there.

"You were holding back last night," I say, against his chest, my voice quiet. "I felt it."

I feel his exhale against my chest.

"I get it," I say.

"No. You don't," Jackson replies, his voice raw, quiet.

His phone buzzes again in his pocket, and he pulls it out.

"I'm on the way out now," he says when he answers.

He pushes his phone back into his pocket and looks down at me, tugging lightly at the end of my braids so that I'm forced to tilt my head up and meet his eyes.

"I like these," he says, toying with a braid. I smile, and he does too before his smile fades at the edges. "We're not your parents, Simone."

My brow wrinkles in shock when I stare up at him. His serious expression doesn't change.

"That was never our path. I'm sorry that I ever let you think it was."

I blink, still too stunned to speak.

He glances at the door. "I don't like leaving shit hanging like this between us," he admits. "We need to talk for real."

My gaze drops to his chest.

"Don't go silent on me," he warns. "I mean it."

I nod, swallowing the lump in my throat. "I won't."

"I'll tell Caleb to call you when he gets to my house." He presses a quick kiss to my forehead before gently setting me aside.

I watch as he crosses the room, pausing at the door. "Try to manifest something good in that class today," he says before sliding out of the room.

Eight

IT'S BARELY NINE A.M. WHEN I make my way to the villa's outdoor restaurant that leads to the beach. I couldn't go back to sleep after Jackson left my room. I just sat there, staring out at the patio, replaying the words we exchanged, replaying the way he felt inside of me, replaying the new way he looked at me.

Sleeping with him just opened up a new can of worms. I know that. All the unresolved shit between us just came rushing out, like a balloon releasing air after it's been popped. But I wanted him. I still do. Our chemistry is intoxicating and I still feel a little buzzed from it, hours later. I still smell his scent in my skin, even after showering.

The sun is glowing bright in the blue sky and the salt-scented air is humid and warm as I walk along the palm-tree-dotted path toward the small restaurant that faces the beach. I spot Logan seated at one of the white bistro tables, sipping from a teacup. I slide into the seat across from her, dropping my clear beach bag, stuffed with my phone, sunscreen, and key, into the seat next to me.

"Morning," I greet her, grabbing the coffee on the table and pouring myself a cup.

She grins, her shades covering her eyes. "How'd you sleep?" she asks.

I sip, enjoying the caffeine and the pureness of the coffee, which is better than anything I've had a in a while. "Good."

"Jackson already went to the airport?"

I nod.

She looks at me, holding back a smile before tilting her chin toward me. "You have a hickey on your neck."

"Shit," I whisper, setting my cup down and grabbing my neck as Logan laughs.

"I'm joking," she says, still chuckling as I flip her the bird. "But at least I know for sure what you were doing last night. Or should I say, *who*."

I sigh, glad my large sunglasses are covering my expression because I'm almost on the verge of tears… again. Logan's smirk immediately falls from her lips, and she leans forward, shaking her head.

"Damn, it wasn't…"

"Of course it was," I say. "It's me and Jackson. It *always* is with us. He's… We…" I shake my head. "Our chemistry is just… *insane*. Always. Like my atoms are fucking attached to his or something. It messes with me. But…" I shake my head. "It scares me."

"What scares you?" Logan asks.

"That our chemistry is always so explosive. Because I wonder if it glossed over shit we should've noticed sooner in our marriage, or even before we got married, you know?"

Logan leans back in her seat. "So what are you gonna do?" she asks.

"Wha*t can* I do?"

"Whatever you want to do, Simone."

"We're divorced for a reason."

"And what is that reason again?" she asks. She begins spreading jam over her piece of toast. "You don't seem to know. I doubt he does either."

"Well, that's fucked up," I say, frowning before I sip more coffee. "You know how we were at the end. Arguing *all of the time*. We couldn't even breathe in the same room without getting into it. We were so angry with each other."

Logan twists her lips but says nothing.

"We kinda got into a little bit this morning again. He's *still* so angry with me…" I trail off, letting go of a breath. "Anyways." I look out toward the beach.

Logan chews in silence as she observes me. "Delroy texted me this morning," she says after a minute, knowing I need the subject change.

"Already?" I ask, though I'm not surprised based on his behavior last night.

"He's trying to have dinner when we get back to Atlanta."

"He seems cool. And smitten."

Logan shrugs, nodding, as my phone buzzes.

"Hey, Mom," I greet Cynthia as she and my dad, Barry, sing an incredibly out-of-tune version of Stevie Wonder's "Happy Birthday" together. "Thank you," I say when they finish.

"How's the beach?" Mom asks.

"It's nice, pretty," I answer.

"I talked to Caleb yesterday. He said Jackson was in the same place as you, working on an article."

There's a hint of skepticism in her voice when she says it.

"Yep. We linked up for dinner," I volunteer. "We had a good time."

"Well, that's fun. I'm glad he was able to make time for dinner with you." She says it casually, but as usual, there's an undertone to her words.

I bite the inside of my lip to keep from responding, frowning as I look toward the ocean.

"All right, talk to you later, Simone. Happy birthday," my dad yells in the background.

He's no doubt off on his usual Saturday morning routine, hunting down obscure car parts for his muscle car. He has a competition in a couple of weeks. I know "later" for him means the next time I reach out to him, since I can count on one hand the number of times my father has picked up the phone to call me since I moved to Atlanta at eighteen.

"So how was the dinner?" Mom asks.

"It was really nice. Relaxing and pretty."

"Caleb said you two were staying in the same resort?"

I sign internally. Jackson is right about Caleb's inclination to be a reporter. "Yeah, it ended up working out that way."

My mom makes a humming noise that I probably shouldn't respond to. I do anyway.

"What, Mom?" I ask wearily.

"Nothing. It's just you two have always been hot and cold. This then that. Up and down like a pogo stick."

"We've been divorced for two years," I say, swallowing my irritation. "That's pretty final."

Her response is to make that humming noise again.

My mom loves Jackson. My entire family loves Jackson. Jackson has always been himself. He's always been certain of who he is, without a trace of arrogance, and that combination is so rare in people, it's hard not to gravitate toward it.

But not talking to my mom about our relationship is something I learned the hard way. It took me way too long to learn it. Way, way too long. Mostly because whatever I shared with her about whatever was going on with us had a way of boomeranging back into my face. I know my mom doesn't mean to do it. It's just her way. When she's wronged, or even when she *thinks* she's been wronged, it stays with her, etches into her skin so that every interaction from that point on is marked by whatever happened before. My brother Tyler says it's because she's a Taurus and they never forget shit. She also has a tendency to project.

"Divorce is nothing but a piece of paper," she says.

It's the same thing she told me hours after I signed the divorce papers, when I called her as a sobbing mess. At the time, as irrational as it sounds, those words gave me some comfort. Like maybe I hadn't made the biggest mistake of my life. Now, it just irks me.

"For you and dad, maybe," I say before taking a sip of my coffee, hoping it will help my stomach unclench. "For other people it's not, like, a game. Or a thing you do to prove a point."

My parents have proven that point twice already. My mom and dad divorced the first time when I was fourteen, just about to enter high school. Mom woke me and Ty up at one thirty in the morning and told us to pack a bag, that we were going to a hotel, and we were leaving my dad, this time for good.

He didn't even notice we were gone until the next afternoon. Where my mom was unforgiving and performative in her anger, my dad was absent and dismissive. It made for a fucked-up combination, and they were both too self-absorbed to see how their toxicity fed off one another's. They were divorced for three years, and got remarried right around the time I was set to graduate from high school. They divorced again when I was in college, right around the time I met Jackson my senior year. Then they got remarried when Caleb turned two, having "found their way back to each other." Now, they're just as miserable as they were when we were kids, only it's quieter because they're older, and less affecting because I'm not there to witness their blowouts.

"Is that what you think?" Mom asks after a moment of silence. "That I was proving a point when I left your dad?"

"No." I sigh. "I dunno. It doesn't matter what I think anyway. I'm not living in your shoes, so I can't judge your decisions."

"You remember how he was. Emotionally abusive and manipulative. Self-centered and self-serving, only worried about his dang-gone cars."

My mom's voice is getting more animated as she lists off my dad's very real flaws. But she kept returning to him. And he to her. It was their cycle of brokenness. I spent a lot of time in my early twenties wondering what her life, what *my* life would be like if she'd stayed divorced the first time. If maybe I wouldn't be so jaded. Or if I wouldn't have always felt so lost in my own relationships. If maybe I would've loved Jackson differently.

But I'm grown, and my decisions are my own. Putting that all at my mom's feet is unfair.

Silence lingers between us, and I feel a dull ache in my stomach forming into a ball. I push my coffee away.

"Anyway, Logan says hi," I say, attempting to turn the conversation to safer ground, glancing at Logan, who's been chatting with our friendly waitress the entire time. "I'm putting you on speaker."

Logan exchanges a look with me before she yells a hello to my mom. I should feel bad about using Lo as a buffer, but in our twenty years of friendship, she's gotten used to it.

I'm half listening as they fall into easy conversation. It takes less than thirty seconds for my mom to begin complaining about her neighbor Cindy, who is a never-ending source of weekend ire for her, until Monday, when she will return to the insurance office and complain about her coworker being petty and rude to her. My mom is a lovely woman—smart, caring, empathetic. But she is deeply unhappy, and hasn't found a way to not blame everyone else for her unending unhappiness.

We hang up, and I nibble halfheartedly on a piece of toast. Logan and I have about fifteen minutes until our manifestation class, and I'm back feeling heavier than I felt before I left Atlanta.

My eyes close briefly as flashes of my night with Jackson flood my brain. His dark moans in my ear. The familiar feel of his weight on me. The feel of his facial hair scratching against my skin. And the look in his eyes. The brand-new look that, hours later, still twists my stomach in knots.

"He told me we're not like my parents," I admit, opening my eyes and glancing at Logan. She looks up from her phone.

"You're not," she says, unsurprised by my confession as she leans back in her chair, straightening out her bright blue cover-up.

"He was holding back last night. I felt it," I say.

Logan raises her brows. "I thought y'all's 'atoms were connected' and shit."

I roll my eyes and laugh.

"He's probably in self-protection mode, Simone."

"He has to protect himself from me," I say quietly, almost to myself, as I grab another sugar packet off the table and pour more into my cup. The coffee is rich and smooth and doesn't need any more sweetener. But I need something to do with my hands.

"Your issues are not just on you. You know that," Logan says. "Shit with you two has always been complicated. Y'all are two complex motherfuckers."

I sigh again, sitting up straight in my chair and shaking off thoughts of last night, determined to focus on the moment.

"I'm at the beach in Jamaica on my birthday," I declare, slapping the table, making the coffee nearly splash out of my cup.

"Hell yeah," Simone exclaims, slapping the table too.

I stand, looking toward where people are gathering by a palm tree at the edge of our villa, near a line of beach chairs that are waiting to be set out. "Let's go manifest some shit, shall we?"

Logan smiles, and I link my arm with hers as we head toward the group.

AN HOUR LATER, LOGAN AND I are at the beach, after having finished our class, which was as whimsical and over-the-top spiritual as I expected. At one point, we were sitting on our mats, facing the water with our eyes closed, instructed to visualize something first, then "receive" it.

"You can't receive something you can't see," the shirtless teacher, whose long locs nearly touched his skinny calves, said. *"There are no wrong answers here. Visualize. Bring that vision to life in your mind. And once you've done that, separate your desires from your needs. They're not the same—unless they are. You'll hear it when you feel it,"* he said. *"Let your mind see what it sees. Don't try to suppress anything. There are no wrong visualizations."*

The first thing I visualized was Jackson and the way his eyes looked when he hovered above me last night, holding his weight on his forearms, his biceps flexing with the effort. And I let myself feel the memory of him inside of me stretching me, of him covering me. And then I felt horny, guilty, and even more frazzled, which I'm certain was not the intent of the manifestation class, so I forced myself to visualize the new teal chairs I want for my office instead. I'm hoping to manifest them on my credit card when I get back to Atlanta.

Logan and I settle in our beach chairs and I pull my phone out of my bag and turn it back on, since our visualization would not work unless we were "detached from all distractions." I gave Caleb the number to the resort before class started, so I was okay with turning it off for an hour. My heart lurches the second the phone lights up. I've missed eight calls and even more texts.

"What's wrong?" Logan asks, noting the expression on my face.

Did y'all see this??? Tristan's text comes through in real time with a link.

I click it and Logan leans over, peering through her sunglasses at my screen. It's Dillon's video, but not the private one Jenna sent me—this one's on ESPN's Instagram. The comments are already in the thousands.

"*Fuck,*" Logan breathes.

My stomach drops as I scroll through the notifications. Three sports blogs have already picked it up. Jenna's given an exclusive interview to *Deadspin,* saying she sent the video to Dillon's team "weeks ago" and nobody cared, so she needed to get the story out there, on her terms, to help women in abusive situations everywhere.

Dillon's already on TikTok, calling it a "misunderstanding" and claiming the video was "taken out of context." His PR team— the one I specifically told him not to use because they're idiots—is apparently handling his social media response without consulting me. Dillon also says his agency, Sage Athletic, already saw the video and thought it was an exaggeration on Jenna's part.

I sit up straighter in my chair, my peaceful post-manifestation buzz evaporating in the humid air. My stomach sinks and then lurches. "Fuck. Fuck, fuck, fuck, *fuck!*"

"Breathe, Simone," Logan says, moving to sit beside me. "We literally just said we were gonna be still in times of conflict so we can hear from God. This is a time of conflict."

"This is a time of *catastrophe!*" I yell, before I look around to make sure nobody heard me. The security guard looks over at us, bored. "What I'm hearing right now is shit just hit the fan."

Logan sighs and glances at Tristan's name, who just appeared on my phone because he's calling.

"Tyesha and Kelly are both citing breach of conduct to get out of their contracts," Tristan's deep voice greets me the second I answer. They're both WNBA players, and both essential to the agency. "They say they can't be represented by an agency that tolerates clients who commit verbal assault…"

"… against women," I finish with Tristan as I read the email they sent aloud.

"I just drafted our official response and sent it over to you. I sent a letter to everyone else we rep, letting them know we don't condone Dillon's actions."

I'm nodding as Tristan speaks. "If we drop him now…" I say, shaking my head.

"We look reactionary and fake," he says.

"But if we don't…"

"We look like we're condoning his actions."

"We're screwed either way." I peer out over the water. The couple from yesterday is out there floating on their backs, looking as if they don't have a care in the world. "I may as well go with what I really wanted to do from the beginning. Have Jared get the paperwork together and make sure it's clean," I say, referencing our lawyer who's on contract.

"Aight. Yo, I'm sor—"

"It's not your fault," I interrupt before Tristan can get his apology out.

"I'll hit you when the paperwork is done," he says. "And happy birthday. I'm sorry this all happened today of all days."

"Me too." I drop my phone back in my beach bag and look at Logan. She stares at me silently. Suddenly, the blue ocean that was so calming just minutes ago is spinning. I feel the familiar rush of heat spread from my belly to my head, and I blink, trying to push past my panic attack. I haven't had one in a couple of years, but when I was a teenager, they'd get so bad, I'd pass out sometimes.

I do not want to be passed out on the beach in Jamaica, I do not want to pass out on the beach in Jamaica, I repeat in my head as I attempt to inhale air, my chest rising and falling rapidly. I try to drag the salty air in through my nose, but it feels clogged, and my heart is beating way too fast.

"Simone…" I see Logan's lips moving, but her voice is muffled, far away.

The only thing I can hear is my harsh intakes of breath, the ringing in my ears. I close my eyes, gripping the sides of my lounge chair as I struggle to breathe, counting to eight in my head as I inhale, and to eight as I slowly let out the breath to another count of eight. I do this four times—in and then out—eyes closed before my heart beat starts to regulate. When I open them, Logan passes me a glass of water—from where, I don't know. Her eyes are round and filled with tears.

"I'm okay," I say, licking my dry lips. "I'm okay."

Logan quickly wipes away the tear that's dripped down her own cheek, her eyes wary.

She's not buying my lie either.

Nine

BY THE TIME SHIT FINISHED hitting the fan and splattering all over the walls of my existence, I lost four clients—five if you count Dillon's punk ass. He put out a statement that splashed its way onto conservative news sites and made the rounds on social.

I am extremely disappointed by Sage Athletic's spineless decision to no longer represent me. The accusations made by my former partner are not only categorically untrue but an example of how professional athletes and entertainers are too often taken advantage of for monetary gain. We are weighing our options and considering legal action.

They don't have a case. But it doesn't matter. Perception is powerful. NFL defensive end Tyrell Braxton, our other biggest client aside from Dillon, left because we didn't do enough to support Dillon when the public "turned on him" for something that happened years ago. And on the flip side, three of our WNBA players, Tyesha Smith, Kelly Lennon, and Crystal Ivanov, all left because Sage Athletic "condones verbal abuse and toxic masculinity."

That leaves me with three total. Lisette Gordon, a veteran franchise WNBA player who's been with me since I launched Sage Athletic, a point guard for Houston, Malika Higbee, and Dante

Harden, a second-string NFL cornerback who's on his way to retirement in the next couple of years.

I've been back in Atlanta for two weeks, and dealing with the aftermath has left a constant, dull ache in the back of my brain and a knot rolling around in my chest, mostly because of regret. I didn't go with my gut, and Sage is on the verge of collapsing because of that.

"So, your fortieth wasn't what you thought it'd be."

I blink, refocusing on the present.

"Even though I told myself I didn't, I think I had all these expectations of what it meant to turn forty in my head. What'd I'd be doing, where'd I be in my life trajectory or something," I answer, folding my hands in my lap.

I found a therapist a few days after I got back from Jamaica. Her name is Zuri Peterson, and I picked her because the photo on her website reminded me of a deeply solemn girl I took Spanish with in college. Then I got paranoid she actually *was* that girl with a new last name, so I did a deep social media dive. Turns out, she's not—which is a relief.

Now I'm sitting in her office. The first thing I did when I walked in was scan for neon signs. Thankfully, there's nothing about "vibes" or "dreaming big." Just plants. Lots and lots of them—flowing over her wooden bookcase, down the side of her desk, hanging from her curtain rod, on her windowsill. She works out of what looks like a converted house not too far from my neighborhood in East Point, and it feels like a beachy forest inside—with all the plants, the soft teal walls, the wicker baskets.

"Negril is beautiful," I offer when it seems as if I'm supposed to be saying something more. "I loved having time to hang out with Logan. The dirty banana rum drink I had was delightful."

Zuri laughs. This is our second meeting, and I already like her much better than Natasha. She feels more qualified to provide me direction because she's in her mid-fifties.

My first time meeting her on Zoom, she did the typical therapist thing—*why are you here, what do you want to work on*, and all that—but it only lasted about ten minutes. Zuri is one of those people who gets straight to the point, which I appreciate, because nobody has time or money for small talk. Or in Natasha's case, Instagram memes.

"Earlier you said you 'went dark.' What exactly do you mean by that?"

I swallow, releasing a silent breath as my heart picks up pace.

"Is that plant real?" I ask, my eyes on what looks like mini-palm tree in the corner of the room behind her desk. So much for not having time to waste on dumb small talk.

"Yep," Zuri says, following my abrupt subject change without blinking. "It was about this big when my mom bought it for me when I moved into this office a couple of years ago." She holds her hands about a ruler's length apart. "The last place I was in was a shithole with a racist landlord. My mom told me I needed to breathe new life into my space and business."

I smile. "Your mom a therapist too?"

"Nope." Zuri shakes her head, grinning. "She's just wise."

"Well, I'm impressed," I say, eyeing the plant, which is hanging from her curtain rod and nearly touches the floor. "I kill literally everything that comes into my house. The last plant I bought didn't even make it out of my car. I'm starting to think it's a sign."

"Of what?" Zuri asks, crossing her legs.

She's wearing a long dress with a blue jean jacket and sneakers. Her thick reddish-brown locs coil loosely down her back, held back by a bright yellow and pink headscarf. She looks like she could easily be playing the acoustic guitar at an outdoor festival or lecturing a group about the power of earthing at a conference in the West End.

"I dunno," I answer with a shrug. "My inability to nurture? My inability to help things in my life thrive? My inability to let things grow without intercession on my part?" I'm rambling now. And I never ramble. I stop and take a breath.

Zuri raises her brows. "You said the word 'inability' three times in a row." She lets that sit for a beat. "Is that how you feel? That you have an inability to nurture or help things thrive?" She tilts her head. "I'm sure Caleb thinks differently."

I expel a breath and swallow, shifting in my seat, then cross my feet at the ankles. Today is the first time in eight days I've worn anything except sweats and a t-shirt. Today I put on jeans, high-top peach-and-brown Dunks, and an off-the-shoulder long-sleeved peach Sade t-shirt. It's the first time in eight days I've done anything with my hair too. My braids are ready to come out but I haven't had the energy to mess with them. Today at least my edges are accounted for, and I'm wearing a brown knit beanie to hide the new growth. I've promised myself to take them out tonight.

I tug on the edge of my braid as I think about my son and the crease that's been etched between his brows all week whenever he talks to me. Not only is he perceptive like his dad, he can read. He's seen every post calling me an undercover misogynist, every TikTok video breaking down why I'm "part of the problem."

"I think he believes he has to protect me," I say, poking my tongue with my cheek.

"From who?" Zuri asks.

"Me." I shake my head.

"How so?" Zuri presses when I don't answer.

"What I mean by 'going dark'… I was just down the past week. I was in bed pretty much the whole time. And I hate for Caleb to see me like that. I kept trying to get up, but like…"

I shake my head, feeling the tears stinging my eyes. I refuse to let them spill out.

"My body felt like it was filled with lead," I say when I know I won't cry. "Like there were cement bricks in my chest and in my feet."

It's hard to look at Zuri when I admit that. To admit that even after our first therapy session, I allowed myself to go back to that place.

"Does that happen often?" Zuri asks. "Your not being able to get out of bed?"

"Not often, no."

"When was the last time?"

I shrug and release a breath, my gaze shifting to the plant her mother bought her. "When I got divorced." I meet her eyes. "And before that, a few times in grad school. It happened when I quit Kingship Agency—that's one of the biggest sports agencies in the country. My old client, Dillon, is actually being represented by them now." I roll my eyes. "Anyway, it was a big deal that I was working there as a Black woman, you know? Like I was supposed to be super appreciative of being one of the only Black women at the agency, and the youngest. Almost like I owed them something for recognizing my talent."

"And you quit?"

I nod. "I just… couldn't keep being disappeared. They wanted to parade me around like I was their Black woman mascot while they continued treating their Black athletes like shit, and I was just over it."

I don't say it, but Jackson is the one who supported me while I was wrestling with the idea of quitting. He's the one who suggested it was time for me to build my own agency.

"Maybe it's time for you to focus on you for once, instead of always thinking about how to stretch yourself to be all things for other people. You

really think they're interested in letting you know how valuable you are? That doesn't suit their end game, which is hoarding you and your talent, making you feel like any success you have is dependent on them. Nah, fuck that."

"Sometimes I wonder if I made the right decision," I say. "Jackson… He was supportive when I started Sage Athletic. He put our family on his back, emotionally, financially… and…" I shake my head again. "When shit like this happens, I just wonder about what. It doesn't feel like it was worth it. The things I lost, the sacrifices that were made…"

I trail off and exhale.

"It's normal to feel overwhelmed by the weight of your emotions," Zuri says after a beat. "When you 'go dark,' it's called—"

"Acute stress reaction," I supply before she can finish.

"You've been told that before?"

"I used to be a cutter," I admit, heat rising to my cheeks. "Back when I was first starting high school. And when my mom found out, she freaked, of course, and I started secretly seeing a therapist."

"Secretly?"

"My brother didn't know. He's a few years younger. He was, like, maybe ten or eleven at the time? And he was doing well in school and playing ball—he was an outfielder and he played corner in football," I explain. "I used to call him Baby Deion. Like Deion Sanders," I add when Zuri's face remains blank. "Because Deion Sanders played both positions too. Anyway, my brother's name is Tyler, not Deion, so obviously he hated it."

"And your dad? Did he know that you were in therapy?"

I shake my head. "My dad was very… absorbed in his own life," I say. "And my mom said he shouldn't know. It was during one of their divorced times, and when I think about it now as an adult with a kid myself, I'm pretty sure she didn't want to seem like she was failing us as a single parent or something. Nobody wants to admit their kid who, on the outside, anyway, is doing well, is actually very much not okay."

"So, you were cutting and seeing a therapist for it, but were told to keep it a secret," Zuri summarizes.

"The self-harm stuff is way in the past," I say, picking at nonexistent lint on my jeans. "Therapy back then helped with that. But sometimes when I'm really overwhelmed, I still get really heavy and it's hard to, like, move."

"It's understandable that when you're feeling overwhelmed you'd rely on old coping mechanisms to deal," Zuri says, leaning forward and forcing me to meet her gaze. "We just need to create new, healthy ones."

I nod, tugging at one of my braids before letting it drop and folding my hands in my lap again.

"You mentioned Jackson. Was your marriage with him one of the sacrifices you feel you made?" Zuri asks.

"Sometimes, yeah," I admit. I lick my dry lips. "We slept together in Jamaica," I blurt.

The first time Zuri and I met, it was because I felt like I was sinking with everything that was going on with Dillon and Sage, especially after my beachside panic attack and Logan's earlier lecture. I barely mentioned Jackson at all during that first session, only that he was my ex-husband.

"We went out for my birthday because he happened to be in town working on a story for this soccer player, Delroy Smith. Do you know him?"

"My daughter loves soccer, but I don't know much about it. His name sounds familiar."

"Well, he's a big deal," I explain. "Super talented and outspoken about things that actually matter. He has investments in the new Pan-African soccer league, the African Football League.

He's very smart and impressive. So Jackson was interviewing him for AndScape. It's gonna be an entire package, and Jackson is writing the cover story. And anyway, Jackson and I ended up hanging out while we were both on the island, and yeah. Sex happened."

Zuri's face remains impassive. Not aloof, just caringly blank. I wonder how she does that. Does she practice it?

"And how'd connecting with him again like that make you feel?"

I pull in a breath and let it out slowly. Seconds tick by and I shrug, shaking my head, pressing my lips together.

"It made me feel everything," I finally admit. "Like I made the biggest mistake of my life giving us up. And then that made me feel like I did something shameful, because I enjoyed it so much and I'm the one who ended things. And then I felt confused because we argued the next morning, and that brought up a lot of our old issues."

I draw in a breath, watching the sunlight from the window cascade over the plants on the back wall. "We have incredible chemistry. It's magnetic and electric and consuming if we let it be. But toward the end of our marriage we couldn't talk without it turning into an argument. And it's like all of that chemistry was channeled into negativity and made everything feel a hundred times worse. That morning, after we were together in Jamaica, I just felt really heavy. That's how I feel now. Really heavy. Trying to sort out what I feel is like trying to gather up the air in my arms or something."

Zuri purses her lips before tilting her head a bit. "And how are things between you and Jackson now?"

"I'm fairly certain they're pretty fucked up," I say with a humorless laugh. "I haven't spoken to him or seen him. He texted me more than a few times to check in on me when all the crap happened with Dillon. But I just couldn't deal." I release a breath. "He used to hate that. He always used to say that I was in my head too much. And that I never talked. And even in Jamaica, he made me promise that we would talk, that I wouldn't go silent on him. And that's exactly what I did."

His texts came not long after Jenna leaked the video.

I'm just landing and seeing everything that's going on. I tried to call you.

And then later that day, after he called for the second time. *Simone. Call me.*

And after I arrived back in Atlanta: *Caleb said you landed safely. Don't worry about dropping him off, I'll come to you.*

And then, when I left the house to "go to the grocery store" to avoid seeing him when he came for Caleb, *Okay, Simone. I'm here if you decide you need me.*

"Is that what your argument the morning after was about?" Zuri asks, snatching me out of my thoughts.

"Kinda. He told me 'we're not your parents.' My parents, they have this kind of, I dunno, explosive energy. Everything is always super hot or simmering just below the surface with them. They've been divorced and remarried twice."

I'm staring at the plant now, not Zuri, as the words continue tumbling out.

"He also implied I never truly wanted to be married to him, which was the first time he ever said that. We didn't get married until Caleb was in the first grade. But it wasn't because of lack of love. I love Jackson. I can barely remember what it's like *not* to love Jackson. But I just didn't want to fuck it up, you know? I didn't want the back-and-forth mess my parents had. I didn't want to fuss and fight and argue all the time in my marriage. I didn't want Caleb to have to deal with that the way me and Ty did, you know? We were fighting all of the time when he moved to Charlotte. He was there for seven months and then he quit. He said he couldn't do it anymore, so he came home. And at first I thought it would fix things, but they got worse. He was depressed and I was too, because we just couldn't seem to get on the same page, no matter how hard we tried. So when it started to feel that way between me and Jackson—like us being at each other's throats all the time, like we were never going to be happy together, when it felt like all we were doing was fighting—I called it. I thought I was doing the right thing for everyone, for us, for Caleb."

Zuri is quiet for a moment. "I think your coping mechanism up until now has been to hold everything in. To zip up everything inside of you to protect yourself because you learned early that, one, feelings make things messy, and two, that your feelings are meant to be stashed away and hidden, which invites those feelings to turn into shame for feeling them at all."

I open my mouth to deny her assessment then close it. My breathing is coming faster, the familiar heat in my chest flowing upward, resting behind my eyelids.

"It's okay to *feel*, Simone," Zuri says, her voice even and soft. I nod as a tear spills down my cheek.

"I hold shit in a lot," I admit, my throat clogged. Saying it aloud seems to make the tears melt, and they come out hot, leaking down my cheeks.

"Holding everything in has never protected you, though, has it?"

I shake my head, licking my dry lips as I wipe my eyes with the back of my hand, happy I didn't go all out and put on mascara today.

"Do you know what it really means when you're holding things in?"

Zuri asks the question rhetorically, but I shake my head anyway.

"That you never fully show up."

Ten

AN HOUR AFTER LEAVING ZURI, I show up to my office. It's been sitting damn near abandoned for the past two weeks. Well, abandoned by me, anyway. Tristan uses it for meetings with the three remaining clients we have. I'm about to find out if it's actually two, because Malika Higbee is sitting in front of me.

Malika's a small forward who mostly rides the bench for Houston, for no other reason than she seems bored most of the time. When she's fully engaged, she's incredible. The team has been seeing more spurts of her talent this year, and I know her signing with us has something to do with it, mostly because being with us gave her confidence. It's one thing to tell someone they're worthy. It's another thing to show them they are.

Malika is seated cross-legged in one of the oversized orange chairs in our small office, which is really just one big room, sectioned off by a minibar in one corner, a couple of desks on the other side of the room, and a small lounge area in the other. She's picking at her fingernails disinterestedly, even though she's the one who called this meeting.

"My mom said I should talk with you all," she offers, glancing up with a small sigh. "She says I need to 'start showing more interest in the 'affairs of my career,'" she says, using air quotes. "She'd probably be mad if she knew that I told you guys that."

I twist my lips and glance over at Tristan, who's perched next to me on one of the stools that overlooks the small bar area, which is stocked with fresh juices and teas. Last year, around the same year I boho'd my house, I did the same in my office. Only my house is softer, muted pale greens and beiges. My office is louder—burnt oranges and turquoise colliding with natural woods and wicker accents.

"But I like you guys," Malika continues, her gaze darting between me and Tristan. "I trust you. And I prefer to be represented by a company that's led by a Black woman, not some random white man."

She looks at me when she says that, and I nod and subtly release a slow breath.

"I appreciate your trust in Sage," I tell her. "In *me*. And I appreciate your coming here and having an in-person conversation before you made a decision."

Malika shrugs as she takes a swig of her green juice. "What ol' boy did was fucked up. But if we're being for real, they've blown this thing up way bigger than what it should've been. Saying you're 'anti-feminist' and you're not an 'ally' and all that…" Malika waves a hand dismissively when she quotes from the posts that've been going around with my picture attached. "If *she* wasn't white, this wouldn't have even been a thing to this level. And this idea that we're supposed to go out of our way to defend white women who have *never* been any ally to us unless it's convenient for them." She waves a hand dismissively again.

I glance at Tristan but say nothing.

"Anyway"—she swallows a sip of juice—"like I said, you've always been honest with me. And, bay-bee, I *know* I wouldn't have anything in terms of endorsements if I wasn't signed with you. Like, *nobody* else was foolin' with me. I haven't forgotten that."

She starts singing Rihanna and Kendrick Lamar's "Loyalty," and I laugh as Tristan chuckles. Malika's a cute girl—perky and honest, like she should be the tell-it-like-it-is best friend in a teen comedy.

When we first signed her, she was averaging six minutes a game. Most agencies wouldn't touch a bench player, but we saw her potential. The nail polish deal came first. We pitched her as an up-and-coming voice in women's basketball with an authentic social media presence. Then the protein powder company. Both deals helped her see herself as valuable off the court, which translated to confidence on it.

Malika stays and chats for a few more minutes, twirling back in forth in the chair as I fill her in on the new terms of the partnership with the nail polish company. Tristan quickly settles the upcoming filming schedule with her so they can plan out her posts for the next sixty days. All of this happens in between her texting on her phone, and the second Tristan's finished talking, she springs out of the seat with the energy of a twenty-three-year-old, off to get her nails done.

"That went better than expected," Tristan says, hopping off the stool and grabbing a water out of the small fridge once Malika is out of the door.

He's dressed casually as usual, in tapered khaki-colored joggers and a matching hoodie. His beard is neat and trim. Tristan has sleepy eyes, the kind that make him look like he's always assessing you but doing it casually.

"Yep," I agree, running a hand over the back of my neck, closing my eyes briefly. "I thought for sure she was coming to let us know she was done."

I open my eyes and look at Tristan.

"Thank you for holding us down while—"

"Nah, we're not doing that," he says. "The clients we lost? Fuck 'em."

I sigh, looking up at the ceiling.

"We keep movin'. We keep building," Tristan continues. "And then one day we'll look back on all this shit and remember all of the lessons it taught us."

I let my head fall and look at him. "That's very *Shawshank Redemption* Morgan Freeman of you."

"Get busy living or get busy dying," Tristan says, bending his deep voice to sound more like the actor.

I laugh. "For real, no more representing people I don't even *like*," I say. "I think maybe our first move should be to build on what Malika just said—that we saw her when nobody else did. And that attention and, I dunno, *belief* in her translated to her playing better on the court. So maybe we need to not focus so intensely on getting heavy hitters right now, and pay more attention to the bench. Who out there has potential like Malika?"

Tristan is nodding. "I like that direction."

"And not just the WNBA, of course. Let's look at the National Women's Soccer League, the Women's Tennis Association, the LPGA…"

"Yeah, I'm feeling that. I think that's an angle we could tap into. It'll be more work, though, because we'll need more athletes to keep us profitable."

"For sure."

"Aight." Tristan claps his hands. "I think we have a plan."

I stare up at the ceiling again, thinking about the loss of income that's about to hit me hard, and how we're going to make this work.

"I'm gonna have to take out a loan." I'm still staring at the ceiling. "I won't be able to stay afloat without one."

I hear Tristan's sigh as I study the patterns on the ceiling, but he doesn't dispute my claim.

"I think I need some wings," I declare, dropping my gaze to look at him. "You down?"

"Hell yeah. I'll drive."

Eleven

WE WIND UP AT A wing spot on Ponce De Leon that's been open for more than two decades, a feat in a city that loves tearing down buildings and is in a perpetual state of building something newer. It's just past five p.m., and the dive bar has just opened, which means we aren't forced to wait because this spot is notorious for having some of the best smoked wings in Atlanta, and is known to run out after a few hours. I'm tucked into a corner of the booth, my legs stretched out and resting on the bench across from me as I tuck into my lemon pepper flats.

"You look cute today," Tristan observes, taking a bite from his wing.

"As opposed to all the other days when I don't," I say around a mouthful of meat.

He rolls his eyes. "You need to learn how to take a compliment."

"Thank you," I say as he shakes his head at me. I suck the citrusy seasoning off my thumb and frown. "It's so weird that you only like drums."

"Drums are underrated," Tristan says, unfazed as he chews.

"Drums are for five-year-olds."

He smirks then shrugs. "Bella put me on."

I laugh at the idea that his toddler convinced him of a better way to eat chicken wings. "I haven't seen her in, like, three weeks. She doing anything new lately?"

"Not really." Tristan swipes through his phone on the table and pulls up a picture of Bella. "Still running around telling everybody 'no way.'"

I smile. "She's so dang adorable."

The last time I saw her, when I asked if she wanted to be picked up, she said, "No way!" in her cute little baby voice, even while stretching her arms up for me to lift her.

Tristan grins. "She's still not trying to hear anything about potty training."

He passes his phone to me, and I smile at the photo of her in pigtails, on a bright yellow kiddy slide at the park by Tristan's house in Vinings. I smile wider at the sight of her. She's a seriously adorable baby, with Tristan's full lips and wide nose, and her mom's large, almond-shaped eyes and thick, coiled hair.

"She'll use the potty when she's ready. Don't sweat her about it. At least you don't have to worry about her whipping it out and peeing all over your couch at random moments like Caleb did when we were training him."

Tristan laughs as he takes his phone from me and sets it back on the wooden tabletop before taking another bite of his wing. "Melissa wants her to start taking harp lessons."

"*Harp* lessons?" I repeat, raising my brows.

"Because the piano is 'too basic.'"

"Oh, wow. That's deep." I attempt to keep my face neutral as I take another bite from my wing.

"What two-year-old do you know taking gotdamn *harp* lessons? And now Melissa's found some woman who she met at Jack and Jill who claims she can teach her."

He takes a swig of beer, nodding in acknowledgment to a shaggy-haired guide who passes by our small booth.

"Well… maybe she'll end up being a harp prodigy," I volunteer, shrugging.

Tristan fixes a bland look on me. "Bella is *two*. She can barely hold her sippy cup, let alone play the fuckin' harp. She don't even know what a harp is." He shakes his head.

"Have things mellowed out with Melissa at all?"

He shrugs. "She's cooled out some. We got the custody situation handled now. We had to get our shit in check for Bella's sake. You know how it goes."

I nod. "Yeah."

"You should be glad things with you and Jackson weren't ever like the messy shit Melissa was on."

I drop my gaze to my wings, my heart rate increasing just at the mention of Jackson's name.

"Things were pretty amicable between us," I manage.

"I heard y'all hooked up in Jamaica."

I pop my head up and look at him, heart racing.

"That you had dinner with him and Delroy," Tristan continues, digging through his tray of wings, oblivious to my reaction.

"Yeah, it was nice." I breathe an inner sigh of relief that he's oblivious to the mess I've made of things with one of his best friends.

"Lo's been kickin' with ol' boy pretty tight since you've been back."

I don't know if it's a question or an observation. "They've been on one date, I think."

"Nah, she's been out with buddy, like, three times already," he corrects me. "He ain't even her type."

"Logan doesn't really have a type."

"No, she has a type. Not physically. But she definitely likes corny motherfuckers she feels like she can boss around."

I can't stop my burst of laughter. "Delroy is actually cool. And that's not true. She thinks if she can boss men around, they're weak. And she definitely doesn't like that."

"Exactly. That's the whole point. She ends up with dudes she can direct, but that ain't what she actually wants in real life. I don't think *she* even knows that's not what she wants, though, which is the fucked-up part."

I decide not to mention that she said almost the same exact thing about him.

"What's up with you two?" I lean back in the booth.

"What do you mean?" Tristan asks.

"I dunno. The way you said that was very… tension-filled." I take of sip of my watery PBR. "Y'all into it again?"

Tristan meets my eyes as he tosses his wing bone back into his tray.

"Nah, we're good. Even when she thinks we ain't. She's my heart, she knows that. That actually might be the fuckin' problem."

He looks off toward the bar area, which is starting to fill up with people drinking shitty beer and talking loudly over the sixties rock music that's bouncing against the wood-paneled walls. His phone buzzes on the table and I get a glimpse of a pretty, woman's face flashing on the screen, before Tristan silences it.

"You're not hanging out tonight?" I ask

Unlike me, Tristan was dating again before the ink was dry on his divorce papers. He's a serial monogamist and hates not being in a relationship.

"Nah. Ol' girl is messy, man."

I chuckle. "What'd she do?"

Tristan shrugs. "Same ol' same. People in Atlanta just be out here," he says, waving a hand over the table. "With nothing to offer and unlimited expectations."

"Quit dating twenty-five-year-olds."

He rolls his eyes. "That was *one* time, Simone," he insists as I laugh. "*Once.*"

I'm still laughing as I pop a crispy tater tot into my mouth.

"This woman is thirty-four," he says, bobbing his head toward his phone. "Old enough to be better."

I reach over to his tray, taking a fry. "Do you ever miss Melissa?" Tristan wrinkles his face.

"Well, not *Melissa* specifically, but being married?"

"I miss not having to be out here," he replies. "I miss coming home to someone. Sharing experiences with someone. But bein' real, Melissa was never really that person for me."

I almost say "duh" but manage to hold it in. Logan definitely would've let it out. That's part of the reason they're always fussing with each other. Tristan stares at me for a beat as he leans back in his booth.

"So, how are you feeling about everything?" That's his way of asking about my silence this past week. "Lo says you started seeing a therapist."

"I'm all right. I was actually there earlier."

"How's that goin'?"

"It's a lot," I reply. "But it feels good to be able to talk through things."

Tristan nods. "For sure," he says, his eyes serious. "I'm proud of you, Simmy."

I laugh. "Why? Literally everybody is in therapy these days. Like a diagnosis is a personality trait or something."

"Yeah, but you ain't everybody."

"I most certainly am not."

"And it sure as hell beats the garden section, right?"

"You sound like Logan, shut up," I say, tossing a napkin in his direction that he bats away with a smirk.

"Oh shit," he says abruptly, tilting his chin up and smiling, his eyes focused over my head, toward the doors of the bar.

I turn to follow Tristan's gaze and spot Jackson with his co-host Alisha Graham just inside the doorway, scanning the crowded bar before his eyes land on our booth. His expression flashes with surprise before he conceals it.

Tristan beckons him over, and Jackson begins weaving his way through the crowd. He's wearing a black Falcons fitted turned backward, which makes his stubble look thicker. His thin black hoodie is tucked under his black leather jacket. He looks good. Better than good. Sexy and virile and masculine.

"What's up, bro," Tristan greets him when he reaches our booth.

"Sup, cuz," Jackson returns, slapping Tristan's hand when he stands and giving him a half hug. "Sup, Simone," he says as I stand, awkwardly sliding out of the booth to greet him with a hug. His clean scent envelops me, but he's quick to release me. I look from him to Alisha.

"Hey, Alisha," I greet her with a quick hug. She smells like Tom Ford's cherry perfume, a scent I love but can't pull off.

Her hair is thick and wavy, parted down the middle and hanging over her shoulders. Her eyes are catlike and expressive, and she has a pert nose, with a doll mouth that's currently curled up in a smile, revealing even white teeth. She rocking what I call the Jemele Hill style—jeans with a t-shirt that says *The Blacker The Berry* under a formfitting black blazer. She looks up at Jackson before redirecting her attention to me.

"Hi, Simone." She smiles. "I feel like I haven't seen you in forever."

The sports circles in Atlanta are pretty small, so we crossed paths briefly even before she started hosting a show with Jackson. She's even interviewed a few of my clients.

"Yeah, I've been around. Just busy. You know how it goes."

"Oh for sure," she agrees. "It's constant, right?"

"Nonstop." I nod. "I like your shirt."

She grins, tugging at the hem. "Thanks. This is actually from Latisha Joiner's line," she says, referencing the popular gymnast who debuted at the last Olympics. "We had her on a couple of weeks ago, so I'm trying to support her."

I nod again. "Dope show today."

Tristan and I listened to them on the way over as they discussed the pipeline problem—the low number of Black head coaches in the NFL despite the high percentage of Black players.

"Thank you," she answers, leaning forward the way she does when she's about to get in deep with someone on their show. "How you holdin' up with the McCarthy Meltdown?"

Alisha is very forthright, which is partly why she's so good at her job. I almost roll my eyes at her use of the hashtag, even though she used it sarcastically.

"I mean, shit happens. You bounce back."

"I really would've rather had you on today. But Jacks keeps saying it's not the right time." She elbows Jackson with the casual familiarity of someone who's spent hours in the studio with him. "But I think people need to hear what really went down."

My gaze briefly connects with Jackson's before he looks at Alisha.

"The situation was too hot and we weren't gonna exploit—" he starts.

"How is letting Simone tell her side of the story when she's out here gettin' cooked exploiting anything?" she cuts in, the same way she does often does in their show.

She glances at me and tacks on a quick "no offense."

I look at Jackson who meets my gaze steadily, a flash of something in his.

She looks between us and shrugs. "You coulda used us to clear your name. Or at least we could've had Tristan on to talk about it."

"I thought y'all weren't doing tabloid-type shit," Tristan says, sliding back into the booth and leaning against the seat comfortably as he looks up at her.

Alisha shares an inside look with Jackson that makes my stomach dip. They have inside looks. And chemistry in spades. They're even matching today.

"That wasn't tabloid shit," she says, directing her attention to me again. "You shoulda come on the show. We could've chopped it up, Black woman to Black woman."

"I'm down to do that anytime," I say. "But not when I'm starting from a position of having to defend myself. I'm more interested in talking about the lack of diversity in the industry that sets stuff like this up to happen in the first place. I'm not in a position to be picky with my clients. And that's not an excuse," I say before she can get started. "It's just the truth. I know I made a terrible judgment call and I'm paying for it now, but…"

I shake my head.

"Are y'all sitting down?" Tristan asks them, glancing around. The place is starting to fill up and seating is scarce.

Alisha slides in the booth next to Tristan. Jackson slides in next to me. He holds my gaze for a second, and I see anger just beneath that new blank stare he's perfected since we split. I look away, fiddling with the napkin holder.

It doesn't matter, though, because I can feel his searing body heat against my side. And I can smell him, triggering memories and fantasies all in the same breath. My chemistry professor used to tell us that our sense smell was the "pathway to the soul." Sitting next to Jackson, breathing him right now, I understand more and more what she meant.

"This is what we should be talking about on the show," Alisha insists, speaking loudly over the swell of laughter that erupts from the table next to us. "Violent athletes, *especially* football players, is a topic that needs to be publicly addressed more often."

"We wanna talk about violence against women perpetrated by athletes, cool," Jackson says, his voice a low rumble. "But we ain't doing it just because something is popping on social media. A valid discussion should happen when things aren't hot, otherwise it invalidates it entirely."

"It doesn't 'invalidate the discussion,'" Alisha lobs back. "What better time to talk about something than when it's relevant and happening in real time?"

"We're the people who are qualified to talk about important things with nuance," he counters. "If we woulda had that conversation last week, it would've gotten lost in the million of other bullshit takes that were floating around."

I feel like I'm in the middle of their show, and it's annoying. I glance at Tristan, who's leaned back in his seat now, watching the two of them showcase their chemistry in real time, before he glances at me, gauging my reaction. I lean forward and put my elbows on the table, picking up a tater tot and dipping it in ketchup. There will be no reaction.

"Again, I'd rather be having this discussion on our show," Alisha singsongs, grinning at Jackson over the menu she's just picked up. "You're being overprotective."

"Aight, Alisha." Jackson returns her grin, shaking his head.

I stop swirling my tater tot and pop it into my mouth, chewing slowly as I subtly release a breath.

"You talk to Caleb?" Jackson turns and asks me, when Alisha starts scanning her menu.

"Yeah, he texted when they got to Huntsville." He's in Alabama on an overnight field trip to the Space & Rocket Center with his engineering club. "Have you?"

Jackson nods. "Yep, a few minutes ago. He said they were on their way to dinner."

"Want one?" I ask, pushing the paper tray of wings toward him.

"I'm good." He meets my eyes for a beat. "Thought we agreed you wouldn't go silent on me."

His voice is low, so Tristan and Alisha can't hear. I open my mouth then close it, shifting uncomfortably in my seat. I know him well enough to know he's pissed. He doesn't get hot when he's angry. He goes cold, almost completely still, like he sinks into himself so that he can observe how fucked up you are without interference. And he has every right to feel that way.

Jackson inhales when I say nothing, and looks away from me when Alisha calls his name. "What's up?"

"I was sayin' maybe we should try to grab a different booth because Carter just pulled up—my cousin," Alisha informs me. "She just started over at CNN as a sports reporter. I've been trying to tell Jacks she's literally perfect for him. She's super smart, she's funny…"

It feels as if the wind has just been knocked out of me, and I drop my gaze to my half-eaten wings. I blink slowly, suddenly lightheaded. I can hear my heart pounding in my ears. Jackson is here for a *date*?

He's staring at Alisha when I'm finally able to glance at him. "I keep tellin' you, I'm good on all that."

Alisha pouts. "Don't be rude to my cousin, Jacks. I'm serious." She looks at me, her eyes narrowing a bit before they widen. "Oh, shit. I'm sorry. This isn't weird, is it?" She looks between the two of us. "Y'all have been divorced for, like, *years* now, right?"

It dawns on me that Alisha never even knew Jackson and I as a married couple. Somehow that revelation makes me almost as sick as the idea that he's here to meet up with another woman. I glance at Tristan who looks between Jackson and me, shaking his head slightly when he shoots Alisha a look.

"You guys can actually have this booth," I manage, leaving Alisha's question dangling and tossing a napkin on my tray. "We were about to leave anyway."

I push lightly at Jackson's shoulder so that I can get out of the booth. He gets up, and I'm able to slide out without having to meet his eyes. Tristan plays along, hugging Alisha and giving Jackson dap.

"See you later," I tell Jackson, meeting his eyes for a split second before focusing my attention on Alisha. "Y'all have a good night."

I hear Alisha shrill loudly as I'm making my way out of the door, passing by a very pretty woman with deep dimples in both cheeks and long braids that skate past her lower back. I pause long enough to see her greet Jackson and Alisha at the booth we just occupied before I push into the cool night air.

Twelve

JACKSON AND I HAD OUR first date at Art Beats & Lyrics, an arts event that started in Atlanta to showcase the works of dope local artists, all soundtracked by hip-hop music. It'd taken him the entire semester I was interning at CNN to ask me out. Jackson wasn't exactly shy, but he was quiet and laidback. And we were friends. We ate lunch together. We walked to the MARTA Station together. We exchanged books—I gave him Nikki Giovanni's *Gemini*, since that's his birth sign. And he introduced me to *The Watchmen*. I'd never read a graphic novel before, and he said it was one of the best things he'd ever read—strong praise coming from him.

We'd talk music and sports. He loved the Braves and wore his Atlanta Hawks fandom like a badge. I liked him immediately. *Liked,* liked him. But I was way too shy, and way too afraid of rejection, to do anything about it. When he asked if I wanted to go out with him, I initially thought he meant as just friends. I was still so excited to be doing something with him that had nothing to do with my internship that I called Logan. She helped me pick out what to wear, an orange maxi dress with sneakers and a cut-off jean jacket.

The way Jackson smiled at me when he came to pick me up was different. I always got butterflies with him, but seeing that he seemed to like the way I looked sent them fluttering all through my belly, up into my chest. It wasn't until he reached for my hand later that night, interlacing our fingers as we were weaving our way through the installations as A Tribe Called Quest poured over us, that it dawned on me that maybe Jackson didn't mean for this excursion to be as homies. I blinked up at him, surprised.

"Is this okay?" he asked, seeming unsure of himself for the first time since I'd known him, glancing at our joined fingers.

"Are we on a date?" I blurted, and immediately felt my cheeks heat. *"Like, do you* like *me, like me?"*

He smiled then, that half-grin he often gave me when he thought I said something cute.

"Yeah, Simone. We're on a date."

When I asked him what made him ask me out, because it had seemed like he wanted to just be buddies, he grinned, showing off a glimpse of a dimple, and my heart started beating faster.

"I never liked you as just a friend, Simone," he said as we weaved our way between colorful paintings and detailed photos. *"I just wanted us to be friends before I asked you out."*

"Why?" I asked.

"Because I knew how much I liked you. And I knew you wouldn't trust us to be anything serious until you trusted me as your friend first. You know how hard it's been to not—" He grinned and shook his head. *"I, like, like, like,* like *you."*

I was twenty-one when he told me that, and he was twenty-three. Just babies. But he was insightful, even back then, because what he said was true. I didn't really trust men. I thought they were all running game—which, for the most part, was true, especially at that age, and especially in a city as wide open with beautiful single women as Atlanta. My skepticism and distrust were deeply embedded in the way I approached relationships and, to some degree, life in general.

But I trusted Jackson. Even back then, he made me feel protected and safe.

I exhale the memory away, staring at the TV. It's a couple of hours after Tristan and I left The Local, and I'm sitting cross-legged in my bed, watching reruns of Med School and Derwin's antics on *The Game.* This is one of my comfort shows. Only right now, I am not comforted.

My phone is in my hand again, and I fiddle with it, scanning through Caleb's last text, telling me they were back at the hotel and in their rooms for curfew because they have an early morning on Saturday. Then I click on Instagram, but immediately close it so that I'm not tempted to doom-scroll and get myself all worked up over the jacked-up shit people might be saying about me and my alleged lack of integrity. Then I pick my phone back up again and do what I've really wanted to do since I got home—go to Jackson's Instagram.

It's pointless because he never posts anything personal, only work—his articles, clips from his podcast. Occasionally he posts something with an athlete, or from a work-related social event with colleagues, stuff like that.

"My life is not for strangers' consumption and judgment." That's always been his approach. *"They consume enough of me through my work."*

That was one of our things after we had Caleb. We didn't post photos of our kid because people are fucking weirdos, and use their kids as lifestyle props. If Caleb couldn't give consent to be on the Internet, we weren't going to take that from him.

But Jackson was out with Alisha, his coworker, so I wondered if she and Carter would make it to his feed. I wanted to read Jackson's body language. I wanted to see if their date, or whatever the hell was happening now, was still going at ten p.m.

When I get to his page, I inwardly sigh. The last thing Jackson posted was a teaser from his show earlier today.

I click out of his page and go over Alisha's, who is just the opposite. She shares carefully curated details from her life—videos of her with her line sisters throwing up the Delta sign at Spelhouse's homecoming. Minute-long clips of her and Jackson debating things on their podcast. Shots of her with the athletes that come on their show sometimes. Photos of her out at dinners with her family, which, now that I recognize her, include a lot of Carter. I pause on one of them at brunch a couple of weeks ago. Carter is a very pretty woman, smiling at the camera happily as she holds her mimosa in the air. Her skin is clear and bright. She probably drinks a lot of water.

Alisha's last post came about an hour ago. It's a photo of her and Jackson at the wing spot. He's wearing a half-grin as she leans in close, throwing up a piece sign and making a silly face.

She captioned the photo: *Your favorite hosts eating our favorite wings.*

I roll my eyes. There's no sign of Carter in the photo, but it irks me just the same. Alisha and Jackson are sitting close, and he looks relaxed and slightly amused. As if he's used to Alisha and her antics but finds them entertaining.

I drop my phone next to me again and stare at the TV, trying to concentrate on the show, but my thoughts are all Jackson. It's not as if I've never thought about the possibility of his dating. I've suspected before that maybe he'd been on a few at least. He's fine as hell. He's smart and talented. He's observant and thoughtful. He's ruggedly masculine without being cocky. And over the past year or so, he's sorta become an Atlanta celebrity, since his and Alisha's podcast has blown up and his bylines have gotten bigger. He even pops up on *Around the Horn* on ESPN occasionally, debating with other reporters and giving his take on the day's sports highlights. So yeah, the idea that some woman would swoop in on him isn't far-fetched. It'd be a miracle if they hadn't.

I close my eyes and exhale, then open them and grab my notebook from my nightstand. Zuri suggested I get one and start journaling as one of my coping mechanisms. I used to journal for a while back in high school, when I was in therapy for that six-month period. But when I started feeling better, and life got busier, I moved away from it. My hand hovers over the notebook before I start writing.

Hello, Journal,

I feel like crying. But I've already cried once today, in the garden section of Home Depot. Yes, I went to Home Depot again, but I don't care. And Zuri told me there's nothing wrong with going to the garden section when I feel overwhelmed, if it helps center me, as long as that isn't the only way that I'm able to handle my feelings, seeing as how Home Depot isn't open 24/7 seven and it's not practical for me to drive there whenever I'm feeling some type of way. I went straight there after Tristan dropped me back off at the office. The store was about to close because it was close to 9. I can't believe I had to witness Jackson on a date. Or a half date. Or whatever the hell that was. I'm trying to truly sit with my feelings, acknowledge them and feel them. I feel torn and confused. And I feel sad. And I feel like there's this churning in my lower belly that just won't go away. I feel... like this is really fucked up.

I close my notebook and stare at the TV, then I kick the comforter off my legs and am out of the bed before I can truly think through what I'm about to do. I throw on a pair of leggings, an OutKast hoodie, and a black skull cap, and I'm driving through the darkened streets in less than ten minutes, on the way to Jackson's. I know popping up over his house to see if he made a night of it with ol' girl is a bad idea. I know it's immature. I know I have absolutely no right to feel this way, let alone act on it. I know I'm on some bullshit. My audacity is on ten right now. But the fire is crawling around in my chest, and sitting in my bed, scrolling Instagram, was not dousing it. I need to see him.

I turn up Nipsey Hussle to help drown out my thoughts as I make the twelve-minute drive to Historic College Park, where Jackson lives in a small two-bedroom ranch.

I slow way down when I turn onto his tree-lined street, creeping down his block at ten o'clock at night like I'm the police. I don't see any cars in front of his house when I swerve and park next to his black mailbox, but that doesn't mean anything. I turn the music low, my heart thudding.

This is stupid. This is irresponsible. This is beyond out of line. But I'm sliding out of my car and walking briskly up to Jackson's front door anyway.

My fist connects with the cool wood when I knock. I'm breathing so hard I'm about to hyperventilate. I glance around at the darkened houses in his quiet neighborhood and breathe in the crisp, damp air. *Really, Simone? What are you doing?*

"*Shit,*" I say aloud, shaking my head as I turn to run back down the steps, hoping he didn't hear me knock, but then the door swings open. Jackson appears in the doorway, barefoot, wearing black sweats and a white t-shirt that stretches across his chest. His face is etched with worry.

"What're you doin here? You okay?" He looks me up and down as I stand on the porch, as if searching for injury, then glances around, like he expects to see an intruder lurking in the bushes.

"No, I'm fine. I'm okay," I say, wetting my lips and stuffing my hands in my long hoodie pocket as I shift my weight.

"Is Caleb—"

"No, he's fine. He's good."

Jackson's brow is still furrowed as he holds the screen door open, waiting for me to step inside his house. I do, noting most of the lights in his small living room are off, except for a small lamp by the slate-gray couch. The TV isn't even on. I can hear sound floating from the back rooms, and see a trail of light floating up toward the living room.

"What's up, Simone?" he asks when I just stand there goofily.

Jackson is still looking at me as if I'm in imminent danger, and I shift my weight, my entire body burning hot with embarrassment as he shuts the front door behind me.

"I was just—" I bite my lower lip, then release it. "I just wanted to see you."

At that, he raises his brows. "You wanted to see me," he repeats.

"Sorry I didn't call," I say. "I know I should've, and it's not cool for me to just pop up on you like this."

Jackson's stance has relaxed a bit now, and he leans against the wall in his small foyer, stuffing his hands in his sweats pockets. He's watching me, gnawing on the inside of his lower lip, his dimples peeking out beneath the stubble on his face.

"Were you busy?" I ask awkwardly.

"Nah, I was working," he answers.

"Do you have company?"

His stance doesn't change. "Is that why you're here? To see if I had a woman up in here?"

"No. I dunno. I— No."

I open my mouth again then close it. I swallow, closing my eyes for a second as I release a breath.

"I'm fully showing up."

This is not what Zuri meant, and I know it. It feels damn near blasphemous using my therapy learnings in this way, during my utterly confused, jealous, horny meltdown.

Jackson doesn't respond to me. He watches me, his lids slightly lowered. He's still angry—I can feel the coolness radiating from him. But there's a new awareness in the air now, and he's also eyeing me warily, like a caged lion sizing up its next move.

My gaze trails over his biceps to his chest, and finally, his mouth. I step closer to him, my heart beating double time, my breaths shallow. Jackson smells like fresh soap, clean, and warm, and *him*. I close the last bit of space between us until we're centimeters apart, his body heat wrapping around me. Tilting my head up, I grab the hem of his shirt, my knuckles brushing his stomach.

"What're you doin', Simone?" His voice is low and gruff.

I sway into him, and Jackson's gaze falls to my mouth. His body heat, his scent—it's making me feel drugged. I push up onto my toes, my chest pressed against his.

He shakes his head. "I don't have the head space to play games with you," he murmurs.

"I'm not playing games," I manage, my lips nearly grazing his when I speak.

His hands are still in his pockets but his breathing has changed, shallower, faster. He has that look in his eyes again, the foreign one that I don't know. I swallow as I fall back onto my heels. Heat spreads through my body.

What *am* I doing? Embarrassment presses down on me, my body suddenly heavy as I step back.

"I'm sor—"

But before I can finish, Jackson moves. His hands slip into my hoodie pocket, yanking me against his chest. His gaze is hot, unreadable—then his mouth is on mine.

He tastes like mint and something undeniably him, and I moan softly at the contact. There's no hesitation in the kiss. Jackson's tongue is warm and demanding, and I meet his energy, tangling it with mine. I kiss his bottom lip, sucking on it, and he moves his hands from my pocket to my hips, dragging me closer, a low sound escaping his throat.

When I slip my tongue back into his mouth, he meets it with his, sucking lightly before pulling me against him, his erection pressing into me.

He turns us in one fluid motion, pinning me against the wall with a palm braced beside my head before dipping down, kissing his way along my neck, then back up. Jackson tugs impatiently at the waistband of my spandex, and I push my hands beneath his t-shirt, trailing my fingertips down his hard stomach. His hand slides beneath the fabric, slipping into the front of my panties, and a soft noise leaves my throat when his rough fingers graze my wetness. The back of my head thumps against the wall, and my hips jerk at the contact, heat rushing through me. I'm on the brink of climax already.

"Is this what you wanted?" he murmurs against my ear, his fingers moving in slow, steady circles. He's hard, rigid, pressing into my thigh. His mouth finds my neck, his tongue mimicking the movement of his fingers. A sharp hiss slips out of me as I stroke him through his sweats.

"Then say it," he demands, pressing harder into my hand.

"I wanted you," I reply, the words leaving me in ragged pants.

My mouth falls open when his fingers move faster, my body tightening and then breaking apart. I'm already coming, *hard*. Bright light flickers beneath my closed eyelids as my mouth falls open. I can hear my near scream somewhere deep in the back of my brain, hear my shallow breaths tangling with his. He presses his mouth to my neck, breathing heavily.

"You make me feel fuckin' crazy sometimes," he says hoarsely, sliding his hand back up. He tugs at my waistband, pulling me against him.

"I don't mean to."

"That's not good enough, Simone," he says.

"Do you want me to leave?" I ask, tilting my head up to meet his gaze, holding my breath as I wait. There's a beat of silence.

"No."

Thirteen

"YOU WANNA READ THIS?"

It's two hours later and I'm lying in Jackson's huge bed, wearing one of Jackson's white t-shirts, half watching *John Wick: Chapter 2* while I finally unbraid my hair. He's in a ribbed undershirt, otherwise wearing only his boxer briefs, and has been typing for the past forty-five minutes. The other time was spent inside of me.

I followed him back to his bedroom and he wasted no time pushing me toward the bed, pulling off my spandex, and sliding inside of me. The hoodie came off unceremoniously after he was already buried in me. So did my skull cap, which Jackson tossed somewhere on his bedroom floor, murmuring how he couldn't do this with me wearing it and nothing else.

This time it was fast, needy, and wild, and I screamed out so loudly that the back of my throat burned when I climaxed again seemingly out of nowhere, which triggered Jackson's guttural moan.

He slides his laptop toward me, and I grab it, placing it in my lap as I start reading the latest edit of his story on Delroy. Jackson moves behind me, pulling me between his outstretched legs as he leans against the headboard. His fingers find my hair seconds later, picking up where I left off, undoing my braids.

"This is really, really good," I say when I'm finished. "Like, *really* good. Especially the part about his aunt, and how you tied in how her influence shaped his thoughts on the Diaspora and his role in bringing people together through the sport."

"That part about what he's trying to do by investing in the African league is clear?" Jackson asks.

"Yeah, I think so. I'd maybe trim that line about the World Cup in his quote, though. It's kinda dangling a little bit."

"Yeah, I thought about that," he says as he finishes my last braid. "That's a good call."

"This might be one of the best things you've ever written," I say, turning my head to look up at him.

His lips twist, like he's debating how serious I am. Jackson has written *a lot* of pieces in his lifetime, and he's one of the best sports writers in the country. I can say that honestly, without bias.

"Seriously," I say, bobbing my head as I reread the last paragraph. "This is really … I dunno, like, nuanced. Almost like the start of a book." I turn to look up at him again.

"You think?"

I nod. "Yep, it has that level of depth."

I set the laptop aside and massage my scalp now that my hair is free. Then I gather up the braiding hair and hop down from Jackson's bed, headed for his small bathroom to throw it away. I didn't fight my urge to snoop earlier when I used the toilet. I found no lingering traces that another woman had been here.

Not that that means anything. Jackson's bathroom is always clean and neat, and it smells faintly of his cologne. The shower curtain is dark blue, as are the toothbrush holder and soap dispenser. He probably got it as a set. The rest of his small house is the same— simple, functional, with dark furniture and few traces of his former life with us, save a couple of photos in the living room of Caleb.

He's always been good at compartmentalizing his feelings. Maybe his home is a reflection of that skill.

I pause, glancing at myself in the mirror. My hair is now puffy and wavy, and I pull at it, shaping it into a style that actually would be pretty cute if I left it like this. My lips are slightly swollen, my skin flushed. And even though it's late, my eyes are bright, like my body perked up from the inside out with Jackson's nearness. I flick off the light and pad barefoot over the hardwood floors back into his bedroom.

His laptop is now on the nightstand and Jackson is stretched out on the bed when I return, watching the movie through half-closed eyes.

"It's so weird when people have Common playing a bad guy," I say as I climb back onto his dark brown comforter, glancing at the TV screen when Common begins acrobatically shooting at Keanu Reeves.

Jackson grins. "Yeah, that's not dude's lane. He always looks like he's about to break out and start freestyling about ending gun violence."

I laugh as I climb across the bed toward him then straddle his waist and meet his eyes. He grabs my hips, watching as I slowly lower myself down to kiss him. I kiss his top lip, then his bottom, shifting my body when I feel the beginning of his erection poking me.

"Why didn't you call me?" he asks against my mouth.

I close my eyes and exhale, then start to get up, but Jackson tightens his grip on my hips.

"Don't move. I feel like I get better responses from you this way."

"Shut up," I say, with a half laugh.

He loosens his grip enough for me to sit up. I release a breath and stare down at him as I trace a finger over his new-to-me tattoo, watching his skin pebble beneath my touch.

"I started therapy again."

Jackson doesn't look surprised. "How're you feelin' about it?"

"Good. It's helping me organize my thoughts, I guess." I pause. "I have a hard time talking, Jackson. Like, when shit gets really heavy, it's my thing to shut down. You know that. And I'm trying to get better with that. I *am* getting better with that, little by little."

"Not with me."

"Yes, with you. I'm here right now, right?"

Jackson fixes a look on me. "Your coming here wasn't about that. It was about you thinkin' Alisha's cousin was over here."

He shakes his head, like the thought of her coming over is preposterous.

"'Jacks' is a stupid fucking nickname," I blurt, staring at him. His lips curl up, but he says nothing. "Carter was pretty. And apparently 'smart and talented.'" I use air quotes like the hater that I currently am. "So it's not that far-fetched to think that you might've found her attractive."

"She was very attractive. And cool—way more mellow than Alisha."

My heart drops, and I look off toward his closed blinds. The room is dark, except for the light from the TV and the small slivers of light peeking through the window.

"So why isn't she here, then?"

"Because like I said earlier, I'm not interested in all that. Plus, what do I look like, tryin' to start something up with Alisha's *cousin*, of all people? Alisha's messy as hell. She don't mean to be, but that's just who she is. And she's nosy. And I have enough messy shit goin' on in my life right now."

"What does that mean? Me?" I shift on him.

"This shit we're on right now? Yeah. It's messy."

"I asked if you wanted me to leave." My heart is racing.

He gives me that same look again. "C'mon, Simone. You knew the answer to that when you asked the question. I want you all the time. And you know it."

He says it matter-of-factly, like he's telling me the sky is blue. I inhale when he says that, heat spreading through my body.

"But this shit…" He waves a hand between us. "What are we doin' here?" His gaze is intense and questioning.

I sigh as I lift my shoulders. "Being in the moment?"

Jackson runs a hand over his face. "I don't want a *moment* with you. This shit ain't… It ain't healthy for me."

I feel myself deflate completely at his words, intermingling with guilt because I feel selfish, and I know he's right. This isn't healthy for either of us. But that high that I get in his presence, that feeling of comfort, drowns out all of our other shit right now.

"Have you been with anybody else sexually? Since we…"

"Divorced?" Jackson finishes for me, raising a brow. I shift on him again, and he looks off toward his blinds. "Why're you asking me that, Simone?"

My stomach knots violently. "So, yes?"

I move to get off him, and this time he lets me. I sit cross-legged on the rumpled bed, taking slow breaths. I don't have a right to feel this way. I didn't have a right to ask him that question, especially when I knew I wouldn't be able to handle the answer.

"A lot?" I ask anyway, my voice barely above a whisper.

"No."

"When?"

"About a year ago," Jackson tells me.

"Who?" The questions are floating up my esophagus and out of my mouth without thought.

"*Simone.*"

"Do I know her?"

Jackson closes his eyes. "This is fuckin' insane," he mutters, almost to himself. "We haven't been married for *two* years. *You* wanted the divorce, remember?"

"I haven't been with anyone," I volunteer. "I couldn't even think about—"

I pick at the comforter, swiping quickly at my eyes. I'm not a crier. Or I used to not be. Now that's all I do.

"You wanna know what happened?" Jackson says, sitting up with his back against the headboard. "It was on the anniversary of our divorce."

He lets that sit with me for a beat.

"And I was fucked up. Fucked *all the way up*. I couldn't get my head together. I don't ever remember feeling that low."

Guilt pangs in my chest, spreading slowly downward, landing in my belly. I rub a hand there.

"Tristan got me up and we went out to The James Room to have a drink so that I could get out of my head about us."

"*Tristan* was there?"

That feels like a betrayal. But Tristan and Jackson have been friends for years, so is it really so surprising he'd be there for Jackson at a low point in his life? One that I caused?

This shit *is* messy. Maybe *I'm* messy.

"This woman I used to work with at CNN back in the day was there," Jackson continues without answering me. "We started talking. And I thought... I thought if I could do something to stop thinkin' about us..."

"Rachel?" I ask, barely able to breathe.

Jackson's eyes snap to mine, and I know my guess is right. She was one of the producers that worked at CNN when I was interning, and I knew she liked Jackson, even back then.

I feel like I'm going to be sick. We stare at each other for long seconds. I try not to let the idea of Jackson touching Rachel, being inside of Rachel… Was it in this very bed? Did they go to her place? Did he leave love bites all over her chest and neck? Did he make the same low noises, like he's being tortured and she's the best thing he's ever felt, with her?

I exhale slowly. I brought this on myself. I breathe in and out for a few seconds, aware of Jackson's eyes on me as I get my head together.

"Did you keep seeing her?" I open my eyes but don't look at him when I ask the question.

"No. She doesn't even live in Atlanta anymore. She's somewhere on the East Coast now, in Jersey."

"So you've been dating this whole time? Like, other people?"

"No, Simone. I haven't been dating. I ain't dragging someone through the mud with me when I'm—" He looks at me. "My heart was broken. *I* was broken. You know how many days I couldn't even get out of the fuckin' bed? How knowing I had to keep it together for Caleb's sake was the only thing that—" He stops and shakes his head. "What do I look like, trying to date someone else? Look at what just happened. All you gotta do is show up and…"

He trails off.

"Why'd you really come over here, tonight?" His eyes are tired, jaw tight. The light from the TV is dancing over his handsome features, and for the first time tonight, he looks drained.

I open my mouth then close it, my gaze trailing to the window before I look at him again.

"Because I miss you." I push the words out before they get lodged in my throat, overrun by my fear.

The second the words leave my lips, it's like something releases in my chest. Like I've been holding that realization in for a long time and it's finally freed. Jackson exhales, running a hand down his face. The sound of John Wick shooting up the people who killed his wife's dog is low, floating through the otherwise silent room.

"So you think I'm on a date with another woman and suddenly you miss me? You know how fucked up that sounds?"

"It's not *suddenly*. And we were together in Jamaica."

"Yeah, and then you cut me off again, for what? Two weeks?"

"I didn't cut you off. I just needed…" I stop. "But that doesn't change what I said. I do miss you, Jackson."

He looks away from me. Silence stretches between us for long minutes.

"Today," he finally says, not looking at me.

"What?"

"You think you miss me today," he says.

I frown. "Jackson—"

"But what about tomorrow?"

I start to speak, but he cuts me off.

"Nah, you don't know *what* you want, Simone. I'm not sure you ever did."

"You keep saying that," I say clutching the comforter.

"I have a reason to keep saying that, don't you think?" His tone is gruff but not loud, his gaze hot.

"So you don't believe I ever *loved* you now?" I ask, sitting forward a little.

"I didn't *say* that," he says. "I just… I don't know what to think when it comes to you anymore."

My chest rises and falls rapidly as we stare at each other. He yawns, running a hand down his face, which means I yawn too.

"You okay if I turn this off?" he asks.

I nod and he reaches over me for the remote on the nightstand, then clicks the TV off. I slide down into the bed next to him, staring up at the darkened ceiling. My eyes are gritty with sleep but feel too heavy to close.

"I shoulda never left for Charlotte," Jackson says, his deep voice quiet in the darkness of the room.

"You needed to go," I counter. "I know what I said in Jamaica, and it was wrong. I know you needed to do that. You wouldn't be doing what you're doing now—your career wouldn't be where it is—if you hadn't gone."

"I was being selfish." His voice is rough with exhaustion. "I knew it would cause problems for us because I know you, and how you think, and what you need to be okay. And I thought I could just do it anyway, the back-and-forth thing every other weekend just for a year, and that it wouldn't break us."

I blink sleepily into the darkness. The silence hovers.

"You know how you told me we weren't like my parents?" I ask a few long seconds later. I turn my head to look at his profile. "I think I was trying so hard to not be like them, I self-manifested that shit right into our marriage."

I laugh, though it dies at the edges. I scoot closer to Jackson, who's lying on his back, and run a finger up the inside of his wrist. I put my fingers in his, and he interlaces them, then turns on his side and pulls me into his arms. I snuggle close, breathing in his scent. I kiss his chest, feeling the steady beat of his heart, even as exhaustion wears on me.

"I always wanted you, Jackson," I whisper against his skin.

"Even when you were handing me divorce papers?"

I release a stuttering breath. "Yes."

Fourteen

IT'S RAINING OUTSIDE WHEN I blink my gritty eyes open, my gaze landing on the rain-streaked window in Jackson's bedroom. The sky is gray in the early morning, and I watch fat droplets slide slowly down the glass. My body is heavy, my thoughts muddled, and I don't feel like moving.

I dreamt of Jackson again. We were in the car on the bridge, only this time he wasn't coaxing me to drive. He was silent, staring out the passenger window while the road melted away in front of us.

I turn my head, my eyes settling on Jackson. He's still sleeping peacefully on his stomach, his muscled back rising and falling with steady, even breaths. I swallow hard and stare up at the ceiling. My thoughts are everywhere and nowhere at once. On the woman Jackson admitted sleeping with, and the reality that my decision is what caused it. On the pull that still exists between us, and the reality that even with it, things are still so cloudy. On how relaxed I am in his presence, and the reality that this is a temporary bubble created in a moment of high emotion.

Jackson is still the only person who has ever made me feel every emotion possible while also making me so comfortable that my mind goes completely blank. In this space, in his bed, that's dangerous—not just because, after what he said last night, I know it's probably not good for me to be here. It's that thought that forces me to get up, carefully sliding my legs from beneath his so I can slip out of bed.

But before I can move, Jackson stops me with a large palm on my thigh. His eyes are sleepy when he looks at me. He reaches around my waist, dragging me back over the warm sheets into his arms so that my back is pressed to his chest. I sigh in his arms and close my eyes, allowing the cloud of sleepiness to cover me. He presses a kiss to the back of my neck. Seconds later, his breathing is deep and even. I let it lull me back to sleep.

I don't know how long we're asleep before a crack of thunder jolts me awake. I stare out of the window but can't tell what time it is—the sky is still dreary, painted a heavy gray.

"You know what time it is?" I ask Jackson, my voice scratchy. He reaches behind him and lifts his phone over his head to check.

"Ten thirty."

"I can't remember the last time I slept this late," I admit.

Jackson is tracing a line up and down my belly, then higher— between my breasts—before sliding lower, between my thighs, and back up again. I draw in a long breath, my skin pebbling under his touch. I press against him and feel his erection poking against my butt. I turn my head and look up at him. Our gazes connect—and he trails a line down my skin again, from between my breasts to where my panties would be, if I were wearing any. I know he feels the slickness between my legs when he drags a finger back up to my belly.

I suck in a breath as he rolls on top of me. My legs fall open for him, my body already ready.

He kisses my ear as he pushes inside me. He slides in partway, then pulls back out. He does it again, and the feeling—the friction of his teasing—is almost unbearable. His eyes stay on mine when he does it again, balancing on his forearm, pushing in further before pulling back out.

"*Jackson,*" I practically pant, frustrated, as I wrap my arms around his neck, arching my hips up. "Stop doing that."

He looks down at where we're joined, then meets my eyes again, a trace of a grin on his lips. I lift my head and bite his lower lip. He lets out a low sound and finally slides all the way in, and I moan loudly. For long seconds, Jackson doesn't move. He lets my body adjust as I clench and unclench my muscles around him. Every time I do it, his eyes get lower, his breathing heavier. He brushes his nose against mine and, finally, starts to move.

Jackson's movements inside me are slow, unhurried, and the torturous pace makes it feel like I'm melting into him but still not close enough. The soft sound of the rain pelting the window fills the room, mingling with the breathy noises slipping from my lips. He feels so *good*. And I tell him so.

Jackson slips his forearm beneath my leg, angling deeper, dragging his lips along my neck as he moves—slow, drawn-out strokes that make me feel hazy and drugged. Every one of my senses is attuned to him—the warmth of his skin, the weight of him pressing into me, the way he's stretching me.

Our damp skin slides together under the heat of the comforter, his pelvis grinding against mine. I run my hands down his back, pressing my fingertips into the muscles flexing beneath my touch. His pace quickens and his breath shortens, warm exhales brushing the shell of my ear. I clench around him, and he groans, gutturally.

"*Fuck, Simone,*" he murmurs as I arch up to meet his steady thrusts, squeezing him again.

The movement is too much, even for me. I turn my head, grazing his skin with my teeth before sucking on his collarbone. Sounds I barely recognize slip from my lips. When Jackson and

I come together, it's always intense—but this is something else entirely. The pressure builds, coiling low in my belly. I can already feel myself starting to pulse around him.

He feels it too, because he groans again, then stills, breathing heavily against my mouth. He thrusts against, just once, and I close my eyes, gritting my teeth, trying to hold back my orgasm.

"I don't wanna—"

"I know. Me neither." He bites my earlobe and holds it between his teeth.

I slide my hands down his back to his ass, pulling him deeper into me. He buries his face in my neck as he grinds just his hips.

"*Simone.*" My name sounds tortured when it leaves his lips, and it sends goosebumps scattering across my skin.

He turns his head, his jaw scratching my cheek, and I meet his mouth. The kiss is greedy but slow—tongues tangled, teeth clashing. I suck on his lower lip, and he pushes a hand through my hair, tugging at the roots to tilt my head, then thrusts into me again. The sensation makes me half gasp, half moan, and my nails dig into his lower back as he finally begins to move faster, as if trigged by the sound. He dips his head, capturing a nipple between his teeth, biting gently. The sound that leaves my chest at the sensation—part pleasure, part pain—is breathy and raw. He sucks harder, then pushes at my leg again with his forearm, digging his fingers into my skin. He releases my nipple, pressing his face into the crook of my neck, driving into me faster, harder. I can feel the heat building in my lower belly, and the pressure between my legs is so heavy it's almost painful. I gasp against his shoulder, squeezing my muscles together, my forehead damp with the exertion of trying to hold my orgasm at bay.

"Now," he rasps.

That single word—both a declaration and a trigger—sends heat pulsing through me. I lift off the bed, arching into him as my orgasm climbs through me—an open-mouthed moan dragging itself out of my chest and catching in my throat, held there by the force of how hard I'm coming. He follows with a hoarse, rough groan.

For long seconds, we just breathe, chest to chest, the steady sound of the rain soft against the windows as we come down together.

He raises his head, shaking it slightly when he meets my eyes. My *wow* is lodged in my throat, but I know he sees it.

"It's me and you," he says.

I stare at him and swallow, brushing my nose against his damp shoulder.

"I don't want to leave," I admit against his skin. I suck on it, enjoying the salty taste.

"Then don't."

WE SPEND THE NEXT FEW hours hanging out in Jackson's bed, eating the leftover chicken parmesan he made when Caleb was over the other day, drinking beer, and watching *Dune*. It feels like the early days, when Caleb was old enough to stay overnight at April's in Brunswick to give us a break.

We'd drop him off on Friday afternoon and head back to Atlanta, then turn around to pick him up on Sunday morning. It was silly to do all of that driving in retrospect, but we were young and hungry for each other. We had to soak each other up as quickly as possible in those hours we had alone. Sometimes we'd be in the middle of a fight—something silly that neither of us could quite remember because we were exhausted. And in that time we were alone, we'd find each other again, and remember.

Back then, that was one of the things that gave me hope, that we could always find each other. In the two years before we divorced, we'd lost that, and it affected the way I viewed everything.

"Caleb will be back in a couple of hours." I reluctantly sit up in the bed, running my fingers through my tousled hair. "I should probably go."

This time Jackson doesn't dispute it. We dress quietly, with me sparing glances at him, the heaviness of the moment weighing on my shoulders with every article of clothing I put on. And once we're dressed, he walks me down the short sidewalk to my car. It's drizzling now, no longer pounding rain. The sky is dreary gray, the street rain-slickened. I hover by my open car door and look up at Jackson.

"I don't know what we do with this," he says, stuffing his hands in his pockets.

I swallow hard because I don't know either. We stare at each other for a beat. I feel tears prick the backs of my eyes, but they don't fall.

"You're gettin' wet," he says, pulling my hoodie up over my head.

He slides his hands into my pockets and pulls me toward him, pressing his forehead to mine for a few beats. I feel his breaths, warm and light, reassuring against my lips, even in this heavy state of confusion I've brought on myself. For long seconds, I let myself breathe him in.

"You should go," he says, causing me to open my eyes. "I'll see you later."

I lick my lips and nod, and Jackson's gaze drops there, but he doesn't lean in to kiss me.

"Drive safe," he says when I finally slide into my car. It smells stale and unused after being in the warmth of Jackson's space for the past day and a half.

I look up at him through the rainy window before he taps my hood, then turns and walks back toward his house.

Fifteen

"A SUCCULENT IS WHAT YOU want."

Forty-five minutes later, I'm at Home Depot, wearing the same day-old OutKast hoodie and spandex I was wearing when I showed up at Jackson's unannounced last night. I still smell like him. I still smell like *us*. I'm standing at the register, talking to a kid who looks only a few years older than Caleb, even though he has a full beard that I can tell he wears like armor.

He nods toward the plant in my hand as I finish explaining my bad luck with plants. I've spent the last twenty minutes wandering the aisles, trying to decompress before picking up Caleb from the school. My thoughts are full of Jackson. Jackson inside me. Jackson telling me he's slept with another woman. Jackson telling me he needs to feel me. Jackson saying I make him feel crazy. Jackson's weight on top of me, our fingers intertwined above my head as he kisses my neck. Jackson telling me I broke him.

"They store water in their leaves, so they don't need a lot of water, you don't really have to worry about repotting them…" The kid is explaining. His voice tilts toward boredom as he lists the plant's pros. "You have to actively *try* to kill it for it to die."

"I've actually killed one before," I admit, smiling, pushing it toward him so he can ring it up.

He raises his brows. "Dang, for real? What'd you do to it?"

I shrug. "Existed near it? I dunno."

I grin when he laughs.

"You're really pretty," he says off-handedly when he passes me back the plant after I tap my card.

I frown, tempted to look around to see who he's talking to. There's nobody else in the store, except one of his coworkers, currently loading a huge bag of potting soil onto one of the wide shelves.

"Thank you," I tell the kid.

"You'll keep this one alive," he says as I make my way out of the garden section, into the late-evening air. "I have faith in you."

He gives me a thumbs-up, and I laugh, returning the gesture.

This time, I remember to take the plant out of the car, and set it on my bedroom windowsill.

Sixteen

TWO WEEKS LATER, I'M AT an "align and awaken" yoga class with Logan in a small West End studio, where soft yellows, pale peaches, warm wood, and sunlight streaming through the large windows make the air feel clean and inviting. It's April, so it's time for my next "fortieth birthday experience." I completely forgot I'd halfway agreed to such a thing until Logan called last night, reminding me she'd be at my house around four so we could drive over to the class together.

And I cried. Again.

It came out of nowhere. I was concentrating on getting into Pigeon Pose and staying there, and then, the longer I sat there, breathing in and out like the instructor gently encouraged, I felt tears leaking down my cheeks. Then, in the next couple of minutes, I was crying, trying to hold in my sniffles so I wouldn't disturb the rest of the non-crying class and failing miserably.

I press the heels of my palms against my eyes before rolling up my mat, willing the last of the tears to stop. The studio is quiet except for soft murmurs and the sound of other mats being rolled up. Logan watches me.

"That was intense at the end, right?" Logan asks.

"Did *you* cry?"

This is embarrassing as hell. I know my nose is red because my eyes are still a little blurry with the remnants of the tears I just shed. I'm glad I'm not wearing makeup.

"I almost did. The lady next to me did too, I think. All of these thoughts just started flooding in, like a wave."

I nod, swallowing hard. "Same."

"I read about this before we came, actually. It's pretty common to cry after a class like this. This lady on Instagram was sitting in her car after her class bawling her eyes out. It just came out of nowhere. She didn't even know why."

I concentrate on slipping on shoes. My chest still feels too open from that last pose. As I pull on my shoes, a memory I usually keep shoved down pushes through. My mom's voice, sharp and angry. The shattering of glass. Blood running down my forehead before I even realized I'd been hit.

I was maybe ten, eleven? She was holding a glass cup while they argued, and in an especially dramatic moment, she threw it at my dad when he said something especially vile, about her "dry pussy." Disgusting shit to say in front of your kid. But when my parents started in, it was like they had no spatial awareness. No low blow was off-limits.

I honestly don't even remember the rest of what he said, only the way my mom's face crumpled and the rage that followed before she flung it at him. She had terrible aim, and the glass shattered against the kitchen wall. I was standing at the counter, trying not to listen to them argue and feeling guilty while I made a turkey sandwich, because the whole argument started because of me. They'd come into the kitchen throwing jabs about whose fault it was that I'd forgotten my science project at home. When my mom threw the glass, tiny shards exploded against the wall, and a few hit me in the forehead.

Blood gushed everywhere, because head wounds always bleed a lot.

My dad ran to grab a Band-Aid, while my mom got a warm cloth, sobbing as she sat me on the couch. Dad glared at her the whole time, even as they both fussed over me.

"Are you okay, Simone?" my dad asked me as he tilted my chin this way and that, making sure there wasn't more glass in my face.

I nodded because it really didn't hurt. I had no idea why I was bleeding so much. I really wished they would just both go away.

"I can't believe you—" my mom said, her voice wobbly, her hands shaking as she pressed the warm compress to my forehead.

"Your crazy ass threw the damn glass!"

"I'm crazy? No, you're the crazy one, Barry, if you think I have to stay here and put up your shit!" she hissed.

They were still arguing over me while I bled.

My fingers tighten around my shoelaces. The memory presses in, thick and heavy, but I shake it off and finish tying my shoes. Just as I finish, the instructor, a tiny woman with a pixie hair cut and sun-worn creases in her face, walks over to us. I fight the urge to run because I truly don't want to have a conversation about my bawling session. I exchange a look with Logan and try to smile at the woman anyway. She places a hand on my shoulder when she reaches me.

"I'm honored you felt comfortable enough to let go in my class," she tells me quietly, staring directly into my eyes. "The tightening and loosening in the chest and hips, the heaviness followed by the wave of lightness and relief…"

The woman is describing everything that happened in my body moments ago. "Yes, that's exactly… Yes," I say.

"The hips store stress and trauma," she explains, rubbing a weathered hand down her own hips. "That's why it's so important to allow yourself to feel everything, and then release it. There's so much healing in the breath work." She pauses and looks me in the eye again. "I hope you'll come back."

I nod quickly, offering her a smile. "It was a great session, thank you."

She gives my shoulder one last pat, giving a smile to Logan before sauntering off.

I look at Logan, and she raises her brows then holds up her hand for a high five.

"Another experience in the books, shawty," she says when I slap her hand.

"We really should come back." I sling my bag over my shoulder, and we walk toward the doors.

We exit the studio into the warm evening air. "That was heavy, though," she says. "I don't think I could handle it more than once a month."

"We're still getting smoothies, right?" I ask, nodding toward the juice shop that sells rapper-themed smoothies, along with African black soap, vegan patties, and any other wellness things you can think of.

"Hell yeah, that's the whole reason why I booked this class." She's already heading in the direction of the small shop, decorated with a huge purple-and-black sign that's shaped like a leaf. I nod and smile as we pass by a couple of guys near the store selling bean pies. There are people milling around when we enter, some shopping in the back, digging through the holistic personal items, though most of the line is up front, staring at the huge black menu of smoothies that lists the ingredients. It smells deeply of lavender and frankincense, and I inhale deeply and glance at Logan, grinning.

"Doesn't this remind you of…"

She nods, returning my smile. "Divine Essence," she finishes for me.

It was a small book shop located not too far from Clark's campus in the West End, and on Saturdays during our freshman year, a group of us would meet up there and discuss the state of

Black people across the Diaspora. Back then, we were young, very idealistic, and maybe even a little smug about our vision for the people. We still hadn't exactly figured out how to put our thoughts about what everyone should be doing for advancement into action. Our "consciousness connections" meeting lasted about six months before our busy lives—school, work, hangovers from clubbing the night before—started interfering with our lofty intentions for the Diaspora. I'm still smiling when I order my sea-moss smoothie.

By the time we make it back to my car, my body is still fluid and looser, but my thoughts are tangled up with a hundred different things. Logan sneezes twice as I start the engine.

"This pollen sucks," I say as I turn on my window wipers to knock off some of the bright greenish-yellow dust from the windshield. All it does it turn it to sludge. "There's some allergy medicine in the front pocket of my bag." I bob my head toward the back seat where my purse is when Logan sneezes again, resting her head against the back of the seat.

She turns and grabs my purse then digs through it until she finds the bottle, then pops a couple of pills into her mouth.

"Thank you," she mumbles before she swallows them with her mango/sea-moss smoothie named for 2Pac.

"I think you're Malika's new Rihanna," I tell her as I change lanes. "She hasn't stopped talking about you since she did the shoot."

She laughs, shaking her head. "That little girl had me dying laughing the whole time."

We got Malika to endorse a new prosecco from a Black-owned wine company out in California, and we had her shoot the promo for it at Logan's wine shop to help her out with some free marketing. A win-win.

"She said when she retires from ball, that's what she wants to do too—open a wine shop. She barely even drinks wine. The only thing she likes is Moscato because it tastes like 'fizzy juice.'" I grin. "She said she just likes the wine shop aesthetic."

Logan laughs. "That was a good look," she says. "They're talking about me hosting one of their pops-ups at their vineyard in the summer. They want me to lead a tasting talk. They're trying to get more retailers to carry their wine."

"Dope," I say, bobbing my head up and down.

"Oh, Delroy said he's gonna call you," Logan tells me, tugging on one of the long French braids hanging over her shoulders.

As part of Sage's big regroup, I finally reached out to him. He just fired his publicity team and is now working with a woman's firm based out of New York. The owner went to Hampton University, and we have a few mutual acquaintances. I figured now was as good a time as any to see where his head was in terms of new representation. And we have nothing to lose. We're barely staying afloat financially at this point.

"How are y'all doing?" I ask, glancing at Logan. Three casual dates had turned into her officially dating him now.

"I like him. I like him a lot, actually. He's honest. And confident without being cocky. And he tells me exactly what he wants, when he wants it."

"So Darren—"

Logan shakes her head. "Ain't it anymore. That chapter is officially closed."

"How do you feel about it?"

Logan looks over at me. "You know he was never it for me."

I smirk. "Dude, he was *so corny*," I yell, glad to be able to let it out. "But that doesn't mean you can't miss him."

"Well, I don't. *Everything* about him was mediocre. And at my big age, I just… can't keep trying to make fetch happen."

"I'm surprised you stayed with him that long."

"Me too," she says, looking out of the window.

I check my rearview mirror as a Hellcat races up behind me, its engine roaring unnecessarily before it swerves into the next lane.

"Why?" Logan says, flipping the car off when it whizzes past us.

"You're gonna get us shot out here," I chastise her.

She rests her head on the seat as I exit from I-20 onto I-285. "And they'll get shot back."

I know she sometimes carries a small .22 with her because "you can't be in these Atlanta streets unprotected," but I'm fairly certain she didn't bring it to our "align and awaken" yoga class.

"Anyway," I say, "I'm glad you've decided to officially allow Darren to kick all of the rocks. No backsies this time."

Logan rolls her eyes and frowns when her gaze drops to my outstretched pinky finger. She hooks it with hers after another eye roll, signifying the silent promise.

"Speaking of backsies..." She grins as she waggles her eyebrows. "Jackson's story on Delroy was so, so good."

"I know, right? I told him I think it's probably the best thing he's ever written."

He's actually been on a mini press run because of it, with guest spots on public radio and a few local sports stations. He made another ESPN appearance, this time on *Pardon the Interruption*.

"So... no more middle-of-the-night hookups?" Logan asks, tilting her head.

I let out a long, silent sigh. Just the thought of the time we spent together two weekends ago makes every molecule in my body start jumping around, dancing in my lower belly.

"Honestly, I dunno what I'm doing anymore," I admit as I pull off at the exit to my house.

There are a few kids standing in the middle of the road, water bottles in their hands. One who looks about ten shuffles up my window with a bottle of water. I roll the window down further and pass him a couple of dollar bills from the small stash I keep in the console for times like this.

"It's getting late," I warn him like I'm his teacher. The sun is about to completely set. "You guys need to head home, right?"

He nods, mumbles, "Yes, ma'am," and looks back at his little buddies before he passes me the water bottle, which is dripping because he just pulled it out of his tiny cooler. I wipe my hands on my yoga pants and put the bottle in the cup holder as the light turns green.

"He's way too young to be out there," I mumble as I make a turn.

"I know, right. The other day I saw this kid who looked like he was maybe seven or eight at the exit off MLK."

I shake my head as we fall silent for a moment.

"I just keep making what feels like terrible decisions," I admit as I maneuver through the backstreets toward my house. "But I'm also trying to 'fully show up.' That's what I've been working on with Zuri."

When I told Zuri about my horny, jealous, confused trek to Jackson's house in the middle of the night, she listened with that calm look of hers, the one that said she wasn't judging but was about to give me some advice that would make me rethink my life choices.

"I know I shouldn't shown up at his house like that. Especially after I hadn't been answering his calls," I admitted. *"He told me I made him feel 'crazy.'"*

"How did his telling you that make you feel?"

I shrugged. *"I don't know. Not great. Our sexual chemistry is like the elephant in the room at all times. But there's so much other stuff between us that it feels messed up to act on it sometimes."*

Zuri nodded. She stared at me for a beat, as if weighing her words.

"But your telling him you missed him was a big step."

She was quiet, and I nodded after a moment. It was a big step. It was terrifying in the moment. But I did it. And after I did, I felt lighter, even if it was only briefly. I felt lighter and it was worth it.

"*You opened up,*" Zuri continued, leaning forward. "*You were vulnerable.*"

"*It was hard at first, but after the words were out, I was glad I was more transparent with him.*"

She nodded. "*It's just important that you identify what you truly want from him and your relationship with him.*" She paused again, like she frequently does, allowing me the space to soak up her words, turn them over in my mind. "*It's good that you were in the moment.*"

"Oh, I *was* definitely *in the moment,*" I said.

"*Do you think you acted on impulse?*"

I drew in a breath and nodded.

"*How do you feel about that?*"

"*I feel like it wasn't the wisest thing for me to do. Like it wasn't necessarily fair to either of us for me to put us in that position, especially so unexpectedly.*"

Zuri nodded, though it wasn't exactly a confirmation of my words, more that she heard what I was saying. "*I want you to think about your patterns. You go from silence, not returning his calls, to showing up unannounced at his door.*"

I nodded, guilt coursing through me.

"*Guilt is not the intention here,*" she said, reading me. "*Guilt, shame—there's no space for it in healing. It's only a marker to let you understand what you're feeling so you can then move on.*"

I heaved a breath and looked at her plants climbing over her windowsill.

"*I think you need to find neutral ground for your next conversation with Jackson, if you choose to have it,*" she said. "*A space where you can have a conversation when you're both clearheaded and less emotional.*"

I blink myself back to the present, driving with one hand on the wheel as I take a sip of my sweet smoothie. "All I did was open a can of worms going over there that night," I say when I swallow.

"Why do you say that?" Logan asks.

"Because now I feel like a lovesick teenager." I laugh humorlessly as I set my drink back into the cup holder. "You remember how I was when we first started dating?" I don't wait for her response. "It's almost like that again, but worse. It's like this longing, from deep in my belly. And when we connect now, it's on some other, just-beyond-words type of…"

I shiver in my seat. Logan's brows are raised as she stares at me. Seconds tick by.

"So, are you gonna try to get back tog—"

"He's still so angry with me," I interrupt. "And I'm still not sure how it would work. The one thing I don't wanna do is jump back into something with him with all this unresolved shit between us and have it come out in our marriage. Again. You know? He was right. We're not my parents. I'll never let that happen."

"But what do you *want*, though, Simone? All that other shit aside. What do you *want*?"

"I dunno. I dunno," I reply. "I miss him, and I can finally acknowledge that, at least."

"So have you two been talking? Like outside of Caleb?"

"Not really. He's busy. I'm busy. And he hasn't really reached out. I just feel so… just ugh. I *ache*," I admit. "Like, literally ache on some romance-novel, 'I want you every second of the day'-type mess."

"You think part of that is because you feel like you can't really have him anymore?" Logan asks after a beat.

I squint at the road. "No. There's too much history for me to be on something that simple."

"You said that's how your parents were, though. The second your mom thought your dad might be serious about someone, she'd want him again. Or when your mom started dating that guy, Calvin—"

"Kevin," I correct her.

"—Kevin, your dad was all over her again."

"No," I say. "It's not that way with Jackson."

We're quiet as I turn onto my street.

"Is Caleb still hanging out with that Tiana girl?" Logan asks, changing the subject when my house comes into view.

"They're back and forth. But I think they've cooled off. She hurt his feelings the other day."

"What'd she do?" Logan sits up in the seat.

"He said she acts like she really, really likes him one minute and then the next won't answer his calls and avoids him at school."

Last week he was moping in the living room, scrolling through his phone and scowling.

"What's up with you?" I asked.

He heaved a breath, irritation etched on his handsome face, and I waited for him to tell me what was on his mind.

"Tiana said she doesn't want a boyfriend," he admitted after a long silence. *"But then she acts like she likes me. We text all the time. We hang out at lunch. She comes over here, and honestly, Mom, we both know she doesn't really even need my help."*

Caleb looked at me for confirmation, and I nodded in acknowledgment.

"So why else would she be coming over here if she didn't like me?"

"Maybe she just needs a friend," I suggested. *"And she trusts you."*

Caleb was shaking his head. *"That's what Dad said,"* he said. *"But then whenever other girls come around, she starts acting all funny, like she gets mad about it."*

"Have you told her how you feel?"

"I try to show *her how I feel so my words aren't actionless."*

I smiled. That was another Jackson-ism. *"But maybe she needs to hear it too."*

"I did tell her. Last week, I told her I liked her as more than a friend. But I also told her it's okay if she wants to just be friends because I like being around her so much. I'd rather be around her than not be around her, you know? That sounds dumb, huh?"

I couldn't help but smile. *"No. That sounds honest. That's always the best thing you can be, real with yourself and what you're feeling, and it'll trickle into the way you deal with other people."*

"I just like her," Caleb said, closing his eyes. *"And sometimes it feels like I'm pretending when I'm around her because I like her so much."*

"He made her chicken parmesan," I tell Logan now. "I walked into the kitchen after I came back from the office one day and there he was, chef-ing it up. He plated it and everything."

Logan is laughing. "Shut up. For real?"

"Yeah, you know that's one of Jackson's go-to meals. He's probably been practicing when he's over there."

"That's too cute." She laughs as I pull into my driveway.

"I feel like he's too young to be as intense as he is with this little girl, though."

I pull into the garage, and we hop out of the car and make our way to the door. We push inside and are greeted by the smell of warm chocolate. I made brownies last night and the pan is on the stove, half eaten. Logan grabs one and takes a healthy bite as I set my bag down at the dining room table. I can hear the TV in the next room.

"I just hope he doesn't end up getting his feelings hur—"

I stop mid-sentence when I turn the corner to the living room and see Tiana. In her sports bra. Grinding on my son's lap.

My mouth falls open in shock. They both notice us at the same time. Caleb looks at us and his eyes go wide. I hear him mutter, "Oh, *shit.*" Tiana springs up, flailing her arms in her haste, and almost elbows Caleb in the face.

"Damn, Caleb. On the couch, though?" Logan asks, a hint of laughter in her voice. "You couldn't go upstairs at least?"

I shoot her a look before turning my attention back to Caleb and Tiana, who are now frantically whispering to each other, looking around for Tiana's t-shirt. *Good Lord.* He finds it in the couch cushions and hands it to her like it's on fire. She yanks it over her head, staring at the floor, chest heaving. I press my lips together, breathing through my nose.

"I didn't know you were gonna be home so soon. I thought you were going over Auntie Logan's," Caleb explains, his words falling together into a jumble because he's speaking so quickly.

"Caleb," I say, tilting my head.

He bites on his lower lip, then turns to Tiana. He honestly seems more worried about gauging her reaction than getting in trouble from me. She looks like she's about to burst into tears. Actually, she looks as if she's already been crying. Her eyes are puffy and a little red, the tip of her nose pink.

"I'll call you later," Logan says, looking at me.

She walks over to the couch and pecks Caleb's cheek, murmuring something quietly to him that makes him sigh.

"Tiana, I'm Auntie Logan." She sticks her hand out, and Tiana shakes it. "Maybe we'll meet some other time in different circumstances."

"Nice to meet you, Miss Logan," Tiana says softly.

"Y'all kids be good now, ya hear." Logan wiggles her fingers and heads for the front door after sparing me another amused glance. A few moments later it shuts soundly behind her, and the three of us are left staring at each other in awkward silence.

Seventeen

"MOM," CALEB STARTS, SITTING ON the edge of the couch cushion, "we weren't… It wasn't like that."

I sigh. "Look, you're sixteen. And I get it. I do. But when you're here together alone, I'm trusting you." I look between them. "This scene I walked in on…" I wave my hand around. "Nah. We're not gonna be doing that. You understand what I'm saying? I'm trusting you both to be responsible. Caleb, I'm trusting *you* to be responsible. This is a young lady. And you need to be mindful of that."

"I *am* mindful of that," Caleb insists.

"You know what Grandma used to always tell me?"

He heaves a breath. "'Kissing leads to other things.'"

"Exactly. You two are *sixteen*. And I know you may feel like you know your bodies and that you know what to do with them, but sex is about way, *way* more than what you're feeling physically."

Caleb looks mortified but still keeps glancing at Tiana. He puts a hand on her back when she starts swiping her eyes quickly, her lips pressed into a tight line, like she's angry that she's crying.

"Hey, you all are *not* in trouble." I move to sit next to them on the arm of the couch. "Okay? I just… This is awkward, if I'm being honest."

Tiana nods quickly. "I'm sorry, Ms. Simone," she says, drying her eyes, her gaze still directed toward the floor. "I better… Would you mind taking me home?"

"Tee," Caleb says, "c'mon, you don't have to—"

"I wanna go home, Caleb," Tiana says, her voice firm when she finally looks up at him.

I meet Caleb's eyes over her head. "You can drive the car. But Caleb—come right back, understand?"

He sighs and nods. The two of them get up, heading toward the kitchen to exit through the garage.

"Bye, Ms. Simone. I'm sorry…" Tiana mumbles before she leaves.

I slide down onto the couch and look up at the ceiling, then pull my phone out of yoga pants pocket and am staring at it, debating what to do, when it starts buzzing in my hand.

"Hi," I answer.

"Hey," Jackson greets me.

"I was literally debating if I should call you."

"Don't debate, just call next time," he says. "What's up?"

"I just walked in on Caleb and Tiana dry-humping on the couch."

I can hear Jackson's sigh. "That was all? They weren't—"

"No, thank the Lord Jesus. You think I'd be this calm?"

He chuckles.

"This thing with them is getting a little heavy. I don't want him getting off track."

"Did you talk to him about his punishment for the school stuff yet?"

"What school stuff?" I ask, sitting up on the couch.

"The school sent an email saying he hasn't been to engineering club for the past few days and that he missed ELA and science two days in a row."

I release a long breath and swipe to my email.

"What is *up* with him?" I say as I read the message. "This is exactly how it starts. One minute he's humping on the couch and cutting class, and the next minute she'll pop up pregnant and he'll drop out of school—"

"Simone." There's a hint of laughter in his voice.

"This isn't funny, Jackson."

"Where is he?"

"Dropping Tiana off at home. I told him to come right back, though."

"All right. You want me to come by so we can talk to him together?"

"Yeah, I think that'd be good."

"Okay, I can be there in about twenty minutes."

I hang up with Jackson and scroll through the rest of my email, but I'm having a hard time focusing. I know Caleb is a teenage boy, and teenage boys have hormones. And I know he likes Tiana a lot. But Caleb is a sensitive kid. And whatever Tiana has going on is obviously influencing him to make bad decisions.

I drop the phone next to me on the couch just as Caleb pushes through the front door. He looks sad. No, he looks *burdened*. Seeing that look on his face makes my own chest tighten.

"Nope, your dad is on the way over, so stay down here, please," I tell him when he attempts to climb the stairs to his room.

"Dad is coming over?" he asks, widening his eyes. "You don't think you're being a little dramatic about this?"

I fix a look on him. "I think we just got an email from your school saying that you skipped class. And I think just twenty minutes ago, I walked in on you and your girlfriend doing way too much on my living room couch. So no, I don't think I'm being 'too dramatic.'"

"She's not my girlfriend," Caleb mumbles, scowling. He climbs back down the steps and slouches in the armchair with his red Hawks hat pulled down low on his head so I can't see his eyes.

"That was girlfriend-boyfriend behavior that I walked in on."

There's a pause as I wait for Caleb to speak.

"When I dropped her off, she said this was 'too intense' and she needed space. *Again.*"

He's still scowling when there's a knock on the door. I get up to let Jackson in.

"Hey," he greets me.

He's wearing a long-sleeved black thermal and black stonewashed jeans, and is so effortlessly sexy that it makes the gnawing in my chest worse. I drag my gaze over the way the fabric stretches across his chest, and I know I should look away, but I don't. I haven't seen in him person in two weeks, and it's like everything in my body is reaching for him. He takes me in too, lingering on my hips before meeting my eyes again. My skin is hot everywhere his gaze touches.

I step aside to let him in, his woodsy scent engulfing me.

"He just got back," I tell him, leading the way down the hall. "He's upset. He said she broke up with him again. Or they were never together and she says they can't be, or something?" I lift a shoulder and make a face. "We haven't gotten to the 'ditching school' part yet."

Jackson bites the inside of his lip and nods. Caleb looks up from his spot in the chair when his father walks in.

"What's up, we're not greeting each other now?" Jackson asks.

"Hi, Dad."

Even that sounds mournful, and I shoot Jackson a look before I sit on the couch. He sits on the other end, closest to Caleb, and leans forward with his arms resting on his knees.

"So what's up, Caleb?" Jackson asks after a moment of silence, as our son pretends to watch the TV. Jackson glances at me and I nod, grabbing the remote from the end table and flicking it off.

"Nothing is up," Caleb finally answers.

"That answer's not gonna work." Jackson looks him in the eye. "Take off your hat, son. And sit up while we're speaking to you."

Caleb immediately does as he's told, taking off his hat, freeing his locs, which have grown a bit and are tied back at his nape. Now that his hat is gone, I can see his eyes, framed by long eyelashes, are weary, almost like he's been crying too, or trying very hard not too.

My heart sinks again. Every motherly instinct in my body wants me to pull him into my lap, and cuddle him until he feels better. I have to sit on my hands to keep from doing that because my motherly instincts are also telling me that's not what he needs right now.

"Why'd you cut class?" Jackson asks.

Caleb's gaze falls to the floor and he swallows. Seconds tick by as Jackson waits for him to speak.

"*Caleb*," Jackson says.

Our son looks from me to Jackson, then back to the floor. "I promised her I wouldn't betray her trust."

I glance at Jackson. "You promised who? Tiana?" I ask Caleb. He nods.

"Well, you're betraying *our* trust with what you've been doing," I say. "So what's going on?"

Caleb sighs. "She doesn't really like to go home. That's why she likes coming over here so much. She says she feels better when she's over here. She says she feels better when she's with *me*. Which is why I don't get why she always switches it up the second we actually start to get closer."

"Why doesn't she like to go home?" Jackson asks.

"Her stepdad is crazy."

At that I sit up straighter, my stomach dropping. Jackson stills. "Crazy how?" I ask.

"He broke her mom's nose one time."

I close my eyes, releasing a breath.

"Her mom threw him out, like, a month ago or something, but he still comes and stays the night sometimes. So whenever he's there, she's scared something is gonna happen. She said she gets so scared that she…" Caleb trails off.

"She what?" I ask quietly.

"You know how she's always wearing long-sleeved shirts?"

I nod, dread knotting my stomach.

"She told me she gets so anxious when he's there that sometimes she cuts herself."

My chest tightens and my heart begins hammering. I knew Tiana had something going on, but I didn't guess it was *that*. I exhale, breathing out memories of my own cutting. The times I'd sit up in my room, feeling so much and not knowing what to do with it. Pressing down on the inside of my thighs with scissors and until I drew blood. The release I felt when the pain echoed through my body. The shame I felt the time my mom walked in my room unannounced and saw the marks on my thighs.

I glance at Jackson, whose expression is serious.

"See, I knew I shouldn't have told you," Caleb accuses. "You're *judging* her."

"Hey, watch your tone when you're speaking to your mom," Jackson warns.

Caleb closes his mouth and sinks further into his chair, frowning.

"I'm not judging her," I say. "I actually understand what she's going through because when I was y'all's age… I used to do the same thing."

The words are like molasses on my tongue, slow and heavy when I admit to my son one of my deepest regrets. Caleb's eyes widen.

"Yeah," I say. I haven't talked about this outside of therapy to anyone besides Tyler, when we got older, and Jackson.

"Why?" Caleb asks, wrinkling his brow.

"Your grandpa never hit your grandma, but they had a very loud, very unhealthy relationship."

"That's why they got remarried so many times, right?" Caleb asks.

I nod. "Partly, yeah. I felt like I was always in the middle of their arguments."

"Did Uncle Ty feel like that too?"

"Sometimes. Cutting was one of my unhealthy coping mechanisms."

"And did you… How'd you stop?" He asks the question almost like he's afraid to pry after I told him something that's so obviously hard to talk about.

"I started seeing a therapist," I answer. "Your grandma found me someone to talk to, and it helped me a lot. And I was able to stop. That's when I started running track, actually. Running gave me a way to release all the things I was feeling inside."

Caleb is silent for a while as he stares at the hardwood floor. Then he looks at me.

"Do you have scars?" he asks quietly, glancing at my leg, as if he can see them through the yoga pants I'm still wearing.

"No." I shake my head. "I never went that deep."

"Tiana has light ones," Caleb says quietly. "She said they might go away, but she's embarrassed by them. That's what we were doing today when…" He bites his lip. "She showed me her scars. And I told her I don't care about that because I still think she's beautiful."

I feel my eyes well up because of this kid and his heart. Jackson grins and looks down at the floor between his knees.

"That's good of you to support her," he finally says. "She's gonna need a lot of that."

Caleb looks off toward the window. The sun has almost sunk completely in the sky, and there are only tiny streaks of pink left. I lean over and flick on the living room light.

"You're an empathetic person," I tell Caleb. "And that's a gift. The world will try to tell you it's not, but caring about someone the way you do about Tiana is a gift. And she's blessed you're in her life." I pause, weighing my words. "But this is *really* serious, Caleb."

His gaze flits off to the side, toward the blank TV.

"She's basically crying out for help," I say.

"She said she hasn't cut herself for, like, a month though." Caleb looks back at me, his eyes hopeful.

"That's really great. But she needs to get help from a professional. Does anyone else know about this?"

He nods quickly. "Her mom does. She set her up to talk with Miss Shameka, the school counselor, about it. She goes there every day before school, I think. And she really is getting better. She told me she feels better after she talks to Miss Shameka. That she feels lighter."

"So is that what's up with the ditching?" Jackson asks.

Caleb sighs again, like we're somehow exhausting him. "She just wanted a break from everything. And I thought I should go with her."

"Go with her where, Caleb?" I ask.

"We went to Piedmont Park and just hung out."

"To Piedmont—" I pinch the bridge of my nose. That's across town.

"Troy came too," he says, as if bringing his best friend somehow makes it better. "Tee said Miss Shameka told her she needs to 'touch the grass' or something? Like, to help ground her so she doesn't get so lost in her thoughts."

"And y'all couldn't 'touch the grass' here, in the front yard? *After* school?"

Caleb stares blankly, and Jackson shoots me a wry look.

"I'm getting an A in both of those classes anyway." Caleb is speaking more quickly now. "So I thought I was responsible enough to decide if I could miss a couple of days."

Jackson looks at me again, a trace of a smile on his lips.

"I actually *do* think you're responsible enough to make that kind of decision," he admits. Caleb sits up straighter, his face brightening. "But you have rules that you have to abide by at school, and so right now, you're not at liberty to make that call."

Caleb's face falls again. "So am I in trouble?" he asks.

Jackson and I exchange a look, and he almost imperceptibly nods his head.

"No," I say. "You're not in trouble. But when stuff like this is going on… heavy stuff like this? You need to involve us."

He nods.

"I'm not playing, Caleb."

"Okay," he says, staring at the floor again.

"Even when you promised not to tell because this was way too big for you to carry on your own, all right?" I add. "Next time she's here, maybe I can talk to her if she'd be open to it."

"She's always talking about you. She's always saying how pretty you are and how she thinks you're cool because of your job. But she's not even talking to *me* right now," he says. "I shouldn't have…"

"Was that your first kiss?" I ask.

Jackson hangs his head. "*Mom.*"

"What? I'm just asking."

"No," Caleb says. "But she hasn't … It was hers."

Sixteen is a little old to have never been kissed, but I was the same way. A slow bloomer. Nervous. Shy. Unsure of myself, especially around boys I actually liked. I had a lot of male friends, grew up around nothing but boys, but when it came to anything beyond the platonic, I was clueless and scared to death.

"Today she said she was a freak," Caleb says. "And I was just showing her that she isn't. That she's beautiful to me."

I look at the floor to hide my smile. When I look up, Jackson is watching me, amusement in his eyes.

"It's like you said, Dad. Your actions need to be louder than your words."

Jackson laughs then. "That ain't how I meant that, and you know it."

Caleb smirks before it falls from his lips. "But it's like whenever I say stuff like that to her, or whenever we start to get closer, she always gets all weird and stops talking to me. Like I'm gettin' in trouble and doing everything I can to show her how much I love her, but nothing works because she just keeps disappearing on me. And then the second I'm finally, like, whatever, you don't like me like that and it's stupid for me to keep trying, she pops back up and she's all over me."

"She's dealing with a lot, Caleb," I say. "And she's just trying to figure it all out. She's hormonal, her emotions are all over the place, and she's feeling so much, she probably doesn't know what to do with it all. But you need to protect yourself too."

"Give her time," Jackson says. "Let her know you have her back. And if it's meant to be, it'll be."

Caleb nods, soaking in his father's advice, and I can see him processing it differently than when *I* tell him something.

"But I'm gonna reiterate what your mom said earlier. You don't keep stuff from us, ever. We gotta keep being open with each other, all right? No secrets."

Caleb stares at Jackson then me, a tiny smile on his lips.

"What?" I ask.

He leans back in his chair, crosses his arms, and tilts his chin up. "I know you stayed the night at Dad's while I was in Huntsville. You share your location with me, remember?"

Heat courses through my body and I look at Jackson. His expression doesn't change much, he just releases a slow breath as he twists his lips.

"*That* was a secret, right?" Caleb asks.

"Nah, that just wasn't your business," Jackson responds.

"It's about our family, though," Caleb counters. "Are you guys finally getting back together?"

"It's complicated," I say just as Jackson answers, "We're still figuring things out."

"Do you still love each other?" Caleb asks, in that plainspoken way only your kid is capable of.

There's silence, and I can hear my own breathing, feel Caleb's questioning eyes on me.

"Yes," I finally admit. I look at Jackson, who eyes are on me, his expression unreadable.

"Dad?" Caleb asks.

Jackson doesn't look away from me as he speaks. "I've never stopped loving your mom." My heart starts beating double time. "That's not how love works."

"Then why did you even get divorced, if you still love each other?" Caleb asks innocently.

"Because love doesn't always fix everything," Jackson answers for me.

"But—"

"Caleb." Jackson gives him a look, and Caleb closes his mouth, looking between the two of us like he's trying to solve a puzzle.

"Well, I think you guys should get back together," he eventually declares.

Before I can think up a response, the discussion is interrupted when Caleb's phone buzzes loudly. His face lights up when he reads the text.

"Can I—" He holds the phone up, and Tiana's name is on the screen. Jackson and I exchange a look before he nods.

Caleb hops up, headed for the stairs, taking them two at a time to his room.

"Well, that was awkward," I say, leaning back on the couch.

Jackson runs a hand down his face and releases a breath.

"Do you think we messed him up? Like him knowing that we…"

"I think it's all right. This ain't *The Parent Trap*," Jackson says, smirking. "He'll be okay."

"He has such a good heart," I say, picking at lint on my pants.

"He's a good kid," Jackson agrees. "You catch when he said he—"

"*Loved* her?" I finish. "I wasn't even thinking about 'loving' anybody at that age. Were you?"

Jackson shrugs. "I thought I was in love with the girl I was with my junior year. Mya Jones," he says, grinning. "But Caleb's more serious and focused than I was at that age."

"I told you Tiana had some intense shit going on." I look out onto the darkened street, where Jackson's truck is parked at the curb. "That cutting… It can go all the way left if she doesn't get the help she needs. I hope this Miss Shameka person can really help get her focused and on the right track."

"I hope she doesn't hurt him in her confusion," Jackson adds.

"Me too."

I get up and close the blinds, since it's dark out and I don't want people seeing straight into the house. I turn and look over my shoulder at Jackson. "You don't think it was a mistake that I told him about my cutting?"

"No. I think it was brave of you."

"Brave?" I echo as I move across the hardwood to close more blinds.

"Yeah. Admitting things you've struggled with to your kid, especially something that heavy, takes guts."

I let go of a breath and nod. "Thank you."

Jackson shifts forward on the couch again, his arms resting on his knees. The sleeves on his thermal are pushed up to his elbows, showing traces of the tattoos running down his left arm. He turns just his head to look at me when I sit next to him on the couch again.

"You okay?" His eyes are assessing when they roam over my face, as if he's seeing me for real for the first time today. "You look like you've been crying."

I run a hand down my face. "I do?"

"I don't think Caleb noticed, but I can tell."

"I went to yoga today," I confess after a few seconds. I wave a hand over my outfit. "It was this class called 'align and awaken.' And I was in the middle of doing some hip openers, and this memory I hadn't thought about in *years* just popped into my head. I broke down, right there in the class. They say your hips store trauma. The instructor came over after class and told me it's a thing."

Jackson has been staring between his legs at the floor the entire time I've been talking. "What was it? Your memory?"

"My parents. Mom threw a glass at Dad after he said some super-vile shit to her. It shattered against the wall and cut me on the forehead."

Jackson looks up at me, his eyes roaming over my head, like he expects the wound to appear.

"Cynthia and Barry, man…" He shakes his head. "I can't even see them getting down like that, honestly. Some of the stories you've told me about growing up… It doesn't even seem like they'd be capable of that kind of dysfunction."

"I know," I say. "It was a big deal at the time but, like, also not. You know how you just normalize things as a kid until you get older and realize, 'Hold up. That was actually *not* okay?'"

He nods.

"Did I ever tell you about this other time when my dad locked my mom out of the house?"

Jackson shakes his head again.

"Me and Ty were younger—I don't even know if he remembers, but we were screaming and crying while Mom banged on the door. She ended up leaving and going somewhere, and when she came back that night, she had to climb through the kitchen window to get in. She bleached his clothes the next week. Like, *all* of them. Took them outside on the back porch and just started pouring. He had to wear the same pair of pants for a month until he could get new clothes."

I release a humorless chuckle. "They were *so much* when they were together. Always screaming, always unhappy, always so *extreme*. They were either all over each other or fighting. There was never any middle ground with them. I always knew how that affected me, and even the way I approached our relationship. But I never *knew*, you know? I dunno. I'm rambling right now."

Jackson is hunched forward, his jaw tightening as he processes what I just said.

"You're not rambling," he says, just as his phone buzzes. Reluctantly, he pulls it out of his pocket, sending a quick text. "I gotta roll, sorry."

I nod, swallowing my disappointment that he's leaving. He gets up, and I follow him down the hallway to the door.

"What are you about to do?" he asks when I step outside with him, hovering on the porch.

"I dunno. Work a little bit, probably. Water my new plant."

"What'd you get?"

"Another succulent. I've had it for two weeks and it's still with us, so I'm doing pretty good so far."

Jackson releases a low chuckle.

I lean against the closed door. The evening air is cooler now, carrying the dampness of spring.

"I missed you," I admit softly.

He steps closer, tugging at the waistband of my yoga pants, pulling me against his chest. He hesitates, then bends to kiss me. I rise on my toes, meeting his mouth eagerly, sighing as our lips connect. I immediately wrap my arms around his neck, pulling him closer as I deepen the kiss. He's minty and masculine and everything I've been craving. He chuckles again at my eagerness, then slows us down, pressing a quick kiss to my lips.

"I gotta go," he says against my mouth when his phone buzzes again.

"Who is blowing you up?" I ask before I can think to censor the question, because it's truly none of my business.

"I'm meeting Carter," he says after a beat. "For an interview."

My heart immediately drops, and I feel physically ill. *Carter? What the fuck?* I extract myself from his arms and lean back against the front door, staring at him in the darkness of the evening. I cross my arms over my heaving chest, the air I'm pulling into my lungs heavy and thick.

"I'm talking to her about the Delroy piece. She's working on a bigger story about soccer players coming to play in the States and she's sourcing me for it."

"She couldn't source you for the story over the phone?"

"C'mon, Simone."

"I know I don't have the right to ask because we're not married, but we *are* fucking on occasion, right?"

I stare at him for a moment and then close my eyes, pressing my palms against the coolness of the door. Long seconds pass while I try to get my head together. I hear the rumble of Miss Samantha's garage door opening next door but don't have the energy to wave.

"I'm sorry." My heart is still beating way too fast when I utter the apology. "That was out of line."

"It's an interview, Simone," Jackson says. "Okay? That's it."

"With a woman who you find 'very attractive' and 'cool as hell,' or whatever you said when we were in bed that night."

I shake my head. How did I end up here? Standing in on front porch tied in knots over my ex-husband. *Messy.*

Jackson sighs and stuffs his hands in his pockets.

"*Fuck*, okay," I murmur. "Okay."

"Simone," Jackson says, stepping forward.

"I know. It's… I know. We don't know what we are to each other. I don't know what I want. I asked for the divorce. I showed up at your house that night and basically… I get it. I know."

"It's just an interview," he says again, like that makes it better.

We stare at each other for long seconds, the tension coiled and tight. Finally, I push off the door.

"I hope your interview goes well."

I open the door, stepping inside, then shut it behind me before staring blankly down the hallway, where photos of Jackson still hang on my wall. I turn and head up the stairs to my bedroom to water my plant.

Hello, journal,

Jackson told our son he still loves me today. And I admitted that I still love him too. But it was all so matter-of-fact, so very "and in other news, rain is wet" that I'm not exactly sure what to feel about it. That is staggering information. But it also felt like it should've been followed up by some sort of meaningful action. And the fact that it wasn't almost diluted the confession? I don't know. That seems to be my permanent state since turning 40, not knowing shit. Who woulda thought that at this age, at this time in my life, so much shit would cause me to have to reflect on who I am? On who I want to become? The choices that I've made? The choices that I'm making?

I also found out today that Tiana is a cutter. And tonight, when I was showering, I felt for scars on the inside of my thighs. I haven't done that in years and years, maybe since I was a teenager. There aren't any scars there now, but sometimes it's like I can feel phantom marks anyway. It was always one of my deepest fears, that Caleb would be a little too much like me, and deal with stress in the same unhealthy way that I did. It was always my biggest fear that I would repeat the same mistakes my parents made, and scar him. Thank God he's more like Jackson when it comes to handling stress. He's a problem solver. And at the same time, he's compassionate. That's a rare combo. It's a combination Jackson has always had, even when we were younger, just figuring life out. He always looked beyond the surface, heard beyond the words people said.

I kissed him on the front porch after we talked to Caleb, like some lovesick teenager. Miss Samantha pulled up and I'm pretty sure she saw us too. Jackson could always kiss, though. Slow and deliberate. Thorough. That's the way he makes love to me, too. In tune with my every movement, all of my breaths and moans.

I admitted that I missed him today. Again. Why do I keep telling him that? What exactly do I expect his response to be? Telling him I miss him is just… words. He's off with Carter tonight. Doing an "interview." Jackson doesn't lie to me, so I'm sure that's all it is.

But it could also unintentionally be the beginning. Because Carter is… possibility. And I am the past that keeps trying to linger in his present.

I'm so jealous I can barely function. I'm so tempted to text him and make sure he's home. So tempted to drive over there again. But Caleb is home. And Jackson is right—this shit is messy. Super fucking messy. This pull I feel to him, the possessiveness I feel, when I'm the one who ended us, is super fucking messy. And honestly, maybe telling him I still love him when I'm so stuck on not knowing what I want is super fucking messy too.

But I do love him. I always have, and I'm starting to know that no matter what, I probably always will.

Eighteen

JACKSON'S INTERVIEW WENT VERY WELL. Unlike his Delroy piece, which took a couple of months to produce, Carter's story about the rise of American soccer went live a few days ago. It was a mixed-media piece, her sitting down with Jackson at a local sports bar asking him questions about soccer and its momentum in cities like Atlanta, interspersed with footage of different players, including Delroy. It was good. Great, even. And I know it raised Jackson's profile even more, because it was circulating heavily on social media. She posted behind-the-scenes photos of their interview—her and Jackson in deep conversation. Her and Jackson sitting on the front steps of the bar, side by side. They looked good together.

Turns out his leaving me to go to her worked out well for him.

I know that's not what happened. I know I'm being melodramatic. But that's how it felt, especially since he didn't call me afterward. He actually hasn't contacted me since he left my porch five days ago, and I feel like I'm running on fumes. I know there are bags under my eyes, which are probably more prevalent because I'm wearing an all-black hoodie, jogging pants, and classic Nike Cortezes, like I'm an extra from *Set It Off* and I'm about to go rob First National Bank.

"I'm tired," I admit to Zuri, sinking into her chair. "I feel very, very… tired."

"You have a lot happening in your life at once."

Zuri's hair is mostly hidden behind a bright purple and pink scarf today. It's a good color on her, makes her look like sunshine, contrasting my dreary state.

She studies me for a moment after my confession. "Physically, emotionally, both?"

"Both," I reply. I close my eyes and exhale, long and slow.

"Have you been giving yourself space to pause?"

"I think so," I say, opening my eyes. "I've been thinking a lot. But also trying to be present." I lean back in my chair. "I've been trying to sit with my feelings more, like we talked about. I don't know if I've given myself space to pause, but I do feel like I've been more aware of my feelings. Or letting myself feel things when something happens instead of pushing it aside. I also cry all of the time now, so there's also that," I admit, laughing humorlessly.

"I went to this trauma yoga class with Logan," I continue. "And it brought up a lot of old memories I'd forgotten about. Or maybe not forgotten about but just hadn't thought about in a long time."

"Do you feel comfortable sharing the memories?"

"It was just the same ol' same. Stuff from my childhood. Thoughts I'd pushed aside, or kinda forgotten, about my parents' fucked-up marriage." I blink, thinking about the screaming matches, slamming bedroom doors. "Lately, I've been realizing that I always kinda blamed myself in some ways when they argued."

"How so?" Zuri asks.

"When I was little, it just felt like every time they'd get into it, I had something to do with it. I forgot my science project at home, so they fought over that. I lost my house key, so they fought over that. I didn't clean my bedroom, so they fought over that."

I look down at my sneakers.

"I know now, as a grown woman, that that wasn't my fault. Couples fight, and when they're unhappy with each other anything can be a catalyst for them, anything can be an excuse. But when I was young, I think I may've internalized this need to be quiet. To hold things in. To almost shrink my emotions so that I wouldn't bother anybody."

Zuri nods, her gaze never leaving mine. "It makes sense that you would protect yourself that way."

I stop talking for a while and stare out of her window. This is one of the reasons why I like Zuri. She doesn't pressure me to talk. She allows my silence to speak to me.

"I've been journaling a lot," I say after a couple of long seconds have passed. "I went on a run for the first time in a while. That felt good. I mean, I woke up sore, but it was refreshing."

I might've also woken up sore because I went for my run after the wild sex I'd had the night before with Jackson. But I don't need to share that with Zuri.

"I bought a plant the other day. A succulent. It's still alive. So my coping mechanisms are coping."

Zuri smiles, as I chuckle. "But you're still feeling tired?"

"Yep." I roll my neck. "I feel cranes-in-the-sky heavy." I start humming Solange, and Zuri laughs. Then she studies me for a beat.

"Let's take some time to sort through what feels the heaviest for you. Are you good with that?"

I nod.

"Okay, so take a minute. Sit with it. See what rises to the surface."

I close my eyes again. The answer comes to the surface before I even get them fully shut.

"Jackson. Everything in my life circles back to him. I just keep thinking about how it wasn't one big, explosive fight that broke us, you know? It was more like this slow unraveling." I open my eyes. "We'd fight, sweep things under the rug, then fight again. We were actually already in a bad place when Jackson got the job offer in Charlotte."

He'd been struggling after getting laid off from a local sports publication when it went under. That's the thing about journalism—it's fickle. Publications come and go, from lack of funding, lack of interest, or a sad combination of both. Jackson is an incredible writer, but working in that industry, where so much of your career worth is based on where you write, whom you're writing for, can be taxing. And when work is low, it can be a gut blow, especially to a person like Jackson. Responsible. Protective. Determined to hold the people he loved on his back.

After he got laid off, freelancing helped, but it wasn't enough to bring in the kind of money he wanted for our family. When he started Uber-ing and substitute teaching, he was sober and withdrawn, sinking further into himself.

Jackson's dad died when he was eighteen, before we met. From everything Jackson and April told me, he had been a hard man— quiet, emotionally distant, but a provider to the core. And that was what he drilled into Jackson's head: a man provides. When his father passed, Jackson took on the role of financial and emotional anchor for April and their mom.

"I didn't want him to go, but I thought the Charlotte job might fix things," I tell Zuri. "That he could make the four-hour drive back to Atlanta every other weekend, and we'd be okay. We had a plan—one year of that, then we'd see if he could transfer back after getting his foot in the newspapers' system. But it was hard because he had to cover games most weekends, which meant our schedule was always screwed up."

I needed him here while Sage was picking up. Caleb needed him. Jackson needed us too. Caleb was playing in a junior basketball rec league, and he had his final tournament one Saturday morning at eight a.m. He was twelve, and even then, sports weren't really his thing, but he was still at that stage where he mimicked everything Jackson was interested in. Jackson had to cover the Hornets game the night before and wasn't sure if he'd make it, since he had to file his story. But he showed up. Exhausted, running on no sleep, but there. And Caleb was so excited, he almost ran off the court in the middle of the game just to greet him.

That almost broke Jackson.

That and the fact that Tristan was there.

Tristan was sitting on the bench next to the team, throwing out instructions to Caleb like he was the coach when Jackson walked in.

I'll never forget the look on Jackson's face when he glanced from Caleb to Tristan.

We argued later that night.

"I told you I was going to try to make it," he said while he undressed, tossing his baseball cap onto our cluttered dresser. There were deep circles under his eyes, and they were red-rimmed from lack of sleep.

"The Hornets game didn't get over until after eleven!" I countered, slipping on one of his t-shirts before plopping onto our unmade bed. *"And then you had to write the story, so you didn't get on the road until, what? Three in the morning? After having no sleep? That's crazy, Jackson."*

"What's crazy is Tristan being there when I can't be. I'm his dad."

"Jackson."

He stuffed his hands into his pockets and leaned against the dresser, eyeing me.

"I don't like that shit, Simone."

"What was I supposed to do? Tell Tristan he couldn't come to the game when he's been helping out? He's the one getting Caleb to practice when I can't, when Logan is busy. He's picking him up, making sure he's good. He was honored to be there—to help us, to help you—because that's what friends do. That's what family does. And you know Tristan is like my brother."

"Your brother is in L.A. and his name is Tyler."

My mouth fell open. Jackson looked at the floor, releasing a breath as he ran a hand down his face.

"You're not, like… jealous of Tristan?" I ask. The idea is so wild that it's difficult to get the words out. *"Right?"*

Jackson shook his head, still looking at the floor. *"This isn't about Tristan. I needed to be there."*

"And how is that my fault, Jackson?" I said, raising my voice.

"Because we shouldn't be split up like this in the first damn place!"

"We agreed! We said—"

"No, you said. And I went along with it, trying to appease you."

"Trying to appease me?"

He shook his head. *"We can't operate like this, Simone. It ain't working."*

"Obviously!"

"Which is exactly why it woulda made sense for us to move as a family. This 'me there and you here' shit—"

"I already told you I can't—"

"Can't what, Simone? Be with your husband? Because we're married now, remember?"

"Come on with that, Jackson."

"No, you come on, Simone. What the hell kinda sense does it make for you to still be living in Atlanta when I'm in Charlotte? Huh?"

"I'm in the middle of trying get Sage off the ground—"

"You can build Sage from anywhere!" he exclaimed, looking at me pointedly.

"You're the one who took this job knowing it was in another city." My voice was shaky, my gaze pointed.

"You think I wanted to be in Charlotte? Away from Caleb? Away from you? I'm doing what I had to do for us, so I can provide for us."

"Well, you know why I couldn't move! My foundation is here."

Jackson's eyes widened.

"Your founda— I'm *your foundation, Simone! Me."* He tapped his chest. *"Our family, that's your foundation."*

"All we ever do anymore is argue," I replied, sweeping a hand between us. *"And shit falls apart, Jackson."*

Jackson's expression fell, his chest rising and falling quickly as he stared at me.

"And there it is," he said quietly. *"The hell does that mean, Simone? You planning for us to fall apart?"*

"No!"

"Then why don't you tell me what you're sayin' right now?" he pressed.

I stared at him, my chest heaving.

"Nuh-uh, don't do that. Don't start with the silent shit, Simone. Tell me what you mean when you say shit like that."

But I didn't respond. I couldn't. When it was obvious I wasn't going to talk anymore, Jackson shook his head and left the room. He slept on the couch that night. Three months later, he quit the Charlotte paper and moved back to Atlanta. And things didn't get better—they got worse. Even with him back home, even after he landed a new, higher-paying gig with *The Athletic.* The memory settles on me, sinking into my skin.

"I think he resented me for not moving with him," I say. "I resented him for leaving in the first place. We couldn't move past it."

I feel tears pricking at the back of my eyelids. My eyes are still closed but I can practically feel Zuri nodding, waiting. I inhale through my nose and then release the breath slowly. When I open my eyes, my lashes are sticking together because they're wet.

"I'm just remembering one of the fights we had, not too long before he came back to Atlanta and quit his job in Charlotte. That was so hard on us. I used to think his taking that job is what tore us apart. Now I'm not so sure that was really ever the issue."

"So what about Jackson feels the heaviest now, in the present?" Zuri asks.

I swallow. "Love."

Zuri narrows her eyes a bit as she waits for me to clarify my thoughts.

"Caleb asked us why we got divorced the other day, if we still love each other. And Jackson told Caleb that love doesn't always fix everything." I look down at the floor. "But shouldn't it?"

"What do you think?" Zuri asks.

"I think Jackson and I hit the lowest point we'd ever hit on our relationship," I finally answer. "But I think the love was always still there. And I think… I think I might've ended my marriage before I gave us a chance to climb out of it. Before we had time to figure out if we could."

Zuri lets the realization sit with me a for a long moment as I study the plant her mother gave her, its leaves curling toward the sunlight in the windowsill. My heart is beating way too fast, the weight of that confession rolling around in my stomach like a ball.

"That's a big thing to admit," she finally says. "So you think you ended your marriage without giving yourselves a chance to course-correct?"

"Maybe." The admission is heavy.

"It's possible that in studying your parents' patterns, you overcorrected in your own relationships."

I nod. "I've thought about that a lot. Especially lately."

"And what about that thought feels the heaviest?"

I poke my cheek with my tongue. "That maybe… that maybe love *was* enough. And that maybe I did go into our marriage, into our *relationship*, with the subconscious expectation of failure."

Zuri leans forward slightly. "I know you're exhausted, but you've already done the hard part. You see your patterns. You've connected them to the trauma you experienced growing up."

I nod.

"You know this isn't just about Jackson," Zuri says. Her voice is lower, carrying the weight of the moment but crystal clear. "But maybe the question isn't whether love was enough to fix your marriage. Because that's the past. I think it's time to start focusing on the present, on your right now."

I look toward the window again, shifting in my seat before I meet Zuri's eyes.

"Maybe your question to yourself right now should be —what are you going to *do* about it?"

Nineteen

DAYS LATER, I'M THINKING ABOUT Zuri's question when I buzz Delroy into my office for a meeting that can potentially save my business. He enters, and I get up to greet him with a quick hug. He's dressed casually, but I can tell his t-shirt is expensive, as are his joggers, and the thick gold chain he wears around his neck. His hair has grown out since I last saw him, into kinky curls, and he's rocking a thick beard now. Delroy is a very handsome man. He and Logan make a striking couple.

"Simone, it's good to see you again," he says as he seats himself in one our lobby area's plush orange chairs.

"You too. I wish we would've had time to take you up on that tour in Jamaica."

"Maybe next time." He smiles.

"Delroy, Tristan is on video call," I say, nodding toward the screen in the center of the wall. "He wasn't able to join us in person."

Delroy looks at the screen. "What's up, man? Heard a lot about you."

"Likewise," Tristan says, his deep voice rumbling through the speakers. "Sorry I wasn't able to be there in person. My daughter is down with a bad case of the flu, so I'm here, listening in, but I'll be in and out because she just woke up and she's a little cranky."

"No worries, man. Of course. How old is your daughter?"

"She's two."

Delroy nods, smiling. "I hope she feels better."

"I appreciate it," Tristan returns, before muting his audio as the sound of Bella's crying floats in the background.

Delroy looks around the office. "I love the vibe you have going on in here." His eyes drift from my fake plants to the posters of athletes against vibrant, paint splattered backdrops. "My aunt always says the way you decorate says a lot about how you see the world."

"And how do you think I see the world?" I ask as I seat myself in the chair opposite him.

"Optimistic. Hopeful. But through a realistic lens. You pay attention to the details while keeping an eye out for the overall picture."

I smile, twisting the mood ring I put on again as a good-luck charm, willing myself to adopt its permanent *cheerful/energetic* setting. "Well, that's all positive, so I'll take it."

"I've been following you since our meeting in Jamaica," he says, easing back in his chair. "Even before you reached out. I'm embarrassed to admit I wasn't too familiar with your work, but once I did some digging, I realized—you're a big deal. You do things differently. Malika Higbee was a bench player, and now college players and half the WNBA are copying her nail polish on game day. And that Olympic gymnast could've taken another endorsement deal, but instead, she's co-launching an apparel line with another brand."

I nod. Shayla Hughes is one of the athletes we've recently added to our roster. So far, we've added five more, all women, all talented, all previously overlooked.

"That's what Sage is about—helping athletes establish themselves beyond their sport." I point toward the large photo of

Malika hanging on the wall with her nail polish. "It's about going beyond what they can bring to a brand or a team for me."

I inhale, my eyes still trained on his. "You know I wanted to be a sports writer at first? That's what I went to college for. I kept interviewing these athletes, and some of the stories they told me were just… *insane.* About being signed to agencies that didn't advocate for them, that seemed more loyal to the team than to the athlete. Or signing terrible endorsement deals because their agents were negligent, or just didn't care.

"All of those stories were off the record, so I couldn't write about them. But I couldn't forget them, either. And I realized maybe journalism wasn't really where my heart was. I still loved the athletes, still loved the game—but I wanted to help in a different way. I ended up switching it up, and studying brand marketing in grad school."

I lean forward. "*That's* what I'm about. Helping athletes move beyond what they've been told they should be. Building self-worth that exists outside of a contract. Being wise in your decision making. Wise enough to recognize what you bring into every room—and choosing based on that truth. Nothing else."

Delroy listens, his expression unreadable, as if he's filtering out the truth in my words.

"Don't get me wrong," I add, "the financial part matters. Nobody wants to be told they're valuable without action. The money? That's the action."

"Why'd you leave Kingship?"

"Because I didn't like being a mascot."

I'm repeating Delroy's words verbatim from when he left the U.K. team. He grins.

"And I didn't like the way they treated their Black athletes. If I'm so 'talented and visionary,' then why wouldn't I use those skills for myself and to help other people who look like me? Why would I feel comfortable using my skills to the detriment of another person?"

Delroy nods. "So how'd you get caught up with the Dustin McCarthy thing?"

"Dillon," I correct him.

"If you're about helping Black athletes get properly recognized, paid, and respected beyond their sport, why even represent someone like him? Surely you knew his character."

I swallow. "I did. The simple answer is we needed the money. We're a fairly new agency. We're running lean. No junior agents. No full-time staff. Just Tristan and I."

I glance at the screen, which is now black. I'm not even sure Tristan is hearing the conversation at all.

"What's the complex answer?" Delroy asks.

I pick at my nail and meet his eyes. "The complex answer is I thought I could handle it. Part of it was that I wanted an athlete of his stature because it meant I'd made a smart decision to leave Kingship. It validated me. I thought that if I was strategic enough, I could sign him, take his money, and keep my principles intact. I was wrong."

Delroy doesn't blink. "So you compromised."

"I fell for the illusion of security in the form of a Caucasian male, yes."

Delroy laughs at that.

"But hard lesson learned," I say. "That's all I can do, right? Take the lesson, sit with it, and then keep pushing."

"I'm going to be honest with you," he says after a beat, leaning forward so that his elbows are resting on his knees. "What I'm building is bigger than football. I love the game, but I know what it really is—a means to an end."

I nod, remembering what he said in Jackson's article. "You said you want to build legacy."

"Exactly. So let me ask you this—what's your end game, Simone? Because your track record is impressive. But you said it yourself—you made a call for security instead of alignment. So what happens the next time you're faced with that choice?"

Jackson's advice floats into my head. "Next time, I go with my gut."

The answer seems to satisfy him, and he leans back in his chair. His chain glints in the light streaming from the office window.

"So what's next?" he asks.

My heart starts racing but I keep my face neutral. "Well, the first thing is if you bring me on as your agent, you need to know you're going to make headlines," I tell him. "You'll be the new Jalen Hurts with an all-Black-woman team."

Delroy grins. "Exactly."

"But you're not hiring me because I'm one of a few Black—"

He holds up a hand. "Let me stop you right there, Simone." His Jamaican accent gets even stronger. "We don't know each other well. But from what you do know of me, do I seem like the kind of person who's concerned with quotas?"

"No."

"Do I seem like the kind of man who places his career and finances in the hands of someone with no substance?"

"No, you do not."

Delroy nods and puts out his hand for me to shake. "Okay, then."

I let out a breath and shake his hand. This is huge. *Huge* for our company. Huge that what was the biggest mistake I've made since entering this career actually landed me one of the biggest soccer players on the planet.

"Tristan, you there?"

"Yep—great to have you onboard, man," Tristan chimes in through the black screen.

"I'm excited about what we're about to build," Delroy says.

"All right, Simone, I'll talk to you later. And I'll be in touch," Tristan says to Delroy, as we hear Bella's little voice in the background. "I gotta jump."

Delroy stands when Tristan hangs up. "I actually have a flight to catch," he says, after I mention our assistant will send him the paperwork. I follow him to the door. "I'm trying to convince Logan to take a few days off to join me." He looks at me hopefully.

"She doesn't like missing work," I say. "And it's springtime, so tasting season is picking up."

He nods. "I understand, but…" He grins and shakes his head. "She's an amazing woman. Just very… complex."

"The best women usually are, right?"

Delroy laughs.

Twenty

Did Caleb tell you he wants a car?

I SEND THE TEXT TO Jackson then stare at the phone, waiting for his response. I haven't really spoken to him since he came over to talk to Caleb. I haven't seen him, either—Caleb has shifted between our houses without any interaction on our part, including last night, when Jackson picked him up before I got home from the office.

I did let Jackson know I signed Delroy, though, the second he left my office. Texting him felt like the natural thing to do. He responded immediately with a phone call.

"For real?"

"For real," I said, sure he could hear me cheesing through the phone.

"Remember when you were on the beach manifesting dope shit on your birthday?"

I laughed. "I don't think that's exactly what I was doing, but yeah."

"I do," he said, his baritone warm in my ear. "This is it. This is God giving you things you hold in your heart, baby."

I fell silent when he called me "baby," and he did too, like it had just slipped out.

"Anyway, I'm hella proud of you," he said after a second.

"Thank you."

A few days later, he sent me a bright yellow, leather-bound journal with *Sage: Profoundly Wise* embossed on it. It showed up to my office right when I was setting up the teal chairs I finally manifested.

My phone dings, indicating another text. My heart starts beating faster, like I'm a lovestruck schoolgirl. I'm beyond ridiculous at this point.

Yes, he did tell me he wants a car, Jackson texts back. *I ignored him.*

I laugh. *Dang. Harsh?*

Want and need are two different things, Jackson responds. *Caleb has no money. Let's get the school year over with, see how he does, and then we can talk about a car.*

I nod, as if he can see me through the phone. *Okay. Makes sense.*

I usually do.

I smirk. *Calm down. Thank you again for the planner.*

All good. Proud of you.

I smile so wide my jaws hurt.

What are you doing? Aside from caring for our transportation-less son? I ask.

Tristan actually just came through. We're gonna go pick up Troy and then go play ball.

You mean play ball with Caleb? Since when does he care about basketball? He hasn't played since that one time with the rec league and that was years ago.

Since Tiana.

I laugh then sigh. *Wow. Okay, well, have fun.*

Jackson likes my message, and I set the phone down on the wooden kitchen table, which is full of marketing plans and potential brand partnerships for the six new players we've picked up since we signed Delroy. I was right: the deal did make headlines. And I did become part of the story in a few of the features, with people questioning if my signing him was part of my "redemption arc."

"We're not concerned with them, Simone," Delroy said when I brought it up as something for him to at least be aware of. "It's big-picture time."

I'm looking over plans when I hear a knock at the door. I get up and open it to see Tiana standing on the front porch. Her hair is in long Senegalese twists now, and she has them swept up into a high ponytail. She's wearing her usual oversized hoodie but with shorts and high-top sneakers, since it's nearing May and getting warmer. She really is adorable. It's obvious why Caleb is so head over heels for her. She shuffles her weight, stuffing her hands into her pockets.

"Hi, Miss Simone."

"Hey, Tiana," I greet her. "Caleb's not here. He's at his dad's for the weekend."

Her face falls and she closes her eyes for a long second.

"I know he usually is, but I thought this weekend he said he'd be here because of that engineering project they got assigned?"

I shake my head. "No, they pushed the project deadline back a week because of the field trip to Georgia Tech. So they'll start it next weekend. Did you walk over?" I ask, glancing out at the street.

She shifts her weight. "Yeah."

"Did you text him first?"

"He hasn't been responding to my texts," she confesses, averting her gaze.

I twist my lips, studying her forlorn expression.

"Well, you can come in anyway. You want some lemonade? I have some from the smoothie shop in the West End I really like. It's really good."

She hesitates at the door and then says, "Okay."

Tiana comes in and takes off her shoes before following me down the hall. She takes a seat at the dining room table, peering at all of the papers I have scattered there.

"We just signed a few new people. I was looking over some marketing and brand stuff for them."

"Josette Lindberg?" Tiana's eyes light up when they fall on the point guard out of Chicago we just signed. "She's so talented. You want her to talk about gaming livestreams?"

I hand her a glass of the lavender-infused lemonade. "I try to lean in on whatever people are interested in," I answer. "She likes gaming. So that's where we'll focus."

Tiana looks impressed. "That's cool. You represent Malika Higbee too, right?"

I nod, taking a sip of my own drink as I join her at the table, and Tiana holds up her fingers, showing off her bright yellow nails. I smile.

"They're not as good as hers. I'm honestly not super into my nails. But hers are always so cute, and Caleb is always telling me I should just try new things, because you never know."

Her gaze falls to the table as she sips more lemonade. I patiently wait for her to say what's on her mind. After a few seconds tick by, it's clear she isn't going to.

"Are you and Caleb—"

"We're in a fight," she says quickly, staring down into her glass. "I was coming over to show him that I—" She lifts her small shoulders.

"That you what?" I ask softly, setting my glass down on the table.

She inhales and looks off toward the window. "Your plant is pretty."

I follow her gaze to the succulent I moved from upstairs to the kitchen a few days ago. It's still alive. "Thanks. I usually kill them, but so far so good."

Tiana smiles and then sighs, sipping more lemonade.

"I do really love him," she says after she swallows. She looks up at me, as if trying to convince me her words are true, before she stares down into her cup again. "He's my best friend. He's…" She sighs. "It's just hard for me to, like, rely on people. People are not—*humans* are not very reliable."

I twist my lips and eye her, sad she has to know that truth already. She's only sixteen. She should've had more time to be comfortably oblivious to the ways of people.

"That's probably true, generally speaking," I agree.

Tiana looks surprised by my admission.

"But you know that old Maya Angelou quote—when someone shows you who they are, believe them?"

She nods. "This girl from my school made a TikTok dance to it."

I burst into laughter. "What? It's not even a song."

Tiana rolls her eyes. "Someone put the words from her interview to an old Pharrell beat, and then she made a dance to it. It was so dumb. Not the words. But the dance."

She pulls her phone out, scrolling through TikTok until she finds the video, then holds it up for me to watch the girl, dressed in pajama bottoms and a tiny tank top, waving her arms around like a cheerleader in her bathroom mirror.

"Wow," I say.

"Right?" Tiana rolls her eyes as she slides her phone back into her pocket.

"Well," I say, "the point was, that quote—it works both ways. It's always applied to people's negative actions. But it can be applied to their positive actions as well. What are you being shown by Caleb, day in and day out?"

Tiana inhales shakily. "He says I never know what I want. And that one minute I act like I like him and then the next I act like I don't. And that he's tired of feeling dumb all of the time."

At that her eyes well up, and I feel mine do the same.

"I don't think he's dumb, Miss Simone. I love him. I really do."

The last part of her sentence comes out in shaky stutters, and I get up and hug her. I hold her tight for a minute, then release her and grab a couple of paper towels from the counter and pass her one, dabbing my own eyes.

"You've been through a lot," I say. "That can make it hard for you to get a real handle on your emotions, let alone for you to express them."

Tiana bites on her lower lip.

"Caleb shared a little bit about your situation at home."

She nods, picking her glass up again and taking a sip. "He told me. He never… He always tells me things. He never hides anything."

Her *unlike me* lingers in the air.

"I was…" I stop, considering my words. "I used to cut as well."

At that, her eyes widen. Caleb clearly did not share *that* bit of information with her.

"My situation wasn't too different from yours. My parents fought all the time. Not physically. But there was a lot of emotional and psychological abuse, and my brother and I witnessed it. I was older, so I was responsible for him a lot of times, or I felt responsible for him."

"It's like that for me with my little brothers too."

"I tried to shield my brother from what was going on in our house," I continue. "But there was never anyone to shield me. I used cutting as a way of… controlling my pain, I guess," I tell her. "I was in charge of how much it hurt, of what I felt, and when I felt it. Nobody else."

Tiana hangs her head when I say that, rubbing her arm absently.

"Therapy helped me understand how unhealthy that was. How dangerous it was for me and everyone who loved me, including my parents."

Tiana lets out a sigh that seems to come from the depths of her soul.

"Do you still talk to them?" she asks softly.

"My parents?" I say. "Yep. I talk to my mom almost daily. We talk all of the time."

Tiana frowns in confusion.

"What they did hurt me. And honestly, I'm still dealing with the aftereffects of it in my own life and relationships to some degree."

I pause as I stare off toward the window. "But I don't hold their mistakes over their heads. They weren't, like, *intentionally* causing me and my brother harm. They were just careless about the way they treated one another, and that carelessness landed on me a lot of the time."

"My stepdad is definitely careless with my mom," Tiana says. "I'm glad they're finally divorcing."

"Caleb told me you've been talking to Miss Shameka at your school?"

"I do it every morning before first period. It's free. And I like her. There was this one counselor at church that my mom made us go to when she first split up from my stepdad, and she was…" Tiana makes a face like she's grossed out, and I smile.

"I had a therapist like that once. Her name was Natasha. I really think all she ever did was recite Instagram memes to me."

She laughs, covering her mouth.

"So you like Miss Shameka?"

Tiana shrugs. "She isn't all weird. She's nice. She mostly just sits and listens. And then sometimes she'll ask me questions and she tells me I don't have to answer right away, that I can write it down in this journal she bought me from the Dollar Tree."

"I have a journal too," I say. "I write in it every time I need a way to sort out my thoughts. And I run, too. I run when my thoughts are very heavy, and I just need to feel a little lighter. I actually end up journaling after my run a lot of times. You're an athlete—maybe running can help you too."

"Maybe. I hate running, though."

"So do I."

Again, Tiana looks surprised, and I laugh.

"You don't always have to like what's good for you," I say. "I actually should say I *used* to hate running. But lately, I look forward to it, especially when there's a lot on my mind. The key is to do the thing, whatever makes you feel lighter, consistently."

We fall silent for a while, and I study her. She isn't looking at me—she's absently running a hand up and down her arm before she stops, picking under her fingernails.

"Do you mind if I ask, when's the last time you—"

"It's been a long time," she answers, looking up at me. Her gaze is direct, and I detect that she's telling the truth. "Since, like, a month before I came over and you and Miss Logan saw me and Caleb…"

Tiana flushes and trails off.

"About that," I say. Tiana bites the inside of her lip, suddenly very interested in the inside of her cup. "I love Caleb. Obviously, he's my son. He's my only child, and I love him without limits or even expectations. But he's a teenage boy. And he's hormonal. So are you."

Tiana swallows, picking at the lint on her shorts.

"I'm not going to keep lecturing you about sex, that's just not… I'm not into that, honestly. I'm just going to say that once it's done, it can't be *undone*. There's no takebacks. So whenever the time comes, and whoever it comes with, go in knowing that you're giving that person something precious—permission to access your body. And that permission shouldn't be given lightly."

Tiana is nodding vigorously, face still flushed, as she studies the contents of her nearly empty cup.

"I don't even think he really likes me any more anyway," she says softly. "He's been ignoring my texts for two days. And I called him this morning and he sent me to voicemail. It's like he hates me."

I bite the inside of my lip to keep from rolling my eyes. "He doesn't hate you, Tiana. That I can guarantee."

"I don't know what to do."

She looks up at me wide-eyed. I don't answer right away. Finally, I exhale.

"You just have to start showing up for him too."

"I don't know how to do that," she says, her eyes vulnerable.

"I think…" I release a breath. "I think you just tell him exactly what you just told me. Keep it one hundred with him, and be one hundred percent present with what you're feeling."

Tiana starts to gnaw on her pinky nail, then realizes she's about to mess up her paint job and stops.

"What if he doesn't believe me? What if he still says he doesn't like me anymore?"

"Well… At least you spoke your truth, right? Because holding it all inside of you gets heavy, right? The only thing you can control is you. How you show up. How you deal with people. Because then you know without a doubt that you did your part. I believe God honors that—us doing our part."

Tiana nods.

"So, there's your answer," I say. "Do your part and show up for him."

Twenty-One

HOURS LATER, I'M LYING IN bed, staring up at the ceiling, listening to Cleo Sol. My bedroom fits the feel of her sound—airy and light. I feel floaty, and maybe a bit drunk.

After Tiana left, Logan and I participated in our "fortieth experience" for the month of May—wine making. I'm not sure it really counted as an "experience," since it was a class she was hosting at her wine shop and I would've stopped by to support her anyway. But she said it did, and this is really all her idea, so I went with it.

"Let's just set an intention before we start this," Logan said, nodding toward the wine-making instructor as I arrived.

"My intention is to get drunk."

Logan looked at me flatly, and I smirked.

"For real, my intention is to be honest with myself and others."

"Wasn't that your same intention from your birthday dinner?" Logan asked.

"No, I wanted clarity then," I said.

"Ain't that the same shit?" she shot back.

We spent the next two hours learning how to make wine, and by the time we finished, we had two bottles each, sealed and labeled with the date, to open months from now when the flavors had deepened, since the instructor said we should let it age for at least a year.

My phone buzzes on the nightstand next to me, and I roll over to grab it.

"Hey," Jackson says.

"Hi." My smile is wide. I can't help it.

"You busy?"

"Nope." I roll onto my back to stare at the ceiling again. "What's up?"

"Caleb forgot his backpack there."

"*Again?* I swear, he'd forget his head if it wasn't attached to his shoulders."

Jackson chuckles. "We need to stop enabling him. But he says he has some big assignment due on Monday that he needs to start working on now."

"So you caved and *are* gonna enable him?" I tease.

He chuckles again.

"Are you on the way? Or are you sending him to pick it up?" I ask.

"No, I'll come. Troy is staying over too, and they just ordered wings and got on the game. It's easier for me to grab it real quick, if that's cool?"

"Yep, I'm here."

Ten minutes later, Jackson is knocking at my door. I head downstairs, flicking on the foyer light and peering through the peephole before swinging it open.

"Hi," I say.

He grins. "Hi."

I motion him inside and shut the door behind him. My eyes sweep over him in his black sweats and a black t-shirt, lingering on his well-defined arms and chest. He looks good. Better than good. I can't stop my unfiltered thoughts from coming under the haze of my wine buzz. I can't stop my smile, either. I feel good. Loose. Unencumbered by my never-ending thoughts.

"What's up?" he asks when I just stand there smiling at him.

"You look super good," I blurt, pulling up the strap on my spaghetti tank.

His gaze sweeps over my short cotton shorts and back to my face. "You been drinkin'?"

"A little bit," I say, pinching two fingers together. "Logan hosted a wine-making class at her shop today. You shoulda come! You would've liked it."

I don't wait for him to reply.

"Oh! Do you want a bottle? I made two. I'm getting you a bottle," I declare, heading quickly down the hall into the kitchen. I grab the extra bottle off the dining room table, which still has scattered papers all over it from earlier, making a mental note to clean it all up in the morning.

Jackson hasn't moved from his spot near the door, and he watches me approach, amusement still in his eyes.

"Here," I say, thrusting the bottle into his hands. "You can't open it for a year, though, or else it'll taste like water—or straight alcohol? Or watery grapes? I can't remember what the instructor said."

Jackson rolls the bottle in his hands.

"We got to name it." I step closer and point to the label on the bottle. "See what I named mine?"

I wrote the word "Penny" on the label.

"Remember when you used to call me Penny sometimes, back in the day? Because you said I was like your lucky penny?"

"I do," he says.

"That was pretty corny," I inform him.

Jackson laughs. "You can't think it was too corny if you named your wine after it."

I shake my head too quickly, and the room tilts slightly. "You're right, I didn't think it was corny. I thought it was super cute. I think *you're* super cute. Today. Right now."

I step closer, breathing in his clean fabric scent, his masculine smell just beneath that.

Jackson bites the inside of his lip. "I think you're super buzzed."

"We've already acknowledged that. Remember in *Forrest Gump* when he named all of his boats after Jenny? I named all of my wines after you."

He shakes his head. "That didn't make any sense."

"It did in theory," I say, tugging on the hem of his t-shirt.

Jackson's gaze dips to my hips, then goes up to my mouth again. I can't get a read on the look in his eyes.

"I should go." He tilts his chin toward the stairs, where the music is still playing. "You gonna grab the backpack for me?"

I shake my head.

"No?" he asks, raising his brows.

I blink up at him. He's so handsome. "But you can come upstairs and get it."

I release the bottom of his shirt and start up the wooden stairs, then stop and look over my shoulder.

"Are you coming?" I ask. "It's heavy. I'm not carrying it."

Jackson sets his wine down on the foyer table and follows behind me.

I stop abruptly and turn so that we're nearly eye level on the steps.

"I have a confession."

"What's your confession, Simone?" he asks.

"I can carry the backpack. It's heavy, but it's not *that* heavy."

Jackson doesn't respond.

"I actually have two confessions." I hold up the number two in his face. "Want to hear the second one?"

I wait for his nod.

"You know the night before my birthday when we had dinner? I was wearing an orange dress."

Jackson patiently waits for me to get on with whatever I'm going to say.

"I think I was subconsciously trying to seduce you."

The corner of his lip quirks up. "Really."

I nod quickly, biting the inside of my lip to cover my smile. "Because I know you like it when I wear orange."

His gaze is hooded as he gnaws on the inside of his lip, grabs my waist to steady me when I lean forward. I feel the heat from his hands on my waist, spreading to my belly and lower.

"You don't have to wear orange to seduce me, Simone."

"No?"

He shakes his head, looking me in the eyes. "No."

"I'm trying to seduce you right now. Is it working?"

He chuckles as I lean forward and barely touch my lips to his. He breathes in, his eyes still open and trained on mine.

"Jackson," I say against his mouth. "Is it working?"

He nips my lower lip, holding it between his teeth for a second, sending heat spreading through my body. I lean forward and kiss him when he releases it, tracing my tongue along his lower lip, the pulsing between legs heavy and almost painful, I'm so aroused.

His exhale is sharp, gaze hot when he meets my eyes. He shakes his head again.

"What?" I ask, kissing him again. "Why do you keep shaking your head?"

"Because you're like a fuckin' merry-go-round that I can't get off."

As if illustrating his point, he kisses my neck just beneath my jaw, then sucks on it. Like he enjoyed the taste so much, he couldn't help but to sample it with his tongue too. He turns his head, and I meet his mouth again, prying his lips open with mine so I can taste him with my tongue. His hands slide from my waist to my hips and he pulls me against him, his erection poking my belly as I suck on his tongue. The sound he emits is low and guttural and sends another wave of pulsing heat down my body.

He lifts me then, and I wrap my legs around his waist as he carries me the rest of the way up the stairs to our old bedroom. I close my eyes and wrap my arms around his neck, running my fingers lightly down it, then make a soft noise as he deposits me on my unmade bed.

Jackson stands at the edge of the bed and stares down at me, his eyes serious when he tilts his chin up, silently telling me to take off my shorts. I do, sitting on the edge of the bed, my eyes trained on him the entire time.

"Spread your legs." His demand is gravelly and low, and I obey, shedding my cotton shorts, heart racing, my entire body thrumming with anticipation. Jackson drops down, yanking my hips closer to the edge of the bed.

My back arches as he spreads me wider, and I feel his tongue is warm and demanding against my wetness. My moan is loud, and I run my fingers over his head, then grab his ears as I unabashedly arch into his mouth.

Jackson knows all of my pleasure points, knows exactly what pressure to apply to make me squirm and moan. I can feel the scratch of his facial hair against my inner thighs, his tongue moving expertly against me. He makes a hungry sound, like I'm the best thing he's ever tasted. That sound flips a switch, and within seconds—literal seconds—I'm coming. Hard.

"I love you." I groan incoherently as I spasm violently. "Baby, I love you, I love you."

My legs are still limp, breaths coming in sharp pants when Jackson lifts his head and looks at me. He climbs up my body and flips us. I lick my lips and meet his eyes as I pull him out of his sweats and sink down on him, too aroused to care that he hasn't even undressed fully. His gaze is dark and heavy with arousal, his hands locking around my hips, teeth sinking into his lower lip as my body tightens around him. I close my eyes at the feel of him stretching me, then place my palm on his chest and look down at him as I finally begin to rock.

He breaks eye contact, lifting his head to take my nipple into his mouth through my cotton shirt. I cry out when he sucks hard, my balance slipping as I nearly collapse against his chest. I'm already pulsing around him again.

Jackson pushes up into me, then flips us again, rougher this time, so he's hovering over me. I claw at his shirt, helping him strip it off, then his pants. My short nails drag down his back as he rocks into me, hard and fast, and I lift my hips to meet each deep stroke. But just as suddenly, Jackson slows, threading his fingers into my loosened ponytail. He catches my gaze, then kisses me, his tongue moving in sync with the slow roll of his hips. This feels even better than before, less frantic, more consuming. I can hear the soft sounds I'm making blending into the mellow rhythm of the music.

"You love me?" he breathes against my ear, still rocking into me, his back flexing with each movement.

"Yes, yes," I pant, tightening my legs around his waist. I'm already close again. "I love you."

Jackson moves faster, chasing his own release, slipping his hands beneath me, lifting me off the mattress and into him as he grinds deeper. I wrap myself tighter around him as he lifts and rocks.

He braces himself on one arm, looking down to where we're joined before he kisses me again. That's it. I come hard, biting his chest as I shudder, and he growls through his own release, murmuring a curse. For a while we stay like that, breaths shallow, tangled.

"I'm starting to wonder if Caleb really even needed his backpack," I say when I'm finally able to speak. "I'm starting to think this really is *The Parent Trap*."

Jackson gives a chuckle that sounds more like a grunt and finally pulls out of me. He heads into the master bath and brings out a warm cloth, helping me clean up, his face serious the entire time. His movements are stiffer, his entire mood seeming to have shifted, and I watch him as I pull on my shorts as he sits on the edge of the bed, then reaches around to find his shirt tangled in the comforter.

"Are you leaving already?" I ask. The ache in my belly at the idea of his leaving is acute, even though I know it makes no sense.

"It's late. The boys are at the house." He doesn't look at me when he answers, pulling his shirt over his head.

"It's nine p.m."

Jackson turns to look at me, his gaze unreadable, just that fast.

"I don't want you to leave," I confess.

"I'm not sure what you're asking me right now, Simone." There's a gruff edge to his voice.

A thought floats into my brain, foggy and elusive until it comes into view, clear and lucid. As soon as the thought forms, the words come tumbling out before I can stop them.

"Maybe you shouldn't leave. Like, ever."

Jackson's entire body stills. He turns to look at me, his frown deepening.

"What?"

I swallow. "I think you should maybe move back in."

The words sound even crazier the second time.

"You think I should move back in," he repeats, like he's making sure I hear myself.

But now that I've said it, I can't stop. I want Jackson. I always have—even when I convinced myself we didn't need to be together.

That feeling knots in my belly, tangled with the wine I had earlier and the lingering haze of the most intense orgasms I've ever had. Well, since the last time we were together, anyway.

Jackson exhales through his nose, running a hand over his head. He stares at the hardwood floor for a long second, then shakes his head, his eyes dark and tired when they land back on me.

"What are you even saying right now, Simone?"

"Why are you so mad?"

He stares at me in disbelief. "Why?" he asks, his voice flat. "Why should I move back in here?"

I lick my lips. "Because I think it's what makes sense."

Jackson closes his eyes briefly, then runs a hand over his head.

"I'm trying to…" I pause. "I'm trying to be honest. To be real and present with you."

"Be *real* with me?" he echoes as he cocks his head. "What about anything we've been doing lately has been real?"

"What does *that* mean?" I ask. "I'm being real. I just told you I love you."

"While we were fucking," he snaps, turning away.

He stands and paces to the other side of the room, exhaling sharply. His words hit me in the chest, and I drag in a breath.

"Okay, then I'll say it now too. I love you, Jackson."

My heart pounds. He stops pacing but doesn't turn around immediately. His jaw is tight when he finally does face me.

"And what does that mean to you, Simone? You want me to move in here so we can play house until some shit happens that you don't like, or some more inevitable life shit happens and you decide you don't want me anymore?"

"That's not what happened."

"Okay, then tell me what *did* happen."

He leans against the wall, arms crossed, eyes locked on mine, and waits. Cleo Sol is still playing in the background, only now the music doesn't sound sexy and soothing—it sounds mournful.

"Exactly," Jackson says. "Look around this bedroom." He sweeps his arm around the space. "There isn't a trace of me here anywhere. You erased me from every aspect of your life that didn't have to do with Caleb. But now, all of a sudden, you want me to move back in?"

"I didn't erase you, Jackson. I haven't even taken your freakin' pictures off the wall downstairs!"

"Maybe you should."

My mouth falls open, and I blink back tears. "Why are you—"

"You want me to move back in here, and then what?"

"And then… I dunno, what do you mean, 'and then what'? We'll just be here, together."

Jackson shakes his head and pokes his cheek with his tongue. "That's not good enough. I said this shit wasn't healthy for either of us when we started it." His deep voice is drained now. "Arguing and fucking, and then back again… nah. We're not doing this anymore. I can't keep doing this, Simone."

"Jackson. We were okay just twenty minutes ago. And then I get honest about what I'm feeling and you just—"

"Are you, though? Are you being honest? Or are you a little wine-drunk and feeling feelings that'll flip by tomorrow when you realize what you said?"

"Is that what you think?"

"Yeah, Simone. That's what I think. Every time you come to me you're emotional. You're jealous about Carter, you're upset that—"

"*Carter?* Who was talking about *Carter?*" I ask, leaning forward on the bed. "What does Carter have to do with anything we have going on this room right now?"

Jackson is shaking his head. "See, that's what I'm saying right there. You want me when you're feeling jealous, or panicked, or scared… and that ain't real."

"You don't think this is real?" I ask, my eyes ballooned.

"I think I can't fuck you and just leave it there." He swallows and runs a hand over the back of his neck. The breath he releases is long and slow as he stares at me. "You have me tied up in knots," he admits. "And I'd just finished untying myself after you left me the first time."

"I don't—" I stop and inhale, swiping a tear from my cheek. "I love you."

He touches his tongue to his lower lip, his chest rising and falling more quickly as he stares at me.

"I can't trust that, Simone." His voice is quieter now. "I don't really trust *you*."

The words land like a punch to my belly, and my entire body sinks at his confession. I open my mouth to say something, then close it. He lets out a long breath, and stares at the floor before looking up at me again.

"I want to, but I don't."

Silence stretches between us, heavy and thick.

"Years of feeling like I was always chasing you, even after we got married. Of always feeling like you were just waiting for the right bad thing to happen so you could dip out on me." He stuffs his hands into his pockets. "I don't know how to undo that in my mind."

"You said you still love me." My voice is shaky.

"I do." He says it so matter-of-factly that it knocks the wind out of me. "I also said love doesn't fix everything."

He walks over to the bed and grabs his phone from the rumpled comforter, then stares at me for a beat.

"Lock the door behind me."

Then he walks out. A few seconds later, I hear the door close. And I cry.

Twenty-Two

"THE HELL YOU MEAN, YOU might not go?"

Tristan turns his head and stares at me as he chews. I can't see his eyes because they're covered by his shades. We're sitting on Fellini's street-facing patio, next to the huge water fountain that has been there since before the '96 Olympics.

"I'm saying, it's not important for me to be there if you're going," I answer as I watch cars amble by on Ponce De Leon.

Tristan exchanges a look with Logan, who's sitting on my other side. She shakes her head, her sleek ponytail swishing with the movement.

"She doesn't want to go to Delroy's 'Welcome to Atlanta' party because she doesn't want to see Jackson."

I frown, lifting my beer to my lips and taking a long swig before tugging at my long cornrows. It's summer, which means the wet heat will make my hair frizzy in two seconds flat, so I like to keep my hair braided.

"What am I missing?" Tristan asks.

Logan shoots him a disbelieving look. "You're telling me Jackson hasn't said anything to you?"

Tristan shakes his head, grabbing his pizza and taking another large bite. "He's been MIA for the past month," he says as he chews. "And we don't gossip like you women."

"Man, fuck outta here," Logan says, laughing as she picks up her beer. She wipes the condensation from the glass with a manicured thumb. "You're the most gossip-y one out of all of us."

"Nope," Tristan says, grinning. "I just share relevant information. I'm about maintaining proper communication."

"Okay," Logan says dryly.

"But for real. What up with you and Jackson?" Tristan asks.

I sigh, concentrating on my pizza. I'm not about to cry again. The past month has been a cycle of crying, journaling, running, and working, on repeat. My journal is almost out of pages.

"Damn, you okay?" Tristan asks as he sets his pizza down, eyeing me. He glances at Logan who twists her lips and sighs.

"Me and Jackson aren't really in the best place right now," I reply.

I pick at my pizza, then finally take a bite, chewing without really tasting much. It's been like this for the past month. Some women eat their pain. My stomach knots and burns, and I have a hard time eating when I'm stressed.

"How long this been goin' on?" Tristan asks, sitting back in chair. "I see you damn near every day, and you haven't said anything."

I shrug. "There isn't much to say."

"What happened?"

I sigh. Tristan doesn't care about my annoyance. He just stares at me, waiting for me to speak.

"We'd kinda been… seeing each other again?"

That doesn't seem right. Jackson and I had been having needy, frantic sex sporadically, with no clear boundaries. And I'd been sitting around, stewing in indecision while pining for him—literally dreaming of him, wanting him every second of the day. Making dumbass declarations of love after sex like a confused teenager.

Tristan doesn't look as surprised by my confession as I expected he would.

"You knew that already?" I ask.

He rolls his eyes. "Simone, Jackson has been in love with you since he met you." He abruptly turns toward Logan. "Yo, Lo, remember what he told me when we all met him the first time at El Bar back in the day?"

"What? When he told you that you were about to be his other brother-in-law?" she says.

"Buddy told me he was gonna marry you on the *very first* day I met him." Tristan laughs. "That shit was hilarious. Who was even thinking about getting married at twenty-one, twenty-two years old?"

"Jackson," Logan supplies.

"Jackson," Tristan says. "Even after y'all split up, he was on one."

"That man doesn't know how to *not* be obsessed with you," Logan agrees. "Even Delroy said he peeped Jackson's feelings for you. He said he was very 'present' with you the entire time we had dinner in Jamaica."

Tristan looks as if he's struggling not to roll his eyes. He grabs his beer and taking another swig. "Anyway, I'm not surprised y'all were hookin' up again," Tristan says. "So then what happened?"

I lean back in my chair, adjusting my shades on my face. I close my eyes and let the sun shine on my skin, appreciating its warmth, since it rained for the past two days.

"I asked him to move back in with me," I say without opening my eyes.

"Why'd you do that?" Tristan asks.

I open my eyes and look at him. "Because I miss him? And I love him?"

"You know he ain't on that type of time. This man lost his marriage, his family. You think he'd be satisfied with some shacking-up shit? *Jackson*, of all people?"

I pick at my pizza, guilt making my body warm more than the eighty-degree heat.

"That dude was…" Tristan shakes his head. "I ain't tryin' to make you feel bad, or say that whatever all went down between you two is your fault, but he was… broken, when y'all split."

I rub a hand over my forehead as I release a long breath. "I know. I don't need you to rehash how much I hurt him. Or set him up with any other Rachels you meet at a bar."

Tristan looks surprised for a split second.

"Look, I didn't have shit to do with that," he says, raising his hands defensively. "And y'all were divorced. For a whole year. You should be glad he didn't pop all the way out and get wild."

"Like you did?" Logan asks, looking at him.

Tristan shrugs. "That was different."

"How?" she asks, smirking.

"I shouldn't have ever married Melissa in the first place."

"Well, no freakin' duh," Logan replies.

Tristan picks up a toothpick and twirls it in his mouth as he leans back in his chair. "Why do you dislike her so much? Why you always have something smart to say about her?"

"Why do you dislike her so much you divorced her?" Logan quirks a brow.

Tristan doesn't respond to that, only studies her over his beer.

"Anyway," Logan says, turning to look at me, "you need to be there, Simone. I feel you, I feel your pain, but this isn't high school. You were married to the man for years. You have a teenage son together. And Delroy is the client that helped save your agency."

I take another bite of pizza and chew in silence. "I'm going," I say when I swallow. "Of course I'm going. This is a big night for him, and for Sage, even."

I connected Delroy with a few brands who are sponsoring the party. Logan's wine shop will be represented there too, courtesy of a wine station she designed with her small team, and sponsored by some of the distributors she works with.

"You know he asked me to move in with him."

I almost choke on my pizza. "He *what?*"

"Yeah," Logan says. "The other day, he said he wanted me to live with him."

I glance at Tristan, who has gone completely still.

"What'd you tell him?" I ask.

Logan shrugs. "I told him no. I'm not trying to give up my space. I like my own bed and my own things."

Tristan visibly relaxes. "It's too soon for him to be asking you that anyway."

"Why? It took you all of, what? Seven months to propose to Melissa?"

"That's different. She was pregnant. What was I supposed to do?"

"Uh, not marry her? You know you could've been Bella's dad without proposing to her emotionally challenged mother."

"I was tryin' to do the right thing," Tristan counters, shifting his toothpick to the other side of his mouth. "I was trying to do right by her. Everybody ain't anti-marriage. Some people *want* to build a life with another person. Be committed. Know when they come home that the person they love will be there."

"You just said Melissa wasn't that person for you, though. So why'd you put yourself through that? We all knew she wasn't the one for you."

"Who all knew, Logan?" Tristan says, staring her straight in the eyes. "You?"

She shrugs.

"Then who is, Lo? Huh? Since you know it all. Who's the one for me?"

They hold one another's gazes. I raise my brows, studying my plate because I feel like a voyeur right now. The air hangs thick between us, and not just because of the damp Atlanta heat. My phone buzzes on the table, breaking the silence.

Hey, just dropped Caleb off at your house with his suit for tonight.

My heart pounds at the sight of Jackson's text. Every single time he's texted me since he left my house that night, my heart thuds in anticipation. For what exactly, I don't know. He's retracted into himself and completely cooled off. He's pleasant—polite, even. And that's it.

Okay, cool. I'll see you later this evening.

Jackson doesn't reply, only likes my message. I twist my lips, watching the cars pass by on the street in front of us as I lean back in my chair, rubbing the condensation on my beer glass with a manicured finger. I followed Malika's advice and got my nails done, gothic red. I don't even know what "gothic red" means, but they're pretty and bright.

Mom, I'm gonna walk to get Tiana pretty soon. You don't have to worry about picking her up, Caleb texts me. I shoot him a thumbs-up.

The kids are coming to the early part of the welcoming reception before the adult party kicks all the way off. Caleb is using it as a date night. He and Tiana reconciled the night everything blew up between Jackson and me. Turns out I give good love advice to people who aren't me.

I look up at Tristan and Logan. "We're gonna be late if we don't leave now."

We're heading to a sound-bath class I signed us all up for on a reference from one of our new clients, another WNBA player. She's very "grand rising" and invested in the company who hosts various wellness classes and retreats.

Tristan claps his hands then rubs them together. "Bet, let's go bathe in some sound."

Twenty-Three

WE WERE SUPPOSED TO POSSIBLY ride over to the party together, but we ended up splitting up after sound-bath class. It was held in a small studio in Grant Park, sunbathed in natural light, with giant, colorful fabric curtains hanging along one wall that made it even cozier and more tranquil.

The instructor, who had thick, springy hair piled on top of her head and deep, coppery skin, sat in front of the curtains, surrounded by pastel-colored crystal quartz bowls, filled with water. Her name was Akeela. She told us she was also Reiki master, and invited us to come have our "life force energy" rearranged at her class next week. I might go get my energy rearranged—I feel like it might need it—but I doubt Logan will come with me. I think she was irritated because Tristan spent the whole time we were there flirting with Akeela when she should've been focused on creating rejuvenating vibrations for us.

"What the hell?" Logan leaned over and whispered as class was winding down, her voice barely carrying over the whispery sound. "I do not feel fucking refreshed."

After class, she rolled her eyes at Tristan and left, saying she needed more time to get dressed and would just meet us at the party. I Uber-ed back to my house, leaving Tristan to flirt in private.

When I got home, Caleb and Tiana were already there, getting dressed. They've been on summer break for the past two weeks and have been hanging out almost every day, him there—now that her stepdad is completely out of the picture—or her at our house, playing Fortnite or 2K with him in the living room. Ever since their little couch romp, they're definitely not going to be hanging out in his bedroom. In my mind, the party tonight feels like a substitute for junior prom, which was held late this year, in early May. They didn't go because, according to Caleb, "it's a consumerist tradition and propaganda," plus Tiana doesn't like crowds, even though she doesn't have any problems on the court. "It's like I turn into this whole other person when I'm playing ball," she told me a couple of weeks ago.

"I feel like Monica in *Love & Basketball* when her mom gave her pearls to put on for the dance," Tiana tells me now as we stand in my bathroom, and I clasp one of my dainty gold necklaces around her neck.

"Are they cursing their mothers in Spain?" I ask, doing my best Alfre Woodard impression. Tiana giggles.

Now that she's started opening up, I'm realizing she's a funny kid.

"We'll get a lot of pictures for your mom," I tell her, since Shelly, who's working third shift tonight, couldn't be here to help Tiana get dressed.

We've met a few times over the past month, and she seems pretty cool—plainspoken and kind.

"You look like a little doll," I say as Tiana tilts her head, studying herself in the mirror.

Her caramel skin flushes pink, and she murmurs a thank you as she continues to inspect herself in the mirror, twisting this way and that. Her phone is on the counter—she used a YouTube video to show her how to get her twists swept up into the perfect bun.

She's wearing a shoulder-less lavender cocktail dress that flares out at her knees. Tiana's not really into makeup, but tonight, she's wearing eyeliner, mascara, a bit of glittery pastel eyeshadow, and soft pink lip gloss. It took some convincing to get her to believe that the faint marks on the inside of her forearm are barely noticeable, unless someone is staring and looking for them, which no one will be. Her mom bought her a small bottle of shea butter scar-removal cream that she carries around and slathers on whenever she thinks about it.

"Mom, we're gonna be late." Caleb's deep voice rings from beyond the bedroom, and I roll my eyes because he's acting like this is *his* event.

Tiana exits the bathroom, and Caleb's concern for our tardiness morphs into a big, cheesy smile as he stands in the doorway. There's no playing it cool with him; the boy wears his adoration all over his face. Tiana smiles shyly.

"You look really pretty," he tells her, still cheesing.

"So do you," she says, her gaze trailing quickly over the black suit Jackson had tailored for him. His locs are freshly twisted and tied back at his nape. He even has some peach fuzz happening on his chin now. "I mean, not pretty. You look really good."

Caleb's smile widens as Tiana blushes deeply.

"I mean, you look nice—handsome."

Good grief.

"All right, y'all, everybody looks great. Let's go."

I shoo them out of the bedroom, which hasn't been properly cleaned in a month. It's tacky, I know. But even tackier is the fact that it took me two full weeks after that night with Jackson to change my pillowcases. The sheets obviously had to go, but the pillowcases carried traces of his scent. And at night, when the house is quiet, and my brain has time to freely wander, find a thought, and stay there, they're all of Jackson. His words ricochet and spin around in my brain, traveling like heat waves down my chest and landing in my stomach.

"You erased me… I don't really trust you…"

I exhale, turn from the rumpled bed, and follow Caleb and Tiana out of the room.

"You look pretty too, Mom," Caleb says over his shoulder as an afterthought as we make our way down the stairs.

"Thank you," I say dryly as I take my time walking down the steps so that I don't trip in my strappy heels.

My black cocktail dress is slim-fitting and backless, stopping above my knees. I pulled my cornrows back into a low bun and concentrated on making my large eyes look soft and dark. My lips are painted deep red, a color I don't wear often because my lips have always been a focal point on my face, earning lustful comments from grown-ass men since I was twelve. And while I don't want to hide my femininity, I was always conscious about not overplaying it, especially working in a field dominated by men. Lately, though, I've cared less about that. I'm forty, and this is what I look like. I shouldn't have to hide myself in any way, to make other people feel comfortable. I feel good tonight. And I feel like I look good. Plus, Jackson always used to tell me I have the prettiest lips he's ever seen. Only when he said it, it didn't sound sleezy—it sounded like… reverence.

The rideshare is waiting outside by the time we get downstairs, ready to take us to the Buckhead hotel where the party is taking place. The entire ride there, Caleb is coaching Tiana on who will be there and whom she should try to meet. I saw him studying the guestlist the other night. He doesn't care about athletes at all, and couldn't tell most of them from a can of paint.

"There'll be WNBA players there, though, right?" he said, looking up from his phone when I asked what he was doing. "I just want to make sure I know who everyone is."

Now, as we creep up I-85, I see why it was so important for him.

"Malika Higbee, Taylor Kennedy, Aria McDonald… They'll all be there," he says, counting the names he's recently memorized off on his fingers. "It'd be good for you to know actual WNBA players before you even go to college. Maybe they could be your mentor or something."

Tiana stares out the window and Caleb frowns, his dimples peeking out.

"Tee, don't you think?"

She sighs and turns toward him. "Okay, but I thought this was, like, our date, Caleb," she says softly.

His eyes widen. "It is."

"Well, I don't want to have to talk to everybody—strangers I don't even know—the entire time."

"They're not strangers, though, Tee. They're famous athletes who do the same thing you might want to do as a career. And it wouldn't be the entire time. It'd be good for you to meet some of them."

"Yeah, it'll be cool to see them in person, I guess," she says, biting her lip.

Caleb blinks, leaning closer to her. "What's wrong?"

"I just don't really… I'm not really comfortable meeting a bunch of people, even if they're basketball players. I don't want to do that tonight," she says quietly. "I just wanna be with you. Okay?"

His eyes soften as he nods. "I just want to be with you too," he says, reaching for her hand.

I turn my head to hide my smile and look out the window as we reach the I-85/I-75 split, crawling through Atlanta's parking-lot-level traffic.

About thirty minutes later, we exit the rideshare and make our way into the polished hotel. The kids' eyes widen when we finally make it to the rooftop. It looks a scene out of a movie. String lights crisscross overhead, glowing against the night sky, with the Atlanta skyline stretching beyond the glass railing. A DJ is set up in the corner opposite the bar, playing jazzy house music, while servers weave through the crowd with platters of mini crab cakes, what looks like jerk wings, and fizzy pink cocktails. The air is balmy but not sticky hot, the perfect weather for this type of event.

Caleb straightens his shoulders and takes Tiana's hand. She quickly wipes the awe off her face, trying to play it cool. There aren't any other kids here, but neither of them seem to care.

I catch a server dressed in all black as she's about to breeze past. "Hi, do you have any nonalcoholic drinks?"

She nods, turning to point toward the bar. "Sure, there are a few mocktails on the menu." She winks at Caleb and Tiana before hurrying off.

"If you two want to grab something to drink, go ahead," I tell them.

"Do you want to?" Caleb asks Tiana, who nods as she takes in the scene—athletes, Atlanta's reality TV crowd, artists, and a few musicians all mingling, drinks in hand, clothes sleek and polished. "Mom, do you want me to bring you something?"

"I'm good, but thank you."

They head off, and I scan the area, spotting Tristan near the row of couches facing the skyline, half hidden behind vibrant green potted plants. I make my way over, stopping to greet a couple of Falcons players along the way and grabbing myself a champagne flute from a passing server.

"Sim-Simmy," Tristan greets me with a high five. "You look good."

"'Preciate it. You too."

He's wearing a dusk-colored, slim-fitting suit. It's a color that Tristan can pull off because he's always had the half-ball player, half-model thing going on, given his six-three height. His beard is full and groomed, his eyes covered by shades because the sun is still making its last hoorah in the sky before it begins to set.

"You just get here?" he asks. "Caleb came with you, right?"

I nod toward the brightly lit bar, where Caleb and Tiana are now approaching, bright red drinks in hand. Tristan lifts his chin in greeting. Caleb mirrors the gesture.

"What's good, kid?" Tristan slaps Caleb's hand when they reach us. "You're fresh out here, huh? Okay, I see you."

Caleb's grin widens as he adjusts his coat. "Uncle Tristan, this is my girlfriend, Tiana."

"Nice to meet you, young lady," Tristan says, shaking her hand. "What's that y'all are drinking?"

"It's called a Sunset?" Tiana answers, looking down into her cup. "It has cherries and—what was it, Caleb?"

"I think lime and agave or something?"

"No alcohol in it, right?" Tristan teases, looking at Caleb, who rolls his eyes. "There's more food over there if y'all are hungry," he adds, nodding toward a lavish spread across the room. "And they have a TV section set up over there with a few of the games on, too."

"Mom?" Caleb asks.

I nod my okay, and they saunter off.

"So, you didn't invite Akeela?" I say, referencing our overly giggly sound-bath instructor.

I follow his gaze to Logan. Her hair is down, thick waves cascading over her shoulders, and she's wearing a red dress that hugs her curves and accentuates her skin tone. Tristan's eyes trail down her body, slow and deliberate, before he lifts his glass and takes a swig of whatever brown liquor he's drinking.

"What's up, good people?" Logan greets us, stepping in closer before lowering her voice. "My zipper is stuck." She tilts her head, indicating the small gap along her side. "I went to the bathroom and now I can't get it back up. Tristan, can you help?" She shifts her weight, angling her hip toward him.

"Ask Simone to do that."

Her face wrinkles. "Why? You're standing right here, and Simone's hands are full."

I glance down at the champagne flute in one hand and my clutch in the other.

Tristan meets her eyes. "Because if you keep pushing your ass in my face like that, I might show you where to sit it."

My mouth drops. Logan's lips part, a sharp inhale leaving her lips when her head snaps up. Her expression is one of shock and something else unreadable that I haven't seen before.

"I ain't your homegirl," Tristan adds before taking another sip of his drink, holding her gaze over the rim.

I glance between them, wide-eyed. *What the hell?* Finally, Logan snaps out of it and exhales.

"Simone." Her voice is lower now, almost stunned.

I set my champagne on a nearby ledge and help her tug the zipper up. Just as it clicks into place, Delroy's booming laugh carries over the music.

"There she is," he says, sweeping an appreciative gaze over Logan before leaning in to kiss her cheek, oblivious to the lingering tension he just walked into. "You are stunning," he adds, flashing a smile. His suit is a vibrant cobalt blue, sharply tailored, paired with a crisp white shirt left open at the collar, revealing a thick gold chain, and polished loafers that match the suit's bold tone. "Thank you for being here with me tonight."

"I'm happy to be here," Logan returns, smiling, her voice less shaky than before.

Tristan watches them before downing the rest of his drink. Then he tilts his chin at Delroy, flashing him one of his signature charming grins.

"What's up, man? This is a helluva way to welcome yourself to the A," he says as he looks around, taking in the party, which is steadily swelling with people. The music has switched to an Afrobeat-house mash-up and there are people dancing near the DJ booth.

"Gotta make a splash. I play the long game," Delroy says, returning his grin. They bump fists before Delroy leans over and kisses my cheek in greeting.

"This turned out beautiful," I say, looking around at the twinkling lights and soccer-ball-shaped ice sculpture. "Lisha knows how to throw a party," I say, referencing the event planner I connected him with.

"It exceeded my expectations," he agrees.

"Simone!"

I turn my head to see Benny Gonzalez, a retired outfielder for the Braves, approaching.

"Long time no hug!" he says, scooping me up in a bear hug.

"Benny, dang! You almost knocked my champagne out of my hand!" I say, laughing. "How are you?"

"I'm good, gorgeous," he answers, pinching my cheek.

I roll my eyes and grin, motioning to Logan. "You remember my friend, Logan?"

Benny nods, leaning in to drop a kiss on her cheek as they exchange a quick greeting. He turns to give Tristan dap, and quickly introduces himself to Delroy.

"Seriously, though, everything good with you?" he asks me.

"Yep, good as it can be. What about you?"

"You know I'm in Miami now, right? Living right on the water." With Benny's money, I would be somewhere out of the country, like the Seychelles or Mauritius, not in Miami. But I think most of his family is there now, so I get it.

"Look who decided to grace us with his presence," Delroy says loudly, smiling.

I look to see whom he's talking about, and my heart starts racing. *Jackson.* He looks incredible, virile, ruggedly sexy, and relaxed. But he's not alone.

He's with Carter.

Twenty-Four

"WHO THE FUCK IS THAT?" Logan murmurs, furrowing her brow.

I can't immediately respond to her question. I feel like I can't even breathe. Jackson and Carter have spotted us and are approaching now. Our gazes connect and I try to slow my breathing, try keep my face void of emotion. I'm pretty sure it's not working.

"All right, Simone, call me. I have some ideas I want to run by you, seriously," Benny says, giving my shoulder a quick squeeze as he's pulled away by some tall guy who I'm fairly certain used to play for the Mets when I was in middle school.

I barely register Benny's absence, though. My heart is beating way too hard, way too fast. *You are not about to hyperventilate on the rooftop,* I tell myself once, then twice. I touch my tongue to the corner of my mouth, draw in a quick breath, and look away, then can't help myself and turn to stare at his approach.

He's cut his hair lower again, just high enough for me to barely be able to rake my fingernails through his waves. His stubble is thick, framing his lips. He's wearing a black fitted suit, with a crisp white shirt that's open at the collar and dark sunglasses, and he looks like a freaking James Bond movie come to life. And Carter, in her slinky gold dress, looks like she belongs with him.

"That's Carter," I finally murmur to Logan, noting the flash of surprised anger in her eyes, just before they reach us.

"What's up, Jackson?" Delroy greets him, slapping his hand and pulling him into a quick hug. "Good to see you, bro."

Logan and Tristan greet him next, before Jackson turns to me. "Hey."

"Hi," I reply.

He drops a quick kiss on my cheek, his woodsy scent lingering as I shift my weight and take a sip of champagne.

"This is Carter," he tells everyone. "She's a sports reporter at CNN, and Alisha's cousin."

Everyone exchanges hellos, while Carter gives Delroy a hug, since they already met for the story she produced.

Logan glances at me, gauging my reaction. But I know how to tuck myself in, how to retreat, and I clear my expression, offering a smile to Carter.

"It's nice to meet you, Simone." She has a cute dimple in her chin when she smiles.

"You too. Is Alisha here?" I ask, glancing around.

"Not yet," Carter replies. "She was finishing something up and said she'll get here late. I was trying to beat traffic, so I left earlier. That was a fail." She laughs.

"Yeah, that's never happening in Atlanta," I reply. "I heard you moved here this year? How're you liking it so far?"

She shrugs. "I'm from L.A., so it's different, taking some getting used to."

I nod. "My brother has lived in L.A. for years—it's probably a bit of a culture shock, even with all the film and TV stuff Atlanta has happening these days."

"Definitely. I was telling Jacks I miss our taco trucks, of all the things to miss."

She laughs again, and I smile politely. I glance up at Jackson. His sunglasses hide his eyes, but I feel his gaze anyway—tracing from my lips, where they linger for a beat, to my hips, then back up. But I can't even look at him right now. My stomach, which was calm, knots violently again. I take another sip of my champagne as Carter steps closer to Delroy and Tristan, drawn into a conversation about the story she just produced about him.

Jackson shifts closer to me. "Where's Caleb?"

I nod toward the opposite side of the rooftop where the food is, then swallow more champagne, subtly shifting away from him.

"Everything go good with them earlier? Caleb didn't have any problems with the suit alterations?"

"Nope." I look down into my glass.

"What, are we not speaking?" I can feel Jackson's gaze on me when he asks the question, and I look up at him, my chest burning.

"Don't play with me right now," I say, keeping my voice low.

"C'mon and talk to me over there," he murmurs, bobbing his head toward the entrance, where it's more private.

I look down into my glass again, drawing in a breath while Jackson stares at me patiently. Finally, I swallow and bob my head.

"I'll be back," I tell Logan. "Can you keep an eye on the kids?"

She nods, exchanging a subtle look with Tristan. Carter doesn't seem to notice us leaving as she talks animatedly with Delroy.

Jackson's hand stays on my elbow as we weave through the crowd, stopping to greet people along the way. People asking about Jackson's podcast, or his last appearance on ESPN. People talking to me about the brand deals I recently landed for Delroy and Malika. People asking us both to weigh in on the Braves season or the Falcons' chances of making the playoffs. Each time we pause, we keep it brief. Each time we pause, his grip stays steady on my elbow.

When we finally reach a quiet corner of the rooftop, a full fifteen minutes later, Jackson leans against the high ledge, hands in his pockets. I raise a brow at him.

"I didn't come here with Carter."

"You literally walked in with her."

"And that's all. I ran into her at the elevators. We rode up together. That's it."

I exhale. "I'm having a really hard time with this," I confess. "Like, a really, *really* hard time."

"Me too." He shifts his stance, hands still stuffed in his pockets.

"You look like Batman."

I don't know if it comes out pissy or not. But he looks so good, it's almost annoying. He grins, biting the inside of his lip. His gaze sweeps over me again, slow, deliberate. Then he shakes his head.

"Why do we keep doing this to ourselves?"

We stare at each other for long seconds. I'm just about to answer when my phone vibrates in my clutch. I pull it out to see Caleb's name on the screen.

"Mom—Tiana, she can't breathe." His voice is panicked. "I think she's hyperventilating."

My stomach drops. "Caleb, where are you?"

"I'm inside, near the bathrooms."

"Okay, I'm coming." I hang up.

"What's going on?" Jackson asks.

"Tiana," I answer, already moving toward the entrance with Jackson on my heels. "They're inside."

We push our way through the crowd, back to the cool hotel lobby. The lights are dimmer inside, the music from the rooftop fainter. I immediately spot Caleb and Tiana near the bathrooms, next to an elaborate abstract painting. They're sitting huddled together on a bench. Tiana is crying, trying to draw in breaths, her small chest heaving, and Caleb is next to her, his hand on her back, eyes wide with panic. When he spots us, he springs from the bench, momentary relief flashing in his face.

"We were just standing there talking to these ladies who said they played basketball, and then everybody started asking Tee all these questions about her playing, and she said she needed some water and some air, and so I said, 'Come on'—and then she was having trouble breathing and said she couldn't get air…" Caleb's words tumble out in a rush.

"It's okay," Jackson says quietly, placing a steady hand on his shoulder. "Your mom's got her, okay? She'll be all right. She just needs a minute."

I kneel in front of Tiana. Her chest is still heaving.

"Tiana?" I say softly.

Her eyes are wild and panicked when they find mine.

"You're safe," I say quietly.

I take her hand and squeeze gently. She squeezes back.

"Can you count with me?" I ask. "Inhale for four." I breathe in slow, counting softly. "Hold for seven." Her fingers twitch in mine. "Now exhale for eight. Let it all out."

She nods, drawing in deep, stuttering breaths. Her cheeks are sparkling with the glitter from eye makeup because she's been crying, and I wipe a tear from her cheek with my thumb. I squeeze her hand again.

"Good—let's count again, okay?"

We go through the counting four more times, until her breathing slows. Her shoulders slump and she closes her eyes.

"You're safe, okay?"

She nods, inhaling shakily, taking full, deep breaths.

I glance up at Jackson. He's standing close, his hands firm on Caleb's shoulders, his face tight with concern. Once Tiana's breathing has slowed, Caleb moves to sit next to her. She turns and buries her face in his chest. I start to stand slowly and Jackson moves to help me up. He wraps an arm around my waist, dropping a kiss to the side of my ear.

"You okay?"

I nod.

"You did good," he murmurs.

We stand there listening to Tiana's soft sniffles, watching our son murmur in her ear.

"I'm sorry," Tiana whispers shakily when she lifts her head from Caleb's chest, meeting my eyes. "I'm so embarrassed. Everyone was having fun and I ruined it." She drags a hand down her face then stares the floor.

"Tiana, you did not ruin anything. Did you see those people out there still wearing sunglasses after the sun's already set?" I nod toward the party, which has gotten even louder. "That's usually my first sign it's time to bounce because it's getting corny."

Caleb smiles. Tiana's lips twitch.

"Do you know how many times I've had a panic attack?" I ask her. "Too many to count. I used to pass out from them, they were so bad when I was in high school."

Tiana's eyes widen. "Really?"

"Yep."

"Do you ever still—"

"I had one not too long ago, actually. I've just learned how to breathe through them, the way we did just now. You gotta learn what techniques work for you."

She dabs her face with the tissue I just handed her from my clutch. Her shoulders are still hunched, embarrassment coming off her in waves.

"Did Caleb ever tell you about the time I threw up all over the basketball court?" Jackson asks.

Tiana lifts her head.

"Yeah, it was my senior year," Jackson continues. "I'd get so nervous before games, I'd get sick. And this one time, it happened right there on the court, after tip-off, in front of the whole crowd… during the playoffs." He pauses, grinning as he lets the significance sink in. "They had to stop the game for fifteen minutes to clean it up because there was so much."

"Gross, Jackson," I say, wrinkling my nose, laughing. Tiana smiles and Caleb rubs her back, chuckling.

"Now that we've just finished talking about Jackson hurling all over the basketball court, you know what I want?" I say. "Some chunky soup."

"*Mom!*" Caleb exclaims, making a face as Tiana giggles.

"I'm kidding," I say, laughing. "I really want a burger. Y'all down?"

Tiana nods. "I am kinda hungry."

"Cool, burgers it is." I clap, and Tiana and Caleb stand.

"I'll drive," Jackson volunteers as we follow him toward the exit.

Twenty-Five

"I THINK SHE WAS JUST overstimulated."

I'm seated beside Jackson in the burger joint, my legs stretched out on a chair in front of me, shoes kicked off because my feet were hurting. Our food—a huge carton of salty, greasy fries and thick burgers—is spread out in front of us. Caleb and Tiana are up front, refilling their fountain drinks. Really they wanted to get away from us so they could bump shoulders, poke each other, and do the other awkward flirting teens do at their age.

"I probably should've thought about that," I say, frowning as I watch them. "I know she doesn't like crowds."

"Don't do that. It's not your fault," Jackson tells me. "If you weren't there to talk her down, I feel like that could've been a lot worse."

I shrug and nod, then look around the restaurant, which is pretty empty, except for a young couple sitting huddled together up front near the counter and an elderly woman, what looks to be her adult daughter, and a baby in the corner. Nobody glanced our way when we rolled up in here in formal attire.

I drag a fry through ketchup and drop it again. I was lying earlier about wanting a burger. My appetite is still nonexistent.

"You should eat," Jackson says.

"I look thinner?"

His eyes flick over me. "You look gorgeous."

The way he says it, the way he's looking at me when he says it, makes me flush.

"But you still need to eat."

I pick up my burger and deliberately take a huge bite. He grins, shaking his head at me.

"Are you gonna go back to the party after this?" I ask after I swallow.

"Hell no. I was about ready to leave anyway."

I laugh. "You'd just gotten there."

Jackson just looks me.

"I know," I say. "That's not your thing."

"I always feel like I'm wasting time at those parties."

"We used to go clubbing back in the day," I remind him. "We were all up and through Buckhead in those clubs twerking to Kilo Ali."

I start Bankhead bouncing in my seat, and Jackson chuckles. "When we were in our early twenties. And that was different. That was for leisure. The party tonight was work. People all up in my face just talking and not really saying anything… Nah, I'm good."

He pauses. "Saw Benny was hanging all over you."

I roll my eyes. "You did not."

"I did."

"Benny's a little extra, but he's good people."

"Benny wants you."

I shrug again. "I put on red lipstick tonight. I'm cool as hell. What's not to want?"

Jackson's lips quirk up, then he rubs a hand over his jaw. For a second, he doesn't say anything.

"We need to talk."

"If it's to talk about how I only want you when I'm emotional, then I'd prefer not to."

He blinks and tilts his head. "Simone."

"Jackson."

"I was in my feelings a little bit that night," he admits, balling up his napkin and dropping it soundlessly on the table. "Especially because you always have me wide open after we connect like that. And that night especially was on some other…"

"Our chemistry isn't a bad thing," I say. "I'm tired of feeling bad about that."

He draws slow circles on my upturned wrist, then meets my eyes. "You're right."

The family that's been sitting in the corner gets up to leave, and I watch the mom swing the baby onto her hip. The baby waves at me as they exit, and I wiggle my fingers at him, smiling.

When I look at Jackson again, his eyes are on me. I pick up a fry and pop it in to my mouth.

"What?" he asks.

"You hurt my heart," I admit quietly.

"And you broke mine."

We stare at each other for a long seconds.

He runs a hand over the back of his neck. "What do you wanna do, Simone?"

I look down at the table and then back to him.

"Go home… with you."

Twenty-Six

CALEB HEADS STRAIGHT UPSTAIRS WHEN we get back to the house. It's just after midnight and we've dropped Tiana off at home. She perked up even more as the night dragged on, smiling and clowning around with Caleb in the car, like the weight of her earlier panic attack floated away the more time she spent away from the party.

I linger at the door for a second, watching Caleb disappear up the stairs. He doesn't say much, just mutters a tired "night" before heading to his room. He's out of my sight in seconds.

Jackson steps around me into the house.

"You want some wine?" I ask as I head into the kitchen.

He follows me, leaning against the counter as I pull down two wine glasses from the cabinet. Caleb's hat is on the counter again, next to a butter knife and a paper towel scattered with breadcrumbs—the remnants of the sandwich he and Tiana made before we left.

I only pour myself half a glass of cabernet, taking a sip that instantly warms me and loosens my shoulders. I close my eyes and roll my neck.

"This is good," I say when I open them, swirling the wine in my glass. Jackson nods his agreement.

"From Logan?"

I nod. "Yo, her and Tristan are, like… *on* one."

"What do you mean?" He leans against the counter, crossing his feet at the ankles.

"I mean, do you know what is going on with Tristan? He's acting like he's still into her."

"I think he is." Jackson doesn't look surprised. "He kinda has been for years. I thought you said in college—"

"Yeah, in *college*. I thought he was over all that? He got married, had a kid…"

Jackson shrugs. "When feelings are there and they're real, all of that is circumstantial. Probably doesn't help that he kicks it with her as much as he does, either."

"I guess. That's still kinda wild if that's what's going on."

I sip my wine, watching him over the rim of my glass. His eyes are tired, his shirt unbuttoned at the top. My gaze wanders over the expanse of his chest before I meet his eyes again. He's been watching me the entire time.

"Can you help me unzip this?" I ask, turning my back to him and looking over my shoulder.

He sets his wine down behind him, steps closer, and slides the zipper down, running a fingertip down my spine when he's finished. His touch leaves a trail of heat on my skin, and I draw in a sharp breath. He presses a kiss to the back of my neck, wrapping an arm around my middle. Warmth spreads across my belly and lower. He kisses my neck again, this time using some tongue, and I soften further in his arms, my arousal a low hum that circulates through my whole body. His big hand is splayed on my stomach, and I trace it with my fingertips.

"I'm gonna go change," I tell him.

I can feel him nod against my skin before he releases me. I set my empty glass on the counter and head up the stairs. I'm tired, but my body his humming from Jackson's touch. I brush my teeth, wash off my makeup, and head into my closet to get my pajamas.

Jackson is sitting on the edge of the bed with his wine when I emerge from closet in cotton shorts and a tank top. He takes me in, his gaze unreadable.

"I'm forty years old. I feel like I should probably start buying matching pajama sets. Cute, silky ones."

He grins, watching as I cross the room and climb onto the bed. I sit cross-legged, facing him.

"Did you see a light on in Caleb's room when you came up?"

"Nah, I think he's knocked out."

"He had a long day."

"We all did," Jackson says.

I stare at him for a beat.

"I should've never asked for a divorce," I admit in one breath. "There aren't enough words to express how sorry I am for doing that to you. To us. To Caleb. To our family."

My voice cracks on that word, and I press my lips together and drag in a stuttering breath through my nose.

"At the time, I just thought…" I swallow, gathering my thoughts. "It just felt like I couldn't see my way out of the dark space we were in. It felt like no matter what we did, we just couldn't get out of the trenches. And I thought that meant it was time to call it. And the reason I thought that is because it's all I knew."

I shrug. "I don't feel like crying right now," I say, "but I'm gonna go ahead and do it anyway." I blink, and the tears come rolling down my cheeks.

Jackson smiles. "Come over here."

I scoot to the edge of the bed, and he pulls me close, pressing a kiss to my forehead. Then one to my nose. I can taste my tears when he kisses my mouth before nuzzling my nose with his.

"I always loved you, Jackson, completely and totally, with every single atom in my body," I say, burying my face in his neck. I inhale his familiar scent, feel his body heat, letting it calm me.

Finally, I pull back and look at him. "I just didn't know how to be all in with you the way that you deserved. And that wasn't about you. It was about me and all of the things I was carrying with me. I was like that Erykah Badu song. A freakin' bag lady."

I shake my head as Jackson chuckles at my reference. "Like, we were *young* when we met. And you were my first love. Honestly, you've been my only love. I think I did, in the back of my mind, go into our relationship, into our marriage, with the expectation that it would fail," I admit. "That you would fail me, or that I would fail you. Or that the 'big, bad thing' would happen, and that would be it. And I was always so terrified of putting Caleb through what I went through, of allowing him to witness all the stuff I did, that I felt like I was doing the responsible thing by ending things. I overcorrected."

I pull away, swiping my eyes with the back of my hand. Jackson leans forward, resting his arms on his knees.

"I love you," I say, meeting his eyes. "What did that girl say on *Grey's Anatomy*? 'You're my person'?"

He grins. "I don't watch *Grey's Anatomy*."

"Well, that's what you are. My person. You always have been. And yeah, I'm coming to you emotional because you make me emotional. I feel all of the emotions with you."

"Simone…" He shakes his head.

I swallow hard, my belly tightening. "I know you don't trust me anymore. And I get why you don't. But all I can do is keep showing up. Keep showing you that you can, right?"

He exhales, staring at the floor. I glance at my clothes, which are piled in a chair in the corner because I've been so busy I haven't had time to fold them. I look at him again.

"You're still so angry with me."

He bites the inside of his lip. "Yeah."

I stare at the comforter, scratching it with my pinky nail. I knew he was before I said it, but it hurts just the same. The pain of his admission echoes through my body, pinging against my nerve endings.

"But I love you more." He looks at me. "I love you more than my anger."

My lips part. "So…"

"I don't want to move back in here unmarried to you, Simone. I don't care what anybody else thinks about that, or what's normal these days… I just don't want to do that with you again. That was part of our problem before, my resenting you a little bit because you didn't want to get married when we had Caleb, and not really saying anything about how much that bothered me."

"I was scared of getting married, period. I was scared of *marriage*."

"I get that now. Back then, though… Back then, I thought it was about me. And it felt like I always had to try to prove myself to you, and whatever I did it was never enough to convince you that I was here, and I was all the way in this with you. I don't want to drag my baggage about our divorce into anything new that we're trying to build. It's gotta be a clean slate."

I open my mouth then close it, my heart racing at the thought that maybe he's open to trying to build something with us again.

"I'm not there yet," he says. "Because when, or if, we do this again, it's forever, Simone."

"I know. I don't want anything else with you."

A few long seconds pass before Jackson gets up and sets his empty wine glass on the dresser before heading into the bathroom. He returns wearing his boxer briefs and undershirt, and I hold the covers up for him to slide into the bed. He flicks off the light, casting the room in darkness. I stare up at the darkened ceiling fan whirling in gentle circles, feeling Jackson's body heat, even though we are inches apart.

"I kept my pillowcases on for two weeks after you came over that night because they smelled like you."

"I thought I smelled something funky," he says, sniffing his pillow.

I laugh and slap his shoulder. "Shut up. These are clean."

We're silent for a time, but I can tell by his breathing that he isn't asleep. I turn my head to look at his profile. The soft light from the barely open blinds dances over his features as he stares up at the ceiling. I rub his ankle with my big toe.

"Do you resent me after you quit the paper in Charlotte and came back here?" I ask quietly, holding my breath as I wait for his response.

"No," he says. "Our family being split up like that—I was miserable in Charlotte. Moving there taught me my boundaries, my limits. The reality of being separated from you and Caleb… I didn't factor in how hard our being separated that way would be on *me*."

And then it happened anyway. We ended up separated. He doesn't say it, but that reality, the effect of my decision, is there, hovering over us in the darkened bedroom.

"We were fighting even more when you got back," I say. "I always thought that might've been part of the reason."

"Honestly? It felt like you were pulling away from me even then. Like you'd already figured out what your life would look like without me, and were already living it. And I didn't handle that very well, feeling like I'd already lost you. I didn't know where to put all the things I felt about that."

My eyes widen in shock. "Jackson—"

"I know," he says. "That was on me. That was my guilt, I guess, for leaving you guys in the first place. Or for not standing my ground and dragging your stubborn ass to Charlotte with me."

He glances at me when he says that, grinning a bit. But then the smile falls from his lips. "When I came back home, it felt like I was trying to fit back into *your* life. Like there wasn't any space for me anymore."

My heart sinks and my eyes well with tears. I turn to stare out of the window, where the streetlight is casting a soft glow through the blinds.

"I'm sorry that I ever made you feel that way," I say when I look at him again. "I didn't... I never thought that's what I was doing."

Jackson shakes his head. "Looking back, now that I've had time and space to really think about it, I know that wasn't on you. That was me. Projecting, maybe. I think that Charlotte just exposed some things we'd been sweeping under the rug."

I swallow and nod.

"It forced our hand because everything was out in the open and we couldn't hide from it anymore," he admits.

"I think you're right."

We fall silent again for long minutes as I stare up at the ceiling fan again.

"What are you thinking about?" I ask, breaking the silence.

"Remember when we first met, I was driving back and forth to Brunswick every single weekend to check in on my mom and April?"

Sometimes I'd ride with him, because if I didn't, we never would've seen each other with our work schedules. Those hours-long road trips were when I fell completely in love with him. Our talks. The way he listened. How comfortable I felt with him. The fact that he wanted to be there for the women who were important to him.

Jackson's mother, Janice, is the kind of woman who seems like she needs to be protected—especially back then, just a few years removed from the unexpected death of her husband. She's quiet, almost sullen. And she's always been sweet to me, even after Jackson and I split, almost as if she blotted out the reality of our divorce.

"You can either roll with the punches or be the punch, Simone," she said vaguely the first time I saw her at one of Caleb's school events. She'd driven up to Atlanta for it, shortly after our divorce.

About five years ago, she moved into a retirement community, and these days she's busier than we are—always off on trips with her new group of girlfriends.

"Those trips were crazy," Jackson says now. "But I felt like I needed to do it. Like it was my responsibility. Especially after I left and came out here. Our issues, the things we need to work on, aren't all on you. My dad dying when I was so young—it put a lot of pressure on me. I dragged some of that pressure I felt into our marriage. I had all these expectations for what a marriage should be instead of just letting us breathe and find our own way, figure out what worked for us on our own terms."

We again fall silent. I roll onto my side and snuggle against Jackson's warm body. He wraps his arm around me, and I kiss his chest, sliding a leg over his.

"Know what I think?" I ask.

"Hmm?" Jackson is half asleep.

"Love is the foundation for everything," I say quietly.

He blinks his eyes open and stares down at me.

"You're my foundation, Jackson."

Twenty-Seven

I WAKE UP EARLY THE next morning, right before the sun peeks over the trees. The house is still dark and silent, and Jackson is shirtless, sleeping next to me on his stomach. I can't help it—I lean over, nuzzling his jawline with the tip of my nose, before trailing my lips to his mouth. I kiss him lightly. He inhales, long and deep, and places a large palm on my thigh, still asleep. I lie there for a few more seconds, breathing his air, enjoying his comfortable touch, then slide from under him and head into the bathroom, and then downstairs.

It's sunny out today, and the light is streaming through the kitchen window, exposing the mess I left from the day before. Scattered dishes, Caleb's stuff on the counters, my empty wine glass. I clean up the kitchen and the dining room. I really need to stop working down here at the kitchen table, dragging my work home with me like this. It almost defeats the point of having an office. With the way things have been picking up lately, it might be time for me to think about hiring a junior agent. Even this morning, my inbox is full of people from Delroy's party wanting to connect, despite the fact that I wasn't there very long. I know that's all Delroy. He's loyal, and when he's in, he's all in. His signing with Sage has been a game changer.

I grin when I see a text from Logan. She sent one last night too, saying she saw us leaving and asking if everything was okay. I pause my cleaning and lean against the counter.

Everything good this a.m.?

Yep.

Jackson still there?

I smile, thinking about him sleeping upstairs. *Yeah.*

So, no Carter? What was up with that?

He just ran into her at the elevators and they came up together.

Oh good. I didn't not want to have to start disliking Action Jackson.

But the real question is… um, TRISTAN???

He was just talking shit. Drunk.

He's never been so drunk he asked me to sit on his face.

He was drunk. And we're not texting about this. You know how messy it would be if D found this? He was drunk and probably just… who knows. It's Tristan. And anyway, Melissa came through with her girls after you left, looking like Real Housewives. I think he left with her.

No way.

Way. It's whatever. If he wants to be goofy, that's on him. Anyway, I'll talk to you later. About to get up and run over to the shop. My new hire is looking kinda shaky.

Okay.

DELETE THIS TEXT.

I laugh and do as she asked, then set my phone on the counter. I finish loading the dishwasher, then decide to make waffles for Caleb. He's rarely at my house on Saturday mornings, and it used to be a thing.

I'm just starting the turkey bacon when I hear someone on the stairs. I smile when Jackson comes around the corner. He's pulled on his slacks from last night and is still barefoot, wearing a ribbed undershirt. His facial hair is thicker, his eyes still sleepy-sexy.

I smile when he crosses the room to stand behind me, peering into the pan before dropping a quick kiss on my neck.

"How'd you sleep?" I ask.

"I think you know I slept," he answers, giving me another kiss on my neck.

He turns to pour himself a cup of the coffee I just finished brewing. We made love in the middle of the night. I woke up with my back pressed to his chest, his hand splayed across my stomach. And when I wiggled, pushing my butt against him in my sleepiness, he moved too, sliding his hand up and cupping my breast. I turned and he rolled on top of me, sliding my shorts down my legs slowly, his movements unhurried. He slipped inside of me and my entire body sighed.

Last night wasn't even about either one of us reaching completion. It was about us connecting in our purest state. My release was long, stretched out, racking my entire body. So was his.

The waffles are finished before Caleb emerges from upstairs. So Jackson and I sit in the living room to eat while we half watch last night's baseball highlights.

"Benny texted me this morning," I tell him. I'm sitting in between his outstretched legs as he lounges on the couch.

"I bet he did."

"Shut up. He said he's starting a nonprofit to help get more Black and brown kids to play baseball in the States. Since a lot of the problem is access to green spaces, he wants to build mini baseball fields in 'unusual places' in bigger cities around the country. That sounds cool, right?"

Jackson nods. "It does. So what's he want you to do?"

"He said he wants to partner with Sage however he can. Have some of our clients get involved in ways that make sense, that kind of thing."

"You gonna do it?" he asks.

"Yeah. I think it makes sense. That's what my gut is telling me. It's working again, by the way."

Jackson laughs, his chest rumbling against my back.

"He actually mentioned you, too. He's ready to work on a memoir about the game and his life, and how it all ties together, or something that sounded very serious and deep..." I shrug at Jackson's smirk. "You should think about doing it, though, because he has *baseball* money."

"I'll hit him up, see how serious he is. You know he likes to do a lot of talking."

"True. He's just really scatterbrained," I say, shifting against his chest as I change the channel, landing on reruns of *The Game*.

"How many times have you seen this episode?" Jackson asks. "You should have it memorized by now."

"A hundred and forty-nine? And I do."

He shakes his head as I relax against him again, tracing a line down his forearm with my fingertips, returning my attention to the TV.

Caleb finally comes downstairs around ten a.m. He smiles at the sight of his father stretched out on the couch and me lounging between his legs.

"Morning," he greets us, grinning.

Jackson and I exchange a look. "Morning," I reply. "I made waffles. They're still warm in the oven."

I sit up when Caleb returns to the living room, motioning for him to sit next to us on the couch. "Your dad and I…"

"We're spending time together," Jackson finishes for me, watching Caleb's face closely.

"Are you still figuring it out?" Caleb asks, looking between the two of us.

"We still love each other. And yes, we're figuring out how to do a better job of it," Jackson says.

Caleb nods, eyes on the TV as he stuffs his mouth with waffle. "Cool," he says around a mouthful of food. "Can we watch something else? This is kinda dumb."

I exchange a look with Jackson who grins. I toss Caleb the remote, then get up, grabbing our plates. I've just finished loading them in the dishwasher when I feel Jackson's arm wrap around my middle. I lean back against his solid chest.

He kisses my shoulder.

"You're my foundation too, baby," he says against my ear.

I smile and stare out of the kitchen window. My succulent is just beginning to bloom.

Twenty-Eight

TWO MONTHS LATER, IT'S LATE August, and I'm sitting at my desk in my office, not working. It's loud and full of people. I just got back from my August "fortieth experience" with Logan—roller skating at Cascade Skating. I never really learned how to skate, and my forty-year-old knees are in no position to take a fall. But I've always wanted to learn, so I did it.

Well, I didn't *learn*. But I did summon every ounce of my Usher energy when I stepped onto the rink. I only fell once—mostly because I spent the whole time clutching the wall while little kids with glowing wheels whizzed past me like pros. Logan is a great skater, and was skating backward while she tried to pull me along by the hands. We probably spent more time laughing than skating.

Afterward, we came straight to my office because Logan was supposed to be meeting Delroy here after his marketing strategy meeting with Tristan. Only instead of it just being Delroy and Tristan, Malika Higbee and one of her friends—Rain or Rainbow, or Cloud, or something—were here too. Malika just dropped by to hang out and "decompress," as she frequently does when she's back in Atlanta on break. The season is in full swing again, and her mom is stressing her out. I have no idea what she finds so appealing about the office—mostly, all she does when she's here is play on her phone.

"You ready, baby?" Delroy asks Logan, crossing the room from the bar area where he was talking with Tristan.

Logan is perched on the edge of my desk, chatting with Malika. Logan's been thinking about expanding and opening another wine shop up in Alpharetta, and Malika is soaking up every bit of knowledge she can, still determined to open her own shop at some point. Logan's been bringing her different bottles of wine to try to expand her palate. Right now, I think they're on chardonnay.

Logan nods, accepting Delroy's quick kiss when he reaches her.

"Simone, you have good taste," Delroy says. "What do you think of this?" He flicks through his phone until he lands on a picture of an ugly green leather couch.

I peer at the screen, raising my brows before glancing at Logan.

"Don't look at Logan—give me your honest opinion."

"I think it looks like an ugly alligator box."

Delroy frowns. "What's an alligator box?"

"That," Logan says, pointing at his phone as she slides off my desk. "We are not moving that ugly thing into the house, D. No."

Despite insisting she needed her own space months ago, Logan is moving in with Delroy this weekend. I was shocked. Tristan was too, although he smoothed his face when she told us over dinner, and gave her a congratulatory hug. He even bought them a blender for their housewarming.

Delroy shoots me an exasperated look, and I shrug apologetically. "You asked for honesty. That couch is not it."

He shakes his head and laughs just as the front door swings open. Tristan grins at the sight of Akeela, the sound-bath instructor he's been dating for the past month. Logan turns toward me.

"Why is she here?" she mumbles.

"Because she's Tristan's new woman?" I answer, keeping my voice low as Delroy saunters off to greet Akeela.

"Melissa 2.0," Logan singsongs, glancing over her shoulder at Akeela again.

"You are so shady." I laugh quietly. "Leave that poor lady alone. She's sweet."

I did end up doing her Reiki class for my July birthday experience. It was calming. I don't know if my energy shifted, but I did fall asleep during her massage, so that was nice.

Logan is still frowning slightly as she watches Tristan embrace Akeela, lifting her up off her feet before setting her down. He's very dramatic with his women.

"I'll see you later," Logan says, wiggling her fingers at me and then telling Malika to call her.

On her way out, she greets Akeela with a quick hug before she nudges Tristan with her elbow and tells him to call her later, before Delroy grabs Logan's hand and leads her out the door.

I slide out from behind my desk and stretch just as Jackson walks in. I can't stop my wide smile at the sight of him. He's casual in shorts in a navy-blue t-shirt with a backward Braves cap on his head, his stubble thick on his face. He looks good. Better than good.

He meets my eyes and grins, flashing me his dimples, before turning to Tristan, dapping him up.

"Okay, we're leaving," Malika says, pushing up from the oversized teal chairs I finally manifested on my credit card a couple of weeks ago. "Tell Tiana to DM me."

"Thanks for talking to her," I say. Tiana says she's going to try out for the point guard position this year, and Malika is giving her pointers about improving her ball handling.

"'Lika loves the kids," she quips, even though she's barely six years older than Tiana.

She throws me a salute, flashing her pink-and-gold nails before she and her friend head for the door, stopping briefly to say bye to Tristan and Jackson, giggling as she passes by him. She was recently on Jackson and Alisha's podcast, and I'm pretty sure she has a crush on him.

I grab my bag from my desk and cross the room, moving toward them.

"Y'all getting into anything tonight?" Tristan asks me and Jackson as Akeela leans into his side.

"I'm tired," I answer, tilting my head up to look at Jackson. "Hello."

He leans down, dropping a kiss on my mouth. "How was skating?"

"I only fell once. What about y'all?" I ask Tristan as we file out of the office. I flick off the lights and turn to lock up.

"About to go grab dinner," Tristan says, as Akeela slips her hand into his. "I'll hit you up tomorrow."

I give him a high five and we part ways in the parking lot. I lift my head to the sky as Jackson hits the key fob. The sun is just starting to set, and I inhale deeply. I feel good. Lighter. Like I'm on the cusp of even better things.

I slide into Jackson's car, and am immediately engulfed by his clean scent. I let myself relax in the seat as he turns up the old OutKast record he's playing and maneuvers onto the street.

"What's up?" he asks, glancing at me as he drives with one hand on the wheel, probably feeling me staring at him.

"I missed you today."

"I just saw you last night at dinner."

"So? I can still miss you, right?"

He grins as he reaches over and runs a hand up my bare thigh, letting it rest there. I put my hand on top of his.

Jackson still hasn't moved in. We're taking things slowly. We started couples counseling about six weeks ago. We see a woman named Crystal—she came on referral from Zuri, whom I still see every other week.

We have state-of-the-union meetings once a week, where we check in with each other and talk about where we are—how we're feeling, what we need. We had a conversation about it recently, after dinner one night. We'd just finished eating, and I was admittedly a little snappy. Nothing loud or dramatic. Nothing heavy.

"What's wrong with you, Simone?" Jackson asked as he leaned against the kitchen counter. Caleb was in the living room, on his laptop, working on some game he was building for his engineering club.

"Nothing."

Jackson sighed, and I turned toward the dishwasher, loading the last of the plates we'd just used while I gathered my thoughts. Everything in me wanted to ignore him, to let my "nothing" hang in the air like it used to. To just let my irritation slide away, without speaking it out loud. Instead, I turned toward him and swallowed hard.

"Okay, something."

Jackson waited for me to continue.

"It feels like you're upset with me. And I think maybe I'm reacting to that feeling."

Jackson stared at me for a long minute, gnawing on the inside of his lip.

"I'm not upset with you."

I raised a brow. *"I can feel you, Jackson."*

"I'm not upset," he repeated. *"I just…"* He shook his head. *"I've been in my head lately."*

"What do you mean?"

"Sometimes I get stuck on all the time we wasted."

I inhaled, his words hitting me in the chest, and let the breath, the guilt, out slowly.

"And I start letting myself think up all these scenarios and situations for how things could've been with us. Where we would be by now. I get frustrated because sometimes it feels like we moved backward, and that ain't where we should be at this point in our lives."

"You think we're moving backward?" I asked, trying to keep my voice level.

"No, not like that. I think we're in a better place communication-wise than we've ever been before," Jackson said. *"But the space we're in…"* He waved a hand around the kitchen. *"Where we're at with it, physically, emotionally… I just never expected us to be here at this point. And it's been fuckin' with me a little bit."*

"I'm sorry," I said, my voice quiet.

"That ain't what I… You don't need to keep apologizing, Simone."

"I feel like I can't apologize enough,*"* I said.

He shook his head, grabbing my hand and pulling me to stand in between his legs.

"When we were in therapy the other day and Crystal said my need to fix things was less about control and more about fear… That's what I've been thinking about lately. You were afraid of us being dysfunctional like your parents. I was afraid of failing us, failing to live up to the idea I had in my head about what our marriage was supposed to look like. That was a lot of fear between the two of us."

He sighed and dropped his chin to the top of my head. For a while I stayed like that, letting the heat from his body, his even breaths, calm me.

"I love you," I said softly, tilting my head up to meet his eyes.

"I love you too."

"Can you—will you stay over tonight? I need to… feel you. You know?"

He nodded, bending to nuzzle my nose with his. *"I think I need to feel you too."*

He absently rubs my thigh with his thumb as he switches lanes now, his eyes on the road. I study the passing cars, drawing in a breath.

"Know what I wanna do?" I ask. Jackson turns and looks at me, eyes curious. I smile at him.

TWENTY MINUTES LATER, I'M LEADING Jackson through Home Depot to the garden section. We pass through the paint aisle, weaving our way around a tired couple staring at paintbrushes who look like they're completely over whatever DIY project they committed to.

We enter the garden section, and I sigh as the smell of fresh dirt and green plants hits my nostrils.

"Isn't this cool?"

"Baby, I've been to Home Depot before."

"I know, but don't you just feel better being here, surrounded by all this greenery and life?"

Jackson looks at me with his brows raised. "Not really, but I'm glad you're feeling it."

I roll my eyes and tug on his hand, leading him to the small plant section. The succulent I bought a while back is still alive and well, thriving on my windowsill. I feel like I've passed my plant-killing phase, and now I want to test the theory out. I want another plant.

"You like this one?" I say, picking up a plant with huge deep green leaves and orange stripes down the middle.

"Yeah, it's cool," he says, watching as I twirl the potter in my hands, examining it from all angles. "Where you gonna put it?" he asks as we head to the register.

"Probably the bedroom."

I repainted it a month ago. A cool mint-gray that feels warm and moody, and more like Jackson and me. More like *us*.

Jackson grins. "I think that's a good place for it."

I smile. And I buy the plant.

Epilogue

Hello, Journal,

I should probably go to bed. It's the middle of the night, and it's freezing out here—but man, this air feels lovely and clean, like it's meant to be inhaled by me, right now, in this exact moment.

It's wild to think that at one point, I actually wanted to skip my leap year. It feels like a decade has happened in the past eleven months, but also like it went by faster than any other year of my life.

I used to say the best year of my life was my freshman year at Clark. It started off rough because I didn't know anybody, and I don't make real friends easily. Then I met Logan, and everything changed. It felt like where I was meant to be.

Then I said the best year of my life was the year Caleb was born. Even though it was hard—and my pregnancy was ROUGH— being his mom felt like the thing I was meant to do, unequivocally.

Now, I think it might be this year—my leap year birthday, my 40th. Even though it started off disastrously and I wanted to leap right over it (get it?), this is the year that brought me clarity. Peace. Love.

Last month, me and Caleb shared my second-to-last birthday experience together—foraging for mushrooms. Of course, he thoroughly researched every mushroom species known to Georgia before we went, even though we'd hired a guide. It's the offseason for foraging, honestly, but neither one of us cared. It felt good breathing the fresh air, being out in nature with Caleb. He's such a good kid. So sweet and intuitive. He's talking about going away for college, maybe to Tuskegee or UCLA. I really hope he chooses Tuskegee, even though it's selfish because I just don't want him so far away, even though Ty's in L.A. and I know he'd look out for him. I'm trying to just flow with it, not impede on his decision. It's hard though, honestly.

Anyway, I don't think I've ever been this excited about what's next. I'm in the moment. Fully present. Ready to experience whatever life brings me. Ready to allow myself to feel it all. Ready to fully show up.

I CLOSE MY NOTEBOOK AND lay it on the wooden table before wrapping my arms around myself, shivering in the cold. But I can't stop my smile as I inhale the crisp air and stare up at the dark sky. I sit there for long minutes, allowing the peacefulness of the night to curl around me, before I slide back inside my room and pad over to the bed, toward Jackson's sleeping form. I climb in and straddle his waist.

"Jackson," I whisper, then kiss his ear. "Baby, wake up and come look at this."

He grunts. "I'm 'sleep."

I grin and kiss his ear again. "I know, but you don't want to miss this."

He blinks his eyes open, squinting at me. "What time is it?"

I shrug. "Like, two a.m.?"

He closes his eyes again and doesn't move, so I drop kisses all over his face. He smiles, eyes still closed. Then, before I know what's happened, he flips me flat on the bed and hovers over me on his forearms.

"*What* is so urgent?" he asks, his voice sleepy as he stares in my eyes. "And why are your lips so cold?"

I smile up at him. "Come outside and see."

"Outside?"

"Just put on your robe."

He shakes his head, eyes full of exasperation, and drops a kiss on my lips before climbing out of bed. He slips on his robe—matching mine—then steps outside onto the patio, facing the mountains.

For the holidays, we all decided we wanted to hang out together. So after Christmas, Jackson, Tristan, Logan, Caleb, Tiana, her mom, her little brothers, April, Tariq, and I caravaned up to North Georgia to a rented cabin.

It's really more like a mini-mansion, with separate bedrooms, three hot tubs overlooking the forest, pool tables, and enough space to get lost in. I invited my parents, but they decided—at the last minute—to go on a holiday cruise instead. Ty, to my surprise, joined them.

Jackson's mom ditched us too. She went with her group of friends to an all-inclusive in Mexico.

The cabin trip has been hectic and fun—and loud. Earlier, Caleb, Tiana, and Tariq were deep into a chess battle that involved way more yelling than I've ever associated with chess, mostly because April and Shelly were cheering them on like it was a football game.

Jackson and I snuck away to the hot tub on the far side of the house and stayed there talking until my fingers got prune-y. He's working on his first book—Delroy's biography. He hasn't even finished it yet, but it's already been optioned for TV, and he's been running ideas by me. He also decided to take Benny up on his offer, and signed on to write his memoir as well.

I sigh, looking out at the view now. The pine trees are dark and stretching toward the sky. The air is crisp and cool, clean.

"Look at how amazing that is." I'm unable to keep the awe out of my voice as I look up at the sky. It's brilliant.

The full moon is hanging low, bathing everything beneath it in soft, silvery light. The stars are scattered across the night sky, shining like jewels against the velvety blackness.

"Have you ever seen anything like this?" I ask, turning to look at Jackson.

"This is beautiful," he says, grinning up at the sky.

I shiver in the cold, and he moves to stand behind me, wrapping me in his arms. I breathe in deep, then let it out long and slow, watching it fog in the cold. We stand out there for a couple of more seconds until I shiver again. Jackson turns me in his arms and pecks my lips twice.

"That was worth it, right?" I ask.

He nods. "Yeah, love. It was worth it."

He pecks my lips again before we turn and head back into the room, which is spacious, with wood-paneled walls, hardwood floors, and a gigantic, white furry rug beneath the king-sized four-poster bed. A fire crackles in the corner. I'm still shivering as I crawl into bed. When Jackson slides in, I immediately crawl on top of him to get his body heat. He pulls me close, wrapping his arms around my waist, pulling me tighter against him.

"Simone." His voice is a rumble against my ear. "I love you."

I lift my head and look down at him. "I love you too." I brush my nose against his, letting his stubble tickle my face. "I feel like we should go make love in front of the fireplace, but I also feel like that might hurt my back."

He laughs quietly and then pushes at my silky pajama bottoms, which he bought me for Christmas. He slides his hands up my bare thighs, and I squirm and laugh because his hands are still cold, making chill bumps break out on my skin.

"Nah, c'mere after all that," he says when I try to roll off him, sliding his hands to my waist and flipping me onto my back.

I'm still laughing when my legs fall open for him. He smirks at me as our gazes connect in the darkened room. I lift my head to kiss him, tracing my tongue along the seam of his lips. He makes a deep noise and then pushes into me, inch by delicious inch, never breaking eye contact. I moan my pleasure when he buries himself deep inside of me. He brushes his mouth over mine, then murmurs, "We can see the fireplace from here."

THE NEXT MORNING, WE'RE HEADING for Fort Mountain State Park, bracing ourselves for the Black Bear Plunge. It's an annual event where people run into the freezing water, dip themselves, and then run back out. Every New Year, people drive out here for it. This year, Logan, Tristan, Jackson, and I will be among those people. It was Jackson's idea. "Let's do this for your last birthday experience," he told me, pointing to a story about the adventure on his phone.

I was surprised. Dashing out into a freezing lake didn't sound like a Jackson kind of thing. But ever since we got remarried, he's been on a kick about trying new things. Stuff we've never done before together. We went to the justice of the peace to get married, and we kept it simple—just us and Caleb. Afterward, we went and got burgers.

"You guys are wild for this," April tells us, coffee in hand, as we prepare to leave. She's a pretty woman, with Jackson's long eyelashes and broad nose.

"It was your brother's idea," I say, taking a bite of toast before sitting at the bar to pull on my boots. "But I'm excited. I think it's gonna be cool."

"Literally," April says, and I laugh.

"You should come," Jackson says, standing next to me.

April frowns in horror. "No thank you. But y'all have fun. I'm getting in the *hot* tub."

She raises her brows and turns to head back into her room as I chuckle.

"Y'all ready to roll?" Tristan asks, clapping his hands as he emerges from the back room, just as Logan turns the corner from her bedroom.

We all head toward the door, zipped up in coats and clad in boots, even though we will be shedding it all in less than hour.

I stop our trail out of the door abruptly, turning to look at everyone.

"I just wanna say that I love y'all," I say quickly, heat rushing to my cheeks.

Logan's eyes soften and Tristan grins, glancing over at Jackson.

"You've been exceptional people in my world this year. And I'm just really grateful for all of you. I just wanted to say that, like, out loud."

Logan releases a breath and hugs me. "We love you too, Simmy."

Jackson tugs at the hem of my coat when she releases me, pulling me back against his chest. I tilt my head up and he drops a kiss on my mouth.

"All right, is our Hallmark moment over?" Tristan asks, smirking. "We're about to be late."

"Shut up, Tristan," Logan says, slapping his shoulder and rolling her eyes. Tristan laughs, tugging on my skull cap as he passes by me.

I SIGH, MY BREATH FOGGING in the cold, and focus my attention on the water. It's beautiful out here, tall pine trees surrounding the clear lake, and there's a big group of people, some in swimsuits, others in shorts and t-shirts, gathered at the shore. We're wearing t-shirts and shorts, but it doesn't matter, because it's frostbite weather anyway.

"This shit is crazy." Tristan looks over at me, his eyes almost fearful, then back out at the freezing water as he shakes his shoulders in an effort to stay warm.

"This is about to change your life," Logan says, the tip of her nose red. "We need to do things to get out of our comfort zone every once in a while."

"There's not another Black person in sight," Tristan says out the side of his mouth. Logan laughs, running in place, gearing herself up.

I smile, bouncing up and down in the cold. It's freezing, but I already feel freer. I'll turn forty-one in a month, and my life is fuller than it's ever been. It's richer, healthier, with Jackson.

I turn to him now and look up at him. As usual, he was already watching me, seemingly in tune with where my thoughts had strayed.

"You ready, baby?" he asks.

I hold his gaze, calm and sure, as people begin splashing their way into the lake.

"Yes."

He grabs my hand, and we run toward the water. We take the plunge together.